DRIVEN BY DESIRE

Book One of Driven Hearts

NIKITA SLATER

ISBN 978-0-9958624-8-7

CHAPTER ONE

"Fuck," Riley grumbled, twisting to make sure she was correct. Nope, she didn't have the right tool.

It was late at night and all the guys had gone home so she couldn't call out to one of the other mechanics and ask them to hand it to her. Damn. With a sigh of aggravation, she pushed herself out from under the car. Shoving her long ponytail out of the way, she crawled toward the toolbox and rifled through until she found what she was looking for. Loud, thumping music filled the garage from where her iPhone was plugged into its port on top of one of the tool benches.

Turning back toward the '69 Camaro, Riley adjusted her lamp and prepared to slide back under. This baby was a thing of beauty. It called to her from the moment it entered her shop, which is why she was still working on it at 2:00am. If she did it up right she'd be able to turn a pretty profit on this little sweetheart and take Cilia on vacation. They desperately needed some bonding time.

The music switched off and a deep voice reverberated through the darkness of the garage. "I'm looking for Mr. Bancroft."

Riley froze for a few precious seconds before her head snapped up, judging the distance between a shadowed man and the gun in her toolbox. He stepped forward into the circle of her light, closing the distance between them. Riley's heart slammed against her ribs as his face became visible and she recognized the most ruthless man in the city. Soloman Hart, mafia kingpin, was standing in her garage, staring down at her with cold intent. He now stood directly between her and her gun. Not that she thought it would do any good against a man like him.

Riley felt incredibly small and grimy next to his large, well-dressed frame. She sat crouched on the concrete beneath him, wearing her usual tank top and grimy, oil-stained overalls with the top left to hang down. Her shiny, dark brown hair was pulled back in a messy ponytail and she wore no make-up.

He seemed to be looking her over, taking in every inch of her with interest. Her eyes narrowed in return. She was used to guys staring. She was a thirty-year-old female mechanic, working in a garage full of men. She looked younger than she was and knew she was attractive. Definitely fantasy material for some guys. Which is why she tended to work in the office and on cars in the back, well away from the clients. Very few people knew who actually owned the garage.

"How did you get in here?" she demanded, pushing herself up and standing to her full height, which was still several inches shorter than him. She crossed her arms in front of her chest and glared at him. She had a damn good security system or she wouldn't have been alone in the shop blaring music in the middle of the night.

He ignored her question and raised a dark, thick brow. "Mr. Bancroft?" The single question sent a chill down her spine, letting her know that the next words out of her mouth better be an answer, because Soloman Hart was not a man known for patience.

Riley pressed her lips together for a moment and wondered how best to answer him. The truth of 'Mr. Bancroft' was complicated. And Riley was starting to suspect she may be in some danger. The likelihood of a man of this caliber showing up in her garage for any reason was slim. Which meant something not good was going down. Soloman had men to deal with his car issues, he didn't handle with things like this himself.

She moistened her lips and then stopped when his sharp eyes followed the movement. Taking a breath, she said, "Mr. Bancroft is dead. He died two years ago."

His brows drew together in a frown that made Riley shiver from head to toe. Yeah, he didn't want to play games with her. His next words confirmed this thought.

"Don't fuck with me, little girl," he growled. "Everyone knows Alan Bancroft is dead. I'm looking for the owner of this garage. Alan's son, Riley Bancroft."

"Okay," she whispered. "Why are you looking for Riley?"

Holy shit, she was going to die! The look on his face suggested that the last person that questioned him instead of instantly giving him the answers he was searching for had died a really extra terrible death.

Surprisingly, he answered, his deep voice clipped as he spoke. "Someone stole one of my vehicles yesterday. It was my favourite and I want it back. Thought it might show up here."

Shock flickered across her face. Who would be stupid enough to steal one of Soloman Hart's cars? Well, that explained why he would show up on her doorstep himself at 2:00am looking for answers. She ran the biggest chop shop in the city. Only very few people knew she ran the garage. She had a very good team of mechanics, mostly inherited from her father, that helped keep her safe behind the scenes. Few people even knew the name Riley Bancroft. Except, somehow Soloman did.

"Wh-what kind of car?" she asked hesitantly, hoping like hell it hadn't gone through her shop. She usually did her homework and found out where the vehicles came from so this kind of shitstorm didn't come down on her head, but that didn't mean things didn't get under her radar once in a while.

"Koenigsegg Regera." His voice held no inflection as he named one of the most expensive vehicles in the world. A car that would be one of a kind in the United States.

Riley took a few seconds out from her terror to be impressed. Damn. Soloman must like him some nice luxury racing automobiles. Too bad the man was such a cold-hearted, ruthless bastard. Under different circumstances she wouldn't mind getting under the hoods of his fleet, see what he had going on up in there.

She breathed a sigh of relief. "Nope, I definitely would've noticed one of those. Never even seen one in person, let alone had one in here."

He nodded, still studying her carefully as though taking in every minuscule expression that crossed her face. Finally, he said, "I'd still like to have a conversation with Mr. Bancroft."

Fuck. That was going to be a problem since there was no Mr. Bancroft. Instead, she nodded her head.

"Sure, no problem. I'll have him call you tomorrow." She'd get one of the other mechanics to call and reassure him that his car was never there and if it showed up he would be the first person they called.

He reached out and took her hand before she realized what he was about to do. He held her fingers in a grip that told her she shouldn't pull away from him. He had a brutal looking tattoo on the back of his hand that begged for a closer look. She resisted the urge. He looked down at the black, chipped nail polish on her fingers and rubbed his broad thumb over the tops of her much smaller nails. She shivered at his touch. Based on his reputation and the few glimpses she'd had of him she'd always considered Soloman Hart cold, but his hand was surprisingly warm.

"What's your name?" he demanded, his voice deep and compelling.

Riley tried to pull her hand away, but he continued to force his touch on her. She turned her body away and said in a haughty voice, "None of your business."

He stiffened next to her and she bit her lip, worried that she was about to find out what made this powerful man so feared among their underworld set. He chuckled lightly, running his thumb over her knuckles. "I think you'll find I can make it my business."

She shivered and dropped her eyes, still refusing to answer. She did not want this man finding out who she was. For more reasons than the obvious. When he was alive, Alan Bancroft had taught Riley everything he knew, but he'd kept her existence on the down low in case they ever needed to pack up shop and run. There was also the complication of her mother. Cilia Bancroft, shady accountant to the super rich, was a handful and best kept out of the notice of men like Soloman Hart.

"You can fly, little bird," he said quietly. He looked down at her, capturing her brown eyes with his bottomless dark eyes. "I will let you go for now."

"F-for now?" Riley asked hesitantly.

He released her hand and stepped closer, towering over her, his chest nearly brushing hers. Riley gasped at his unexpected movement and tried to move back. Her leg bumped against the car she'd been working on and she was forced to stand still next to him. Her head swam as his subtle, masculine scent enveloped her. It made alarm bells go off in her head. He didn't immediately move away from her.

"For now," he confirmed, his gaze roaming intently over her. "I think the day will come that we will see... a lot more of each other."

Her mouth opened and she stared at him. Was that a threat? He was looking down at her with something she couldn't entirely define. Speculation? Possessiveness? But how was that possible? He didn't even know her. Though she'd seen him before, they were just meeting officially for the first time.

His eyes brushed over her one last time and she had a keen awareness that she was being granted some kind of reprieve. But it came with a time limit. One that would quickly run out. Her heart slammed against her ribs.

"Do you know who I am?" he asked.

She blinked and then nodded slowly.

"Say my name," he demanded.

Riley gaped up at him for a moment and then, desperately wanting the dark man to leave, gave him what he wanted. She licked her lips and whispered, "Soloman."

He turned and strode away from her, resetting the alarm before leaving the garage.

Soloman slid into the passenger side of his second favourite vehicle. Turning to his friend and bodyguard, he said, "Did you catch that?"

Roman nodded. He had been standing in the shadows near the door where he'd disabled the alarm and unbolted the lock to allow his boss entry to the garage. Though Soloman didn't need back up, the two rarely worked separately, especially since Soloman's climb to the top had earned many enemies. Both knew it was better to have a loyal man guarding each other's backs than to go it alone.

"I want her," Soloman said quietly, not taking his eyes off the passing street lights.

Roman grunted, but didn't say anything. He already knew. The boss rarely pursued women, beyond having them brought in for a quick fuck. That he even asked for this one's name was surprising. "I'll find out who she is."

Soloman nodded. "I want to know everything. There's something about her… I think I might keep her for a while."

Roman grunted. He'd get their information guy out of bed and working on the problem of the chick immediately. Find out who she was so the boss could get laid. Soloman Hart wasn't used to being denied. No one needed to be around the man when he wasn't happy. Much better to just bring him the woman's information and then the woman herself all wrapped up and tied in a bow. Fewer people would die that way.

"And find out where the fuck Riley Bancroft is," he snapped, drumming his fingers restlessly on his leg. "I want my goddamned car back."

CHAPTER TWO

"Cilia, I'm here!"

Riley wasn't overly surprised when no one called back. It was usually a fifty-fifty chance that her mom would be home when she said she would be. Cilia's schedule was about as predictable as the woman herself. She was probably tracking the migration pattern of sea turtles again. Cilia was convinced the little bastards were plotting to take over the planet due to their extreme longevity.

Cilia Bancroft was special. A super genius, actually. She loved Riley. Or at least Riley hoped she did. She just wasn't able to show it in a classic motherly way. She was a really good accountant, but sketchy as fuck. She usually managed to con rich people out of shit tons of money and walk away from them after a few years. They would beg her to continue services, never knowing that she'd stolen their money.

Riley was proud of her mother's talents, but she worried too. Cilia was addicted to gambling, but her autistic brain made it impossible for her not to count the cards and weigh the odds. The challenge of winning, of pitting herself against an opponent drew Cilia to the tables. The danger of being found out appealed to the beautiful widow and terrified her daughter. Luckily, Riley had sufficient contacts in the gambling world to get her mom blacklisted from the legitimate casinos in the city. The underground gambling clubs had been a little more difficult, but she had pulled sway on her dad's reputation until Cilia's money was no good anywhere in the city.

Unfortunately, Riley's machinations against her mother's addiction had created a rift between the two women. Though Riley continued to doggedly care for her mother, despite Cilia's coldness toward her only daughter.

Riley set an armload of groceries on the counter and began pulling food out of the reusable sacks. Cilia wouldn't bother eating if food wasn't brought to her. Like a child, the food had to be either easily eaten or pre-made. Which was probably for the best. Riley shuddered at the thought of her mother using a stove. Knowing Cilia, she would turn the element on, dump a pile of newspapers on it and walk away.

The front door slammed shut as Riley was finishing reorganizing the pantry. She frowned at a pile of used dog toys next to the cereal and wondered if Cilia was going to get a puppy. Should she start buying dog food now, too?

"Grocery day?" Cilia asked absently, wandering into the kitchen. The hems of her jeans were soaking wet and her usually flawless blond hair was chaotic and windswept. She slammed a bucket full of what smelled like sea water on the counter. She had been down to the ocean.

"Yeah, Cilia, I told you I would be by. Remember?" Riley answered, stepping away from the bucket. Experience told her that she didn't want to know what was going on in there. "What's with the dog toys? Are you sure you should be getting another pet? Or do we need to discuss Hamstergate again?"

Cilia gave her a sharp look. "They belong to the neighbour dog, of course. It's a barking experiment."

Without explaining further, she turned to the sink and

tipped the stinky contents of her bucket. Riley turned away and stealthily snuck the toys into one of her grocery bags. It wasn't the dog's fault her mother was always experimenting on the poor creatures of the world. Speaking of which, she most definitely did not want to know what was happening in the sink, judging from the odd sucking sounds.

Edging toward the front door of her mother's bungalow, she asked, "Want to go out for supper or drinks on Friday after work?"

Cilia's back stiffened. "Can we go to Merchant's?"

An underground casino lounge.

Riley sighed in resignation. "No, mom."

"Then I'm busy," Cilia answered coldly, not turning around.

Riley left, letting the screen door slam behind her. She loved her mother, but the woman was beyond frustrating. She emptied her grocery bag of dog toys to a very happy, wiggling boxer cross, reached over the fence to pat his head and then crossed the street to her roadster and drove back to the shop. She needed to get one of the guys to make a call for her.

She got Wendell to help her with the call. He was a mechanic similar in age to her, loyal to both her and her father and not in the least gossipy. He'd been hired at the age of fifteen after his older brother, a shop mechanic, was killed in a gang shooting. He and Riley practically grew up around cars together and had an easy, almost sibling-like relationship. She even went to the occasional Sunday supper with his parents, wife and kids, something she missed in her own life. He did raise an eyebrow when he found out who he was making a call to. Apparently, he had a few qualms over lying to the most lethal man in the city, but ultimately agreed.

"It's not like he'll ever find out it was you," Riley begged.

"Yeah, okay," Wendell agreed, eying Riley's curves under

her loose overalls. "Only because I think its a damn good idea to keep your identity out of this particular guy's hands."

They put the phone on speaker after dialling. Riley waited breathlessly, hoping it would go to voicemail. It didn't. Soloman Hart picked up on the third ring, his deep measured voice answering as though he had been expecting the call.

"This is Riley Bancroft," Wendell said, looking at Riley as he spoke. "I was told you wanted to speak with me, Mr. Hart."

There was a long pause before Soloman's deep drawling voice answered. "Yes, thank you for getting in touch. Did your... mechanic tell you my reason for visiting?"

"Yeah, she did," Wendell assured him. "As she told you, man, we haven't seen your ride in the shop and we'll definitely be in touch if the Regera comes through here. Something one of a kind like that, it'll stand out around here."

"Yes, that would be why I made the visit myself. Do me a favour and ask around your circles... Riley? I want that car back," Soloman said coldly.

Riley's heart pounded against her ribcage. She knew she wasn't imagining the way he paused before he said her name. Why did it feel as though he was toying with Wendell? Fuck, did he know the woman he spoke with in the early morning hours was Riley herself? If he did, then he'd found out way faster than she thought possible. Meaning his reach went even deeper than she had previously expected. No, she needed to believe he had no idea. That he didn't care enough to find out.

"Of course," Wendell reassured him, watching Riley's face with a frown.

"I want something else," Soloman continued, his voice taking on a definite edge. "The name of that woman mechanic I met last night. She refused to give me one when asked."

Riley's eyes flew to Wendell's. He put a reassuring hand on her arm and gave Soloman the name that they'd talked about before the call. "Her name's Katie Pullman," he said with a forced chuckle. "Not sure why she refused to say. She's usually a pretty big flirt. We have trouble keeping her away from the clients. You must've spooked her."

Riley held her breath while they waited for Soloman's response. They'd given him Wendell's sisters name. A quick check using resources that he undoubtedly had access to would quickly uncover the lie. Luckily, Katie was travelling for work and would never know her name was used in vain. Though she *was* a giant flirt and did tend to cause havoc in the shop when she deigned to saunter through with her mini skirts and lacquered nails. She also happened to be Riley's best friend.

Riley hoped that telling Soloman the woman he met was a flirt would put him off wanting anything more to do with her. Perhaps it was a mild attraction and he would lose interest and move on to greener pastures if he thought she was easy. Dude looked like he enjoyed a challenge. She crossed her fingers and prayed he was already moving on.

"Must've," he finally agreed, after a moment of thought. "I appreciate your help with my problem, Riley. Let me know what you hear."

"Will do," Wendell agreed and hung up.

Riley sighed in relief and leaned back against the window of her office, closing her eyes. "Thank god that's done. Hopefully that's the last we hear from him."

Wendell put his hand on her shoulder and squeezed it affectionately. She looked up at him and into two very concerned blue eyes. "Time to think of a plan, Riles. Because that man didn't believe a word I said."

Soloman leaned back in his chair and placed his phone carefully on the desk. He cracked his knuckles and turned to look out across the landscaped yard. He should have been extremely angry, but satisfaction was the only emotion he could conjure. Riley Bancroft just made a very big mistake in lying to him. By playing dirty with him she was giving him the opening he needed to take what he wanted.

For now, he would play her games. Give her a chance to get to know him better and come to him willingly. Eventually, she would give him what he wanted. If she continued to resist him, then he would crush her games and burn her world until she had no more choices. He hadn't become one of the most feared men in the city for no reason. She would learn.

He looked down at the file his information guy had put together two hours after Roman had contacted him. It contained everything he needed on Riley Bancroft. He didn't need to open it to remember the contents. He did pull the pictures out. One was her driver's license and the other was her passport. Both resembled her, but neither did justice to the gorgeous, vibrant creature he'd encountered in the garage.

He looked down at the pictures and then closed his eyes, conjuring her image and the vanilla scent combined with motor oil that he'd smelled on her when he'd stepped up to her. He'd been nearly overwhelmed by the urge to take a fistful of her ponytail, jerk her into his chest and take those plush lips in a hard kiss. Fuck, they were so plump, they begged to be crushed beneath his own thinner, harder lips. She had the type of mouth that made men everywhere picture a dick sliding between the red, lush pillowy softness and into the moist depths of her mouth. It made him want to put his fist through a wall, or a dude's face, and lock her up where no one could see her.

Soon. He would bring her home and show her who she belonged to. For now, he would play the wooing game and lure her into his trap.

Though he'd memorized the words, he flipped open the

file anyway. Glancing down at her information, he reread each word in an attempt to soothe the impatient beast rearing up inside him with the need to go find Riley Bancroft. First, he would spank her for lying to him, then fuck her into submission.

She was thirty years old. The only child of Cilia and Alan Bancroft. Alan Bancroft had passed away two years earlier from a sudden heart attack, leaving his extremely lucrative repair and detail shop to his daughter, Riley Anne Bancroft. Further digging had revealed that the garage was also a chop shop. A fact Soloman had, of course, already known.

The dating and medical information had caused Soloman's blood to boil, forcing him to examine closely what exactly it was he wanted with this girl he had spent barely five minutes with. She was on birth control and went to the clinic for regular blood testing, and yearly pelvic exams, which suggested she was sexually active. The information guy had also dug up a dating profile. Though there seemed to be no one serious in the picture, she dated semi-frequently and had a thing for clean-cut jocks. That was about to change.

The mother, Cilia Bancroft, was a high-functioning autistic that lived on her own and had a gambling problem. She worked as an accountant to the rich and was currently black-listed from every casino and poker game in town thanks to her grown up daughter. Very interesting. This piece of information would come in very handy considering he owned several of the places Cilia was currently not allowed to step foot in. Perhaps it was time to make Mrs. Bancroft's acquaintance.

CHAPTER THREE

Riley was exhausted. It had been a ridiculously long day and all she wanted to do was take a hot bath, have a cup of chamomile honey tea and fall into bed. Engaging the locks on her '71 Triumph Spitfire, she clutched her pepper spray and ran up the stairs of her outdoor apartment building to her third-floor condo. She let herself in, disarmed the alarm and dumped her purse and spray into the nearest chair. It was her favourite 'holding shit' instead of actual sitting on armchair. She had one in her bedroom too for clothes that weren't dirty enough to go in the laundry, but not clean enough to go back in the closet. She flipped the light switch on the wall between her living room and her kitchen.

"Holy shit!" she gasped, staring in surprise and dismay at a massive flower arrangement on her countertop. It was a huge assortment of tiger lilies, red, yellow and orange gerberas, and yellow daisies surrounded by greenery. She'd never seen anything like it.

Turning on her heel, Riley quickly relocked the door and set the alarm again. Then she shook her head and swore again, realizing that whoever put the flowers on her counter would have gotten through all of her security anyway.

"Fuck!" she yelled, covering her mouth with one hand.

She grabbed blindly for the pepper spray in case the intruder was still in her condo. Her fingers closed over the can and she held it tightly against her chest and glared at the flowers like they were going to eat her. Then, realizing she had no choice, she reached out and snatched the card from the prong sticking out of the top.

"Please, please, please be from Cilia," she begged out loud, knowing she was asking for the moon. Cilia didn't even give birthday or Christmas presents, let alone random flower arrangements that must have cost a fortune. But Cilia was one of the few people with a key to her place and the code to her alarm system.

The card was handwritten:

Call me.
   S

She automatically flipped the card over and saw a phone number on the back. She knew exactly who it was from. Riley stared at it for a full five minutes, her heart thumping in fear and anticipation. Would she be crazy to call the number? Would she be crazy not to? One did not exactly ignore a summons from Soloman Hart. She suspected she knew why he wanted to talk to her and she wasn't too eager to have this conversation. If he found her place then he'd found out who she was. After several more minutes of debate, she picked up her iPhone and punched in the number. It wasn't the same one that they'd used at the shop. Was this his personal cell number?

He answered on the first ring.

"Hello, Riley." His deep, rich voice sent a shiver coursing through her body.

"Soloman," she said coldly.

"You received my flowers."

"Obviously," she said through gritted teeth, glancing sideways at the massive arrangement. "You have a thing for breaking into places uninvited."

He chuckled, but there was little warmth in his voice when he said, "You lied to me, Riley Bancroft. Do you know what happened to the last person that lied to me?"

"No," she whispered, her eyes glued to the bright flowers. She was guessing they hadn't received an expensive gift.

"His family will not have the closure they seek, but I won't go into details since I plan on us spending time together in the future. I don't want you to become too afraid of me. I will tell you that you have tread on my patience in a way I don't allow in others," his voice was quiet, chilling. "I'm warning you not to lie to me again. Do you understand, Riley?"

She could feel the adrenaline spiking through her as he spoke, even though she wasn't in immediate danger. She forced herself to breath as evenly as possibly so she wouldn't pass out. Reaching out, she took hold of the edge of her couch and pulled herself down until she was sitting. Carefully, she set the can of pepper spray between her legs. She knew neither he nor one of his goons would be in her apartment at the moment. Not his style.

"Yes," she gasped into the phone. "I understand."

"Good," he said. "I want you to understand the rules, Riley, so you don't get hurt."

Anger flared within her chest. Fuck him and his rules! She didn't plan on getting any closer to this terrifying mafia asshole. Instead, she said in a tight voice, "Fine, thank you for enlightening me. And thank you for the flowers. Th-they're beautiful."

It nearly choked her to thank him for the flowers, but she'd lived and worked in the criminal world long enough to know how things went with these bosses. Even when they did horrifying things, you thanked them so they didn't do something even worse. God, maybe she should sell the shop, move out of town and go legit. The shop had moved some seriously decent income in its time and for the most part she and her dad had managed to stay out of trouble. The shop had also allowed her to have fun with her obsessions: racing and gaming. She could easily game without the shop, but not so much the races. Still, it wasn't worth her life.

"Have dinner with me Friday night."

"What?" she asked incredulously. She couldn't have heard him right.

"I'm asking you out to dinner," he pressed.

Riley covered her face with her hand and thought hard about his request. More of a command actually. Shit. What should she do? Should she have seen this coming? The man was a fucking predator. She'd felt it in the garage. The way he looked at her and touched her. Everything about him was terrifying. There was no way she could handle a man like him. But did she have a choice? There was only one way to find out.

"I... I don't think so. No," she said, making her voice as strong as she could. She waited breathlessly for his reply, praying he would just accept her answer, like the guys that usually pursued her, and hang up.

"Reconsider, Riley," he instructed her, his quiet, deep voice compelling her to give in.

Oh god. She put her head down on her knees for a moment and then she stiffened her spine. She was not a weakling. She would not let some man, no matter how scary he was, push her into a corner and terrorize her into a date. Glaring at the flowers, she said clearly and coldly, "I said no."

He didn't say anything for a moment and then he said in a warmly amused voice, "Then let the games begin, Riley Bancroft."

What the fuck did that mean?

CHAPTER FOUR

"You're clear, Reaper. Shift now and take the inside," Wendell's voice buzzed in her ear.

Riley felt the vibrations of the car, the blood pumping through her veins and the music blasting all around her. She placed her fingertips against the gearshift, let the car drift a few extra seconds and then moving her feet in tandem with her hand, switched gears. The car screamed around the cliff edge, biting through grass and dirt as it left the road for a few seconds before regaining the asphalt and overtaking the lead car.

"Fuck, Riley!" Wendell's voice shouted in her ear. "That was a fucking stupid move. You could've gone over. Goddamnit woman, are you trying to die?! And my fucking tires are toast, aren't they?"

Grinning, Riley turned the music up and ignored Wendell's tirade. That's why they called her the Reaper. She flew in like an angel of death to take out her competitors. He knew as well as her that she wouldn't've beat out Roadkill for the lead if she hadn't pulled that last stunt on the cliff edge. Of course, Wendell didn't care where she placed in the race. All he cared about was seeing their cars in action, watching their sleek lines eat up the road under her skilled hands. All this from his safely staked out spot high up on the cliff with a pair of binoculars.

Riley cared about this race. She needed it if she wanted to get noticed for the big bi-annual race that was worth two million dollars, possibly a sponsor or two, and a shit ton of prestige. The Sparrow Hawk Cup was an invitation only race and she intended to get an invitation this time. She felt Roadkill tight on her ass, ready to retake his lead the second she gave him the opportunity. Yeah, no fucking way.

She swerved to block him when he would've passed on a curve, bumping his left front fender with her right bumper. She winced as they collided and sent him into the guardrail for a few precious seconds before he regained control. She had enough lead time on him now that he wouldn't be catching up. Wendell was going to kill her for messing up his car.

"I'm going to kill you for fucking up my car!" Wendell shouted in her ear.

She grinned and tapped the brakes as she reached the set of lights at the bottom of Old Bay Road, they're unofficial finish line, then spun her tires and headed to the all-night diner up the road the crew had agreed to meet at. A crowd of people were already gathered to greet them. Riley grinned as she got out and accepted the well wishes and congratulations.

"You little bitch!" Roadkill, who had pulled up behind her, lunged for her. Riley screamed as he grabbed her by the waist, tossed her in the air and mock body slammed against the side of her car. "I had that fucking race before you nearly went suicide over that cliff. And what the fuck was that little love tap you gave me? Thought this was a no contact race? You owe me a new light, Reaper."

Riley laughed and punched him in the arm. The blond Australian was her biggest competition in these races. It was usually a toss up between them. Four others had been racing with them, but they hadn't even come close to touching Road-kill or the Reaper.

"All's fair in love and racing, bitch," she grinned up at him. He gave her a smacking kiss on the cheek, slapped her ass and went to find his girlfriend Lula who'd been watching from the top of the cliff.

"Hey!" she called after him, "don't forget, gaming Saturday! Katie's in town for a few days and wants to go to King Me for some old-fashioned first-person shooter. Bring Lula!"

"You're on!" he shouted back before disappearing into a group of friends who had just arrived from the starting point.

Riley went to one of the outdoor windows of the diner and ordered two cups of coffee and two pieces of pie to go. She turned her back on the window while she waited and crowd watched. Rita Flannigan, bubblegum pink hair like a beacon in the night, was striding toward her. At over six feet tall and wearing leather from head to foot she was impossible to miss.

She greeted Riley with a grin and slapped the $2,000 prize money into Riley's palm. Giving her a wink she said, "That was ballsy, Reaper. Let's hope you caught the right eyes tonight. Let me know if you hear anything from the Sparrow, kay? We're all dying of curiosity. Been a long time since a lady's gotten into that circle. The boys think its too dangerous and that's why women can't get near it. I call bullshit. If anyone can do it, you can. You killed it on that cliff tonight and made all the little babies at the top pee a little."

"Amen to that," Riley said through a mouthful of pie and gave Rita a high five. "I'll call if I hear anything."

"You got a car?" she asked curiously.

"Uh huh," Riley nodded, gazing into the darkness. Her eyes narrowed a little. Wendell joined them just then with a tirade about safety and expensive tires. It wasn't anything she hadn't heard before. She held up her peace offering of pie and coffee, which shut him up for a minute as he immediately filled his mouth with delicious lemon merengue.

Riley's phone rang. Glancing down, she saw that Scott was calling her. She rolled her eyes, grabbed her phone and slid off the table. Wandering toward the street, she took the call. "Hey Scott."

He laughed, "I knew you'd be up. You're such a night hawk, baby."

She smiled tightly. They'd only dated a few times, but something about this guy rubbed her the wrong way. Why would he assume she'd be up at 1:00am in the morning? He didn't really know her that well. And even having made that assumption, she didn't think it was cool of him to trespass on her time like that after only a few dates. They weren't good friends. Guys seemed to think because she had this edgy personality that it somehow also made her easy. This was probably some kind of booty call, which made her want to accept just so she could knee him in the junk and explain to Scott in detail how to treat women with respect before walking away from his ass. Dude wasn't worth her time or her breath though.

She was about to tell him to go fuck himself when a shiver of apprehension slithered down her spine. Scott was busy waxing eloquent on all of her amazing body parts and trying to convince her to come over to his place when Riley lifted her eyes and saw the one person she was hoping to never see again. Soloman Hart stood next to a sleek, black Audi S7. As soon as she caught sight of him, he began crossing toward her, like a predator stalking its prey.

Her heart stuttered in her chest as he neared. It was like the shadows shifted around him, accommodating the menacing presence surrounding the man. Riley could hear a hush from behind her as the crowd of people began to recognize him. Men of Soloman's wealth and caliber did *not* hang out around the likes of the racing circles. He wore another

expensive suit that did nothing to distract from his musculature and height. He didn't wear a tie tonight though, as
though it had been pulled off and tossed aside. The buttons of
his white shirt were open at his tanned throat, displaying a
wealth of skin and tattoos.

Riley stumbled back a step. He kept coming at her, stepping right into her space. She would have fallen, except he
reached out to steady her. His long, hard fingers wrapped
around her arm and pulled her upright into the heat of his
body. She struggled to breath as she stared up into his sinister
face, so close to hers.

His dark eyes took in every flickering emotion as it
happened. She closed her eyes and forced herself to concen-
trate. She knew they had an audience. That everyone in her
racing circle would be talking about the Reaper and the mafia
kingpin. *Fuck. My. Life.* This was so not going to be good for
her social life. People would either be clambering to find out
what was up with her or running in the other direction.

"Riley, are you still there? Are you coming over, babe?"
Scott's voice grated in her ear, snapping her to attention. She
opened her eyes and looked up at Soloman, whose face was
inches away from hers. She stood on top of the curb, while he
stood in the street. He was still a few inches taller than her.

He was so close to her, she knew he heard every word of
her conversation with Scott. She tried to jerk her arm away
and step back, but his fingers tightened, threatening to bruise
if she tried to get away from him. She narrowed her eyes, but
stopped struggling for the moment so she wouldn't accidentally drop her phone.

"No, I can't come over," she finally told Scott.

"Too bad." He sounded disappointed. "Hey, you want to
go out Friday?"

Riley was about to refuse, but looking up into Soloman's
face she read the anger and denial written there. An imp
within her decided if he wanted to play games with her, then

she was equal. He shook his head once in warning, a frown biting deep between his dark brows. She tilted her chin and gave him a cold stare. She would show him that she could do exactly what she wanted, date exactly who she wanted. She was her own woman. She was free to say no to Soloman Hart and yes to Scott… whatever his last name was.

She moistened her lips and said, "Sure Scott, let's do something Friday."

Before Scott could make any plans that Soloman might hear, Riley cut him off, "I have to run, Scott. I'll call you tomorrow. Bye!"

She pressed the disconnect key on her phone and slid it in her pocket. Then slowly raised her eyes to Soloman's. The glacial look there was enough to convince her that maybe she should have played things a little differently. Maybe not forgotten who she was messing around with. But dammit, she was a thirty year old business owner. More than capable of making her own decisions. She wouldn't be bullied!

He let go of her arm and stepped away from her. Riley felt as though she would collapse to the ground without his warm, solid presence keeping her upright. He lifted his hand. She flinched, but he only touched her bottom lip with the barest hint of pressure.

"Mistake," he said in his deep, cold voice before turning and walking away from her.

Riley stared after him, frozen in fear as he climbed into his car and drove away without a backward glance. Why was this man pursuing her so hard? He wasn't known for being a woman chaser. A thrill rushed through her, similar to the feeling she got when her car screamed around a hairpin turn. Belated adrenaline slammed through her and her heart thumped against her chest, as though she were anticipating some kind of race. Fuck, she hoped her date didn't turn up dead before Friday night.

CHAPTER FIVE

Riley checked her phone again and frowned. Weird. Scott had left for the washroom ten minutes ago and had yet to return. She took a quick sip of her mojito and glanced around the crowded Mexican restaurant. She nearly choked when she caught sight of Roman Valdez, Soloman's shadow and body-guard, leaning against the bar watching her. Motherfucker. Well that explained what happened to her date. Roman's lips twitched in amusement and his finger stabbed the air as their eyes clashed. He was marking her for the boss.

Fuck. Fuck. Fuck. Time to go!

In a rush of movement, Riley shoved her chair back and reached for her black, silver-spiked clutch purse. She stood up on her three-inch stiletto ankle boots and took one step away from the table. A body blocked hers. With a gasp of trepidation, she looked up, knowing exactly who was trapping her against the table. Soloman Hart placed one hand on the back of her chair and one on the table and leaned into her, forcing her to either sit back down or let their chests collide.

Her ass hit the chair hard enough that her tight black mini skirt slid up her thighs a few extra inches. His eyes dropped to follow the smooth, creamy length of her long legs from her ankle boots to the edge of her skirt. Her cherry red blouse was deceptively modest in the front, reaching up her neck in a high halter, but leaving her back completely bare to show the angel tattoo that spread from her shoulder blades all the way down her spine.

"Going somewhere?" he asked, his voice deceptively quiet. He took the seat opposite her, stretching his arm around the back of her chair so she couldn't leave.

She dug her nails into her thighs and stared daggers at him. "What did you do to Scott?" she demanded angrily.

He flashed her a tight-lipped feral smile, his teeth flashing white against his lips for just a second. She got the feeling he didn't often smile. The air of menace surrounding this man was almost a living thing. His tanned skin and dark hair gave him such a sinister look, it was a wonder anyone would do business with him. She shivered in her seat and took a quick sip of her drink, looking for some liquid courage as she faced off with him.

When she set her drink back down, he picked it up. Lifting it to his lips, he drank deeply, draining the contents while watching her closely. He placed the glass back on the table and said quietly, "I simply instructed him to look elsewhere for female companionship from now on. That you are taken. He understood."

"Fuck that!" Riley snarled, narrowing her eyes at him.

He shrugged negligently. "He needed a little convincing. The little fucker clearly thought he was getting laid tonight and wasn't willing to let go of the idea easily." He shook his head and allowed his eyes to roam her curves. "Not that I blame him, but you shouldn't play with men outside our circles, Riley. He had no idea who I was. I had to explain."

She went white and swayed in her seat. "Oh my god. What did you do to him?"

His eyes pierced hers. "He'll live."

She pressed her fingers against her lips and took a quick

breath, her stomach dipping sharply. God, she hoped Scott was going to be okay. Soloman reached out and took her hand, removing her fingers from her lips. He placed them on the table and traced the delicate bones and veins through her skin, marvelling at how soft her hand was, despite her work as a mechanic. She tried to pull away, but he captured her hand in a hard grip.

"Don't play that particular game with me again, Riley," he said, his voice hard. "The next guy won't be so lucky."

She nodded in agreement. She wouldn't risk anyone else while Soloman was in the picture. He was right, it was too dangerous. This was her fight. She stared at his hand as it claimed hers. The ink on the back drew her eyes. The tattoo was so complex, so brutal. His was a hand that could do so much damage. The thought of that hand caressing her, after he'd used it to do god knows what to her date, terrified her on a primitive, instinctual level.

Two plates of heaping burritos, rice and fried beans with a side of chips and salsa arrived at the table. She used the food as an excuse to tug her hand away from his and back into the safety of her own lap. Riley and Scott hadn't ordered any food so Soloman must've taken the liberty. Riley crossed her arms over her chest and raised an eyebrow at him.

"You don't seriously think I'll eat with you?" she asked incredulously.

His lip quirked and he reached for a napkin. Before she realized what he was doing, he smoothed it over her lap before doing the same for himself. "Yes, I do," he answered easily, picking up his knife and fork.

"Fuck this," she snapped, tossing her napkin on the table and shoving her plate a few inches away. "You can scare off my date, but you can't force feed me in the middle of a busy restaurant."

His shoulders stiffened and he glanced at her from beneath thick eyebrows, giving her a look that clearly said he could force feed her if that were his intention. She bit her lip and tried her hardest to maintain a glare, knowing she was probably failing.

"Eat," he commanded.

She crossed her legs and looked away from him, refusing to pick up her fork. Unfortunately, her gaze clashed with Roman's, who was watching them from across the restaurant with amusement. She checked the urge to stick her tongue out at the shady asshole and dropped her eyes.

Soloman sighed heavily and rolled his shoulders under his suit jacket. Leaning back in his seat, he eyed her. After a moment, he said, "I'm trying to keep this pleasant, Riley. You really don't want to play rough with me."

"Yeah?" she snapped, tossing him a haughty glare. "Then maybe you shouldn't have threatened my date, huh? Excuse me if I don't find it appetizing to break bread, so to speak, with a man that has to bully me into a date."

His fist came down on the table, causing her to jump and nearby patrons to glance toward them. Riley uncrossed her arms and looked down at her lap, unable to bring herself to look at the sinister visage of the man after she'd finally pushed him to snap. She could feel the tension rolling off him as he struggled not to grab her. This was a man unused to be denied the things he wanted.

"Be *careful*, little girl. You don't want to fuck with me," he said from between gritted teeth.

Fuck it. In for a penny, in for a pound. Riley leaned across the table and let him see every ounce of annoyance she was feeling. "Actually, I really do. You've been pissing me off from word go, Hart. It gives me immense pleasure to fuck with you," she hissed in his face.

CHAPTER SIX

Her chocolate brown eyes snapped liquid fire at him, turning his dick to stone right there in the fucking restaurant. He wanted to reach across the table, yank her to the floor, tear open his zipper and shove his cock into that sassy little mouth. No one had *ever* spoken to him the way Riley Bancroft was speaking to him. Just the thought would mean death.

Yet, he wanted more. He wanted her to keep talking, so he would have an excuse to take her home, strip her bare, beat her ass and then fuck her raw. She was everything he never knew he wanted in a woman. Damned if he hadn't been waiting thirty-nine years for her to come along. His cock was nearly bursting his seams to take a piece of her, but he knew he needed just a little more patience. She was still too scared of him. And while the bastard in him thrived on fear, the man that wanted to keep her was willing to bide his time and create the correct balance between fear and intrigue.

She would have to learn her place. In order to do that he would have to teach her to respect him. He would also show her all the things he could give her, starting with the incredible chemistry he felt sizzling between them each time he was near her. The sparks that ignited in the air between them the very first time he stepped foot in her garage and saw those delicate white Sketchers with the Sharpie doodles drawn on them sticking out from underneath the car she was working on.

She was still too frightened to recognize the incredible potential of their attraction for what it was. He would show her. Even if he had to break apart her world and force her to see it. He wasn't a subtle man. There was a reason he owned this city. He would own this woman too.

When she continued to ignore the food in front of her, he copied her action and placed his own napkin on the table. Very well, if she was ready to leave, then so was he. Besides, he had an appetite for something other than the Mexican fare they were currently presented with. He stood, tossing a hundred-dollar bill on the table. She looked up sharply. Clearly, she had been expecting him to react negatively to her rude comment.

"Let's go," he said, pulling her from her chair with a hand on her arm. She stumbled on her incredibly high boots and reached for her purse. Fuck, she had the most beautiful legs he'd ever seen. All sexy, smooth curves.

She had no choice but to follow him when he took her hand and began pulling her around the tables toward the exit. She dragged her feet in a clear show of reluctance, but ended up outside in the warm summer evening air. He walked her quickly toward the far end of the lot where his S7 was parked. Roman had the back door open for them.

Riley dug her hand into her purse, which was awkward considering Soloman had her other hand in his warm, solid clasp. She dug her heels in and tried to force him to stop walking.

"I'm not going with you!"

He stopped and pulled her around so she was facing him. He gave her a pointed look. "Your date gave you a ride here. Get in the car. I'm giving you a ride home."

She twisted her hand out of his grip, yanked something out of her purse and held it up to his face. He saw right away it was a can of pepper spray. "I said," she growled at him, cocking her hip to the side and staring at him coldly, "I'm not going anywhere with you."

Lust sizzled through his veins, screaming at him to show her exactly how he'd made it as one of the evilest bastards in town. He could have that can out of her hand and her on her knees with her hair twisted around his fist in seconds. But the sight of her standing there, facing off against him, beautiful and fearless, convinced him that he wanted to keep Riley Bancroft. Long term. Beating her in a parking lot in front of potential witnesses didn't work with this plan. He needed her whole and unbroken if he planned on taking her as his wife.

He nodded toward Roman who stepped up behind her. When she felt the body heat against her back she glanced over her shoulder, her eyes lighting up with worry. Now she was sandwiched between two men who were both half a foot taller than her, even with the heels, and outweighed her by a lot. The tiny can of pepper spray would be absolutely no help. Soloman put his hand out and waited. After a moment, she gave him the can.

"Good girl. Now get in the car." He tried to make his deep voice sound soothing. She shook her head.

He sighed. He really hadn't wanted to go after the people she cared about if at all possible. He should have known she wouldn't give him a choice. Truth be told, he was enjoying the hunt too much anyway. He wanted her resistance. He took her chin in his hand to make sure she was listening.

"Your friend, Katie Pullman? The fake name your buddy Wendell gave when he was pretending to be you." He paused and waited for her to nod in acknowledgment. Fear lit her beautiful eyes. "Little Katie's been on our radar for a while. My guy Roman here has had a thing for your girl for years. He backed off when she married her artist and moved up the coast. Now it seems she's divorced and coming home. Guess how we know all this?"

"No," Riley whispered, shaking her head. "Please leave Katie out of this."

"Yes, Riley," he said in a hard voice. "You brought her to our attention with your little stunt at the shop. Now get in the car."

Fuck. She didn't have a choice. Now they were threatening Katie. If she didn't go with Soloman, Roman would go after Katie and do to her what they were doing to Riley. Katie was tough, but the divorce had been hard on her. She was fragile, she wouldn't be able to handle the pursuit of someone like Roman. Riley turned on her heels and glared up at the big, muscular bodyguard, throwing every ounce of hatred she felt for the man into her look. He stared back at her coldly before stepping aside so she could slide into the open vehicle.

Riley buckled her seatbelt and pointedly ignored Soloman who took the seat beside her. Roman got into the driver's seat. She stared hard at the back of his head and finally said in an accusing voice, "I didn't know you knew Katie. And she's my best friend."

He didn't speak for a moment as he pulled the Audi onto the road. She was forced to take a moment and appreciate the gorgeous black leather interior of the $120,000 vehicle. Finally, Roman spoke. "Knew her brother."

"Wendell?" Riley asked, confused. She was pretty sure she would have heard from Wendell himself if he'd ever hung out with Soloman's terrifying right-hand man.

"Dexter," Roman grunted.

Riley fell silent. Dexter had been Katie and Wendell's older brother, the one that'd been killed in a gang shooting. Now she understood. Roman had been part of the same gang as Dexter. The one that'd been taken out by the Red Brotherhood in a gang war that lasted a week. Rumour had it that a single guy had taken out half the Brotherhood in bloody revenge for the death of his best friend, Dexter Pullman. Then he'd quietly disappeared. Everyone thought he'd been killed too. Now Riley suspected he had just gone to work for Soloman Hart.

Soloman picked up her hand and laced his fingers through hers. She tried to draw away from him, but he tightened his hand to the point of pain. She subsided, deciding that handholding was not the hill she wanted to die on. She turned fiery eyes on him and dug her nails into his hand. He gave her a feral smile and jerked her toward him until her face was inches away from him.

She gasped and brought her hand up to brace herself against him. Her hand landed on his hard chest, sliding against the fine fabric of his suit jacket. She felt his pectoral muscles clench under her fingertips and jerked back in response. He brought his hand up to catch the ponytail at the back of her head and hold her still, forcing her to stay within the circle of his body instead of subsiding into her own seat.

"Just let me go," she begged him quietly, searching his eyes out in the darkness. What she saw there made her heart sink. Gleaming possession combined with ruthless intent ensured that he would not let her go. "This won't work, Soloman. We're from different worlds. I like fast cars and video games. You like... I don't know, expensive suits and... and breaking people's kneecaps and stuff. Stomach turning shit like that."

He chuckled coldly, releasing her just enough that she could relax back into her seat. He continued to keep his hand in her hair though, running his fingers through the chestnut waves, smoothing them out along the back of the seat. "We'll work, Riley, don't worry about that."

"I don't want to *work* with you," she snapped, shrugging

her shoulder in an attempt to push his hand away from her hair. He merely dropped his long fingers onto her shoulder and began teasing the bare skin. She shivered as sensations cascaded down her arm, tingling throughout her body. She bit her lip to keep the gasp of pleasure from escaping. She did *not* need him to know that he affected her.

Roman's deep voice startled her from the front seat. "Katie in town this weekend?"

Riley's body tensed and she glared at the back of Roman's head. "That is none of your damn business," she hissed.

Soloman's hand tightened on her shoulder in warning, wrapping around the delicate bones and holding her still. "Tell him," he said quietly.

She turned angry eyes on the dark man sitting next to her. "I came with you! You said you wouldn't…"

"Roman will pursue Ms. Pullman or not, regardless of your feelings on the matter." When she opened her mouth to protest he brought his hand down on her thigh, wrapped his long fingers around the smooth, bare skin and slid her skirt up a few inches until his fingers were close to her panty-covered crotch. She gasped into the darkness and clenched her legs tightly together. He responded by flexing his fingers, biting them deep into the muscle of her leg until she wondered if there would be bruises in the morning. Moisture flooded her pussy, while fear and adrenaline sizzled through her veins.

Soloman leaned in until his hot breath tickled the long hair escaping her ponytail. "Answer him," he growled.

For one long, frozen moment Riley couldn't remember what he was talking about. Her entire focus was centred between her legs and the pounding question of whether he would close his hand and crush her leg or slide his fingers further up. She licked her lips, but refused to answer, staring at him stubbornly, daring him to do his worst. She was an adrenaline junkie, she could handle the likes of him.

Eyes locked on hers, he slid his hand up further until his small finger was a hair's breadth away from her aching pussy. She tried to clench her thighs together, but he jerked her leg open and gave her a look of such heated warning that she knew if she dared disobey he would do something much worse. She bit back a whimper as he pressed his fingers full against the soaked crotch of her lace thong.

She couldn't hold back the moan of half fear, half arousal that passed through her parted lips. She thought he might retreat now that he'd successfully intimidated her, but he didn't. His eyes still held hers. Still dared her to refuse Roman's request as he pushed her panties aside and very lightly brushed his knuckle against the soft folds of her labia.

He leaned over and growled for ears alone, "Bare."

Finally, chickening out, she gasped, "Yes, she's in town this weekend."

He moved her panties back into place, slid his hand back and gently smoothed her skirt down. Her muscles refused to relax though. He ran the back of his knuckles over her thigh, then across her arm before settling back into his own seat. He continued to watch her with speculative, gleaming eyes. Fuck. These assholes were pissing her off. They just caused her to throw her best friend under the bus. She would have to warn Katie that Roman was targeting her, and he was a giant, scary fucking bad guy. Then she'd encourage Katie to take another job out of town for a while.

The car pulled up outside of Riley's apartment building. She sighed in relief, never happier to see her home. She'd been half afraid that Soloman was taking her back to his place. She reached for the door, but he captured her hand in a hard grip and pulled her out his side of the car, forcing her to stand too close to him while he leaned down to speak quietly to Roman. She thought she heard something along the lines of twenty minutes. Well that was good, right? He couldn't do much to her in twenty minutes?

Turning back to her, he placed a hand at her back, allowing his fingers to linger inside the edge of her red top, and guided her toward the building. She was reminded sharply of the difference between him and the man who had picked her up for the evening. Scott was about the same height as her when she wore heels, had sandy blond hair, enjoyed sports, and liked to smile and joke a lot. Soloman carried shadows with him everywhere he went. A sinister intensity followed him, warning others to stay away or suffer the consequences. Riley badly wanted to stay away.

When they reached her apartment, she pulled away from the hand that was stretched across her bare back and turned to face him. "Well that was interesting," she said, bitterness creeping into her voice. She dug her apartment keys out of her purse, but made no move to go inside while he was still standing there. "Thanks for the kidnappy ride home."

The edge of his lip quirked at her sassiness. "I'm coming inside, Riley. We have a few things to discuss."

She gasped. "Fuck that! You are so not coming inside my home. I've had enough of you, Mr. Hart!"

"Soloman," he growled, stepping into her space and forcing her to step back until her back hit the door. He reached out swiftly, took her wrist and twisted until she dropped the keys into his other hand. She cried out, but he hadn't really hurt her. He knew exactly how much pressure to apply without harming a beautiful hair on her head. He took her arm, unlocked and opened the door and pushed her inside. She stood gaping at him as he punched in the alarm code.

Her eyes were wide and luminous in the glow of the single lamp she had left on in anticipation of coming home late. She was caught between anger and fear. Her hand came up to cover her mouth for a moment as she decided which was going to win. He rolled his broad shoulders and cracked his neck, waiting for her to decide.

She backed away from him. He slowly stalked her as she walked backward on her heels toward the desk her lamp was on. Her ass hit the edge at the same time as she jerked the drawer open. He could have stopped her, but he just watched as she pulled a taser gun out and pointed it at him.

"You creepy, stalkery son-of-a-bitch!" she snarled, spreading her legs and bringing both of her hands up to hold the weapon steadily on him. "Why the fuck are you doing this to me? I can have your ass for this shit! Lay one more finger on me, asshole, and I will fucking cross the line with you. You think you're badass? You think you're untouchable? Well, I know people in this world, too, and I can have you dealt with, fucker. I'm Riley Bancroft, I'll have your ass before you can have mine!"

Her heart thundered as she waited for his response. As the rush of anger began to recede, she started to silently berate herself. Her options were pretty slim. She was probably going to die just for threatening Soloman Hart. People died for looking at this guy funny and she was pointing a weapon at him.

He didn't threaten her though. He did something she'd never seen him do. Probably no one ever saw him do. He started laughing. It was a quiet, sinister laugh, that shook his large frame. His eyes shone with pride as he took her in from her ankle boots to the long curls cascading from her high ponytail.

"You just solidified your fate, little girl. No fucking way I'm letting you go now," his deep voice shivered through her until she was gasping with dismay.

He moved so fast she didn't have time to blink. He grabbed her wrist in one hand and her neck in the other, cutting off a startled scream. He lifted her off her feet with an easy strength that terrified her. He could crush her throat under those long fingers with just a little more pressure. She tried to kick out at him, but he shook her once, twice, then walked backwards with her until she hit the edge of the desk. He smashed her arm against the wood until she was forced to drop the taser. It clattered to the floor.

She looked up at him with wide, tear-drenched eyes, expecting to die. He forced his hips between her legs until her skirt rode up her thighs, nearly to her hips. He let go of her wrist and wrapped both huge hands around her fragile neck. He didn't choke her, but the threat was definitely there. She brought her hands up to clutch his forearms over his smooth, expensive suit jacket. He jerked her upright until she was sitting up on the desk. She was nearly eye to eye with him now.

"Now, you will listen to me, Riley Bancroft," he growled, the smile leaving his lips as darkness leaked back into his eyes. She was so close to him she could feel the heat rolling off his big body and enveloping her like a cage. She could smell the subtle spice of his cologne and see every nuance of the scar that slashed through his lip, causing it to droop a little. She opened her mouth to tell him to go fuck himself, but his fingers tensed, cutting off her air supply for a few precious seconds. When he allowed her to breathe, she gasped and choked, glaring at him.

"No more talking," he snarled, his flat eyes taking in every tiny expression she made as though memorizing and keeping them. "It's my turn."

He stepped closer, pressing himself into the cradle of her thighs. She felt the bulge of his erection straining against his pants and struggled to tilt her hips away from him, but his hold was unbreakable. She was forced to feel every solid inch of him pressed intimately against her.

When he spoke, his breath fanned across her lips. "You will become mine, Riley Bancroft." Her eyes flared wide in anger, but she didn't speak, aware that the hands on her throat could and would tighten. "I'm not talking about fucking that delicious body, although I will definitely be doing that too. I plan on keeping you, which is why I haven't just taken you to my bed and scratched this itch. You need to get used to the idea of being in my life. So, we're going to get to know each other. Go out a little, until you're more comfortable in my world. Understand?"

Her eyes narrowed. He relaxed his hold on her throat.

"I asked you a question, Riley," he said impatiently. "When I ask a question, I expect an immediate response."

She raised an eyebrow and licked her lips, drawing his dark gaze to her full lips. "Oh, am I allowed to speak now? I didn't want to risk strangulation."

He stiffened and brought his hand to her ponytail, clenched his fingers in the soft, smooth strands and jerked her head back. She cried out and arched back to relieve the pressure. Her breasts shot forward into his chest, drawing an involuntary groan from him. He flexed his other hand into her shoulder blade and leaned against her, biting into the flesh between her neck and shoulder. She yelled, her hips jerking up against him as pleasure and pain flooded her body.

"You want to play games with me, little girl?" he growled in her ear, his hot breath sending tingles racing through her. "I don't have to give you the time I just promised. I could throw my cards down now, chain you naked to the bottom of my bed, bring in a priest that doesn't care if the bride is reluctant and then fuck you into submission for as long as it takes to break you to my way of thinking. That what you want?"

She whimpered. *Bride? Did he say fucking bride?*

"I understand!" she gasped, clutching him like she was drowning and he was her lifeline. "I want more time… please."

He moved back a little and took both of her hands in one of his. He looked down into her desperate face, taking in the shock. He nodded in satisfaction. Gently, he leaned forward and kissed her shaking lips, taking her gorgeous, lush mouth for the first time. He ended the chaste kiss quickly and stepped away from her, leaving her sprawled half on the desk. She had to bring her hands down to clutch at the wood on either side of her hips so she wouldn't fall. Her skirt was pushed up nearly to her hips, exposing her black, lace thong to his hungry gaze. His eyes were drawn to her open legs.

Feeling exposed, she tried to close them, but he growled, "Don't move."

She froze.

"If I don't get to fuck you tonight, I will at least look at what is soon to be mine." His dark tones slithered all down her spine and into every part of her body. She wanted to protest, but she was too happy that he was finally making a move to leave.

"I want to see you tomorrow," he said, his eyes never leaving her body.

"No," she answered immediately.

"Riley," his eyes snapped to hers and his voice held a hint of steel warning. "Do not make me repeat myself."

She sighed and, despite his threats, slid off the desk and tugged her skirt down. He allowed her to adjust her clothes without further comment. "I already have plans with friends tomorrow, Soloman."

She hoped using his given name would help sooth him. He made a displeased sound and she was afraid he would demand she break her plans, but he only asked, "Another date?"

She laughed bitterly. "No, I learned that lesson. I'm seeing Katie and a few other people for gaming. You know what that is, right? Where people get together and play video games, like first-person shooter or racing. You know, like Need for Speed or Battlefield. Or sometimes we go old school and play Legend of Zelda." She made it sound like he was so old and out of touch he couldn't possibly understand what she was talking about.

He gave her a cold look and then slowly nodded his head. "Fine, I'll call you then. We'll go out another night. Make sure you answer my call, Riley."

She narrowed her eyes at him but didn't say anything. She really didn't like his tone. He reached for the door and then looked back at her one more time. His face was in shadows, but she could see the glint of his dark eyes. She shivered.

"One more thing," he said, his deep voice stern. "No more racing, Riley. It's too dangerous."

Her jaw dropped and fury shot through her, stiffening her limbs before she hid her reaction. He took in every part of her and nodded slowly. He knew she was angry and he knew she wasn't about to listen to his arrogant demand.

"You will not like the consequences if you disobey me in this," he growled at her, his voice wrapping around her from across the room. "It's one thing to talk back to me, to ignore my summons, but it will be something else entirely to put yourself – to put *my woman* – in danger. Stay away from Sparrow Hawk."

She desperately wanted to tell him to go fuck himself. In fact, she had to bite her lip to stop herself from screaming at him so loud the neighbours would probably call the cops. She vibrated with fury as he turned and walked out the door, closing it softly behind him. She ran toward it on shaking legs and slammed the bolt shut, knowing in her heart that he could easily get in any time he wanted. She turned around and leaned against it, closing her eyes while she calmed down.

Finally, when she felt her legs would hold her, she strode down the hall toward her bedroom, shoes clicking with purpose. She slammed the light switch on with the heel of her hand. Going to her knees on the plush carpet next to the bed, she reached underneath. Shoving shoeboxes and junk aside, she reached for the thing she wanted, a steel lockbox.

"Okay, you scary motherfucker," she whispered into the empty room, pulling the lockbox out and sitting up. She flicked the correct numbers into place and opened the lid. Flipping through forged passports, money and a gun, she pulled out a burner phone. She plugged it in and leaned against the wall, waiting for it to charge enough for a call. "You want to play rough, I can play rough. This is some next level shit."

Heart beating with adrenaline and anger, she dialled a number she had hoped never to use. A crazy as fuck car buddy that she usually avoided. The guy was a psychopath that had a thing for Riley. He liked to bring her the occasional high-end stolen car as a 'gift.'She usually tried to fly under his radar, which worked fairly well since he was a gangbanger from another county and kept busy with guns and drugs. She didn't like the idea of bringing his focus back to her, but she was reaching the point of having to decide which evil was worse. And Soloman Hart was definitely worse.

"Nobody puts hands on me without permission," she breathed angrily as she waited for Shank to answer.

CHAPTER SEVEN

"Shift, shift, shift, Riley!" Katie screamed, jumping up and down on the couch next to Riley, nearly causing her to drive into the ditch. "He's going to beat you if you don't get out of there!"

"Do you want to drive?" Riley growled, grabbing Katie by the ankle and yanking her down on the couch. Katie went flying and landed on her butt in a flurry of hot pink painted toenails, fingernails and mini skirt. All male eyes in the vicinity were on the blond to see if they could catch a glimpse of panty as she fell.

"Oomph!" The breath whooshed out of her as she landed. "Bitch!"

Riley looped an arm around Katie's neck and gave her a smacking kiss on the cheek as she continued racing her virtual McLaren against Roadkill's Lamborghini in Need for Speed. An eruption of sound went up around them as Riley beat him out. He won the first two races so she wasn't exactly on a winning streak. Still, she was pretty pleased with herself. She shouted and laughed, pointing at him as he took the ribbing with good humour.

He pointed back at her. "This isn't over, Reaper. Next time I'll toss you off the cliff myself."

"You'd have to catch me first, Aussie!" she shouted after him as he grabbed his girlfriend and headed across the bar to get another drink. He gave her the finger over his shoulder.

Katie laughed and picked up her cosmopolitan. "As much as I love watching you kick Roadkill's ass, I'd rather play a shooter next. I suck at these ones."

"You're on, Kit Kat. Let's go find one," Riley agreed, hopping off the couch and holding out a hand for her friend.

She needed a quieter space anyway so she could talk to Katie. They hadn't had two seconds to themselves since they'd arrived at the bar. They found a quiet corner with one of Katie's favourite games, Star Wars Battlefront, ready and available for play. Plunking down next to each other, they picked up the Playstation controllers and entered their information. They played for a few minutes before Riley broached the subject she needed to discuss.

"I need to ask you something and I don't think you're going to like it, so promise not to get mad at me, okay? We don't get enough bestie time when you come in for the odd weekend for you to be pissed at me."

Katie gave her a quick frown and then returned her focus to the game. "I'm not going to get mad at you. Trust me, after the years of shit you've pulled, I'm pretty immune to your surprising me. I mean, I kind of want to slap you silly every time you enter one of those stupid races, but I haven't yet, have I?"

Riley gave her a crooked smile. "Good point."

"So, what's up, Grim Reaper?" Katie only called her that when Riley got serious, which wasn't very often. They usually reserved Katie's weekends home for good times.

Riley sighed and glanced at Katie's lovely, blond profile. It always amazed her that the sophisticated, poised woman came out of the same hood as the rest of them. She was so much better and had risen so much higher. Yet she kept coming back to them and diving into their crap with a grin. She was priceless. Which is why Riley would do anything to protect the sweet, delicate beauty.

"Do you know Roman Valdez? And I don't mean as just a friend of Dexter's, but as something else. Something more?" Riley asked quietly.

Katie stiffened on the seat next to her. Slowly her thumb went to the pause button on her controller and her head turned toward Riley. Her sky-blue eyes held utter and complete shock. "Wh-why do you ask?" She shook her head and closed her eyes for a moment. "I mean, when did you see him? You did see him right… that's why you're asking me this?"

Riley nodded and glanced away from the intense longing in Katie's face. Fuck. There was definitely something going on between Roman and Katie. And apparently it went both ways. This was so not good.

"I saw him last night. He works for Soloman Hart."

Katie gasped and covered her mouth with a hand. Her eyes went even wider. She whispered, "I wondered what happened to him… after D-Dexter."

The aching in her voice was impossible to miss. It was like something had been wrenched away from her and was now just within reach. Riley reached out and took Katie's hand in hers. "Katie, these are dangerous men. They don't fuck around. It's bad enough that I somehow got mixed up in whatever this is that I'm mixed up in. I'm trying to get out. I need you to listen to me, okay?"

"Oh my god," Katie gasped, appalled. "What kind of trouble are you in? What are we going to do?"

Riley loved that her friend was talking like they could both solve the problem of Soloman Hart. She reached out and hugged her best friend. She missed having her in the same city. They had grown up just a few blocks from each other.

Riley was two years older, but they had been fast friends since Riley was fourteen and Katie was twelve, when Riley had beat the shit out of two school bullies that had flipped Katie's skirt up on the playground.

"I need you to please, please stay out of things," Riley begged. "I want you to take another business contract and leave town for a while. As much as I love seeing you, I need you to be scarce right now until I can sort this thing out."

She looked into Katie's face to make sure she understood and agreed. Katie nodded. "I don't like the idea of leaving you alone to deal with someone like him. Jesus, Riley, this is Soloman Hart we're talking about. *The* Soloman Hart! Your dad would lose his mind if he knew you got mixed up with that guy. He's so dangerous. People that mess with him disappear."

Riley swallowed and nodded. "I know. That's why I can't have you around right now. He doesn't play nice. He'll go after the people I'm closest to. This Roman guy is his right hand and… and there's something between you two."

"There's nothing!" Katie protested. "Not really, and not for years. I shouldn't leave you just based on something small like that. He had a thing for me, but we never acted on it."

"It doesn't matter," Riley continued. "He wants you. He made it clear that he planned on going after you, regardless of how you or I feel on the matter. And Katie, this guy doesn't mess around. If you think Soloman Hart's reputation is ruthless, Roman is just as bad. He's a legend on the streets these days. You need to leave town and do it now. Just pack up and go once we're done here."

Katie shivered under Riley's hands. She nodded and said, "Yeah, I'll go if it means that much to you. I already know I can't handle Roman. It's why I never tried. I have another job lined up for Paris anyway. I can leave tomorrow morning. But first, let's play. I need at least a few hours of bestie time to tide me over."

Riley arched a brow and grinned. Reaching for her controller, she said, "Paris? Ooh la la. Fancy little darling, aren't we? Bring me back something good."

Katie laughed and hit the play button on her controller. "I always do."

Several hours later, Riley was one of the last to leave the gaming bar. She was a night owl and loved gaming. It was rare that she got to hang out with her friends though, so when a chance like this came up, she liked to make the most of it. She waved at Lula and Roadkill as they got into a cab. Riley slid in behind the wheel of her Spitfire, having only drunk orange juice all night. She turned the key in the ignition, but nothing happened.

"Impossible," she grumbled with a frown. She kept all of her vehicles in excellent condition, but especially this one since it had belonged to her dad and it was the first car he ever gave her. There was no chance the engine wouldn't fire. She turned the key again. And again, nothing happened.

She pulled the hood release with a sigh and climbed out of the car. She was forced to use the flashlight on her phone since she hadn't parked close enough to a streetlight to be able to properly see what was going on under her hood. Frowning, she checked the battery connections, starter and distributor. But where the hell was the starter coil?

"What the fuck…?" she mumbled just as an arm snaked out around her waist, lifting her off the ground.

She opened her mouth to scream, but a hand slammed over her mouth, cutting off the sound. She felt herself being bent over her car and dry humped from behind. She screamed into the hand smashed against her lips and wriggled wildly.

Terror thrummed through her veins. She kicked out at the man holding her, but her Sketchers did next to nothing against the strong hold. Finally, the guy quit humping her after one last thrust, lifted her away from the car and dropped her. Riley spun around and drew her fist back in a punch when she saw who had been holding her.

"Shank!" she gasped, her face screwed up in disgust.

He grinned down at her, his crooked teeth gleaming in the dim streetlights. He was wearing baggy ripped blue jeans and a grey T-shirt that moulded to his hard, lean muscles. His head was shaved and tattoos showed on every visible part of his body, including a grinning skull plastered across his face. Most of his tats were emblazoned with gang images. He reached out to grab her again and she threw up a hand to push him away.

This was exactly why she hesitated to call on Shank. He was crazy as fuck. Everything he did was extreme, including sabotaging her car so he could sneak up on her and scare her. Then he would touch her at every opportunity. She was so going home to burn her clothes and shower after this. Which was really too bad because she was wearing her favourite pair of flower-embroidered skinny jeans.

"What the fuck did you do to my poor baby, you sick bastard?" she demanded angrily, shoving him back and stepping out of his reach.

"Oh shit, Reaper baby," he groaned when her fingers bit into the muscles of his chest. He stepped up to her car, bent over and reached into the engine. "I love it when you play rough with me. Gives me memories for the cold nights, you know?"

"You make me sick," she snarled.

"Yeah, keep talking, pretty little angel. You know I like it like that. Just gonna picture those lips wrapped around my…"

"Keep it up motherfucker and I'll cut it off."

He grinned at her, his eyes roving over her curves. She shivered and wondered if calling on Shank was just plain stupid. How did she imagine she could control this man? He was as psychotic as they came. The only reason he was still alive is he was just too mean to die. In fact, she was pretty certain he had that phrase tattooed somewhere on his body.

He dropped her hood and patted the roadster affectionately. "Good as new, angel. Now tell me what made the Reaper come calling on her favourite bro?"

Riley sighed heavily and rubbed a hand across her forehead. The damage was already done. She'd called on Shank and brought his focus back on her. For better or worse she was back in his spotlight until gang life called him back. She may as well make use of his crazy ass self.

"I'm having a problem with a guy," she mumbled.

"Yeah?" he said hopefully, cracking his knuckles. "Just point me in his direction and I'll take care of it, sweetheart. He won't be a problem for much longer. You and me? We meant to be, darling. I always knew you'd come around eventually."

He grabbed her around the waist and tried to bend her backward over the car. Riley punched him in the shoulder and wiggled out from under him. "Not a chance, Shank!"

He looked like he was going to reach for her again. She held a hand up. "No touching, dude!" she snarled. "I am not now, nor have I ever been, interested. Fuck, man. How can I be any clearer? I called you because you have a certain reputation for low down psycho shit and surviving things other people don't usually."

He dropped his hands and looked thoughtful. "Yeah, those are valid points. Though it does hurt my feelings a little that you aren't willing to consider me for more. I'd make a great husband. We both agree, I'm very durable."

Riley put her face in her hands and started laughing at the absurd thought of marriage to this man. She snapped out of it when she felt his fingers curve around her shoulders. She jumped back and threw his arms off her. "I said no touching!"

"Okay, okay!" He backed up a few steps. "So, who's the guy?"

She chewed on her lip for a few seconds and then said, "Soloman Hart."

His jaw dropped as shock registered on his pock-marked, tattooed face. A bark of laughter left his lips. "How the fuck did you get mixed up with that guy? Jesus fuck, Reaper. You want me to kill Soloman Hart? I know I'm into some insane stuff, but that's some next level shit."

"I don't want you to kill him. Well... not really. Too dangerous, for both of us," she said, glancing around the empty parking lot as though expecting Soloman's sinister frame to be standing in the shadows watching over her.

Oddly, she was more afraid of him finding her alone with another man than finding her plotting his downfall. Soloman could take care of himself. She was starting to think she was the one that couldn't take care of herself and she just hadn't known it until he came along and started breaking into her life.

"Just mess with him a little, take his attention away from me until I can think of a way to get out from under his thumb."

"Baby, it's gonna take a bomb to divert attention away from you," Shank said, laughing. "Because you da bomb. Get it?"

She rolled her eyes and walked around to the driver's side of her car. "I don't care what you do. Fuck with his business interests or whatever. Just be careful. Dude is one dangerous motherfucker."

He placed a hand over his heart. "You worried about me, angel?"

She rolled her eyes and shook her head, but smiled. "Just don't get caught."

He nodded, his eyes dropping to her chest. "You gonna owe me for this one."

She shivered and crossed her arms. She would never in a

million years give Shank what he really wanted from her. Not *ever* happening. "Don't worry, I can pay you."

He nodded and stalked toward his own car, a '69 Dodge Charger. How she missed that beauty in the shadows she did not know. His car was what had originally drawn them together. She'd boosted it when she was twenty-three. He'd hunted it down at her shop before she got a chance to flip it. In return for her life, she'd had to boost three more cars and give him the profits. She'd gotten to know the weird psycho and his crew in the process. He fell a little in love with her, but she was able to keep him at arm's length. Thank goodness he lived in a different county. He was one scary son-of-a-bitch when he wanted to be.

CHAPTER EIGHT

Riley rubbed at the headache building in her temples. She shoved her office chair away from her desk, rolled toward the door and smacked the light switch, turning off the bright overhead lights. She closed the door while she was at it, muffling the shop noises. She sighed in satisfaction. That felt so much better. Closing her eyes, she sat in the darkened office and just enjoyed the feel of the fan blowing across her bare arms and shoulders for a few minutes. The accounts weren't going anywhere.

Neither was the gift-wrapped box shoved to the edge of her desk. She was pretty sure it was the prospect of the box that was giving her a headache. The beautiful, tastefully wrapped silver box with a white bow had been distracting her from the moment it arrived in the garage. She'd quickly signed for it and whisked it away from the curious eyes of her mechanics. A quick peak at the hand-written card had confirmed her suspicion.

Riley,
Wear this tonight.
Yours,
S

She hadn't opened the box. It was too small to be clothing unless it was intimate apparel, in which case she was going to drive to his estate home on the edge of the city and burn it to the ground. Which would be extremely dangerous. Or it was jewelry, which wasn't something she wanted from him. Which is why she'd had the box for three hours without opening it. And managed to complete exactly two out of the fifteen invoices she needed to finish.

She groaned when her iPhone began playing House of The Rising Sun, the Sons of Anarchy version. She opened her eyes and reached for it. Her breath caught in her throat when she saw the number. She hadn't been brave enough to put his contact information into her phone, but she'd memorized the number. She'd been secretly hoping he would just never call her back. She let it go to voicemail. Seconds later it began ringing again. She cursed the man for ruining her favourite song.

Helplessly, she swiped her black painted fingernail across the screen and lifted the phone to her ear. "Soloman," she acknowledged.

"Hello, Riley," he said, his deep voice caressing her name with satisfaction.

"What do you want?" she asked coldly.

"Why haven't you opened my gift yet?" he asked, a chiding edge to his voice.

She sat up straight, her elbow hitting the edge of the desk with a thump. She sucked air in through her teeth and rubbed her elbow while looking around in consternation. What the fuck? How did he know she hadn't opened his gift? Did he have eyes on her or something, or did he think he just knew her that well? Either option wasn't particularly acceptable. She glanced up at the camera she kept in her office in case of break-ins.

"I'm not interested in your gifts," she said coldly. "You can take it back."

He didn't say anything for a moment, then he spoke, more forceful this time, less indulgent. "Open it, Riley. Do it right now."

The breath caught in her throat. She knew he wasn't in the shop, she would have seen him. Yet her body went cold as though he were right there, commanding her to obey. She had the urge to reach for the box. She clenched her fist against her thigh, curling her hand against the faded, oil-stained denim. She shook her head, her ponytail swaying against her back.

"No."

"You do not want to play right now, Riley. I am reaching the end of my patience with your resistance. Remember my words. I will drive down to your little shop right now, shut it down and bring you home, where you can serve me on your knees. Is that what you want, little girl?" His words were rough, but they wrapped around her like smooth silk bonds.

She shivered and opened her hand, sliding her spread fingers along her thigh, wiping away the sudden dampness. She shook her head again and whispered into the dim interior of her office, "I don't want that."

"Good girl," he purred. "All you have to do is open the box and look inside."

Without speaking, she reached out and pulled the box across her desk. Papers fell to the floor as she tipped the box into her lap. She ignored them. Bracing the box against her stomach, she jerked the bow open and flicked the top off. Her eyes widened when she saw what was inside. She held it up with shaking fingers so she could see it in the little bit of natural light filtering through the blinds.

"Oh my god," she gasped, staring in dismay at one of the most incredible pieces of jewelry she'd ever touched.

"Wear it tonight with something appropriate," he instructed.

She shook her head, eyes wide. It was beautiful. It was barbaric. She couldn't possibly wear it around him. Everyone would know it was a stamp of ownership. *His ownership*. She dropped it onto her desk as though it were a handful of spiders.

"No," she said clearly.

"No?" he repeated, his voice taking on a steel edge. "No, you won't wear it, or no, you won't come out with me?"

Taking a deep breath, she answered him, eyes never leaving his gift. "Take your pick, Soloman. I don't want to play this game with you. Just… just take this thing back and leave me the fuck alone."

"This is not the answer you want to give me, Riley."

She hung up on him and turned her phone off.

CHAPTER NINE

Finally, her headache was completely gone. Riley lay back in the tub enjoying the scent of vanilla and lavender candles permeating the steam coming off the hot water from her bath. Lorde's Pure Heroine album played from her phone through a Bluetooth speaker, filling the small washroom with music. Her hair was piled high on her head so it wouldn't get wet. Her shoulders and breasts were covered in vanilla scented bubbles. She was in heaven, which was saying something considering the day she'd had.

She'd been pretty worried that Soloman would make good on his threat and show up at the shop to drag her away. Plus, the cops had come sniffing around about a stolen Mercedes SUV. Wendell had done his usual dog and pony show of giving them the correct paperwork for all of the vehicles in the shop. He was really quite remarkable at shaking his head in commiseration and looking innocent. The SUV had been in the part of the garage they didn't take the tourists to. Underneath the lifts there were false concrete pads. Her dad had done such a good job of building the shop, law enforcement had never been able to find the extra space.

With a lazy sigh, she lifted one leg at a time and dragged a loofa across the silken skin, debating whether or not to shave. Though she had dark chestnut hair, she'd thankfully inherited light coloured hair on her arms and legs from her blond mother. She didn't have to shave her legs more than once per week to stay nice and smooth. And despite her somewhat racy reputation, she hadn't actually been to bed with a guy in almost two years, so her shaving regime had fallen a little to the wayside. She was choosy about men and she had a business to run. Though she liked to have fun, she rarely found anyone actually worth taking home.

When her music cut out and House of the Rising Sun began playing she scrunched her eyes shut and groaned. With a sigh, she reached for her phone, knowing she wasn't going to enjoy this conversation one little bit.

"Soloman," she growled.

"Roman is outside waiting for you. I want you to meet me at one of my clubs," he said, his voice sounding chill to her ears, as though he knew she would deny him again and was preparing to play hardball with her. She sat up in the tub, splashing the water a little. "Do not... wait, are you taking a bath?" His voice took on a surprised tone.

She smiled despite herself. She got the feeling he hadn't intended to ask her that. "None of your damn business, Soloman," she replied haughtily, purposely splashing the water a little more so he couldn't miss the sound.

He cleared his throat and growled, "Invite me over, Riley, right fucking now, and I will forget your constant disobedience and the punishments I have racking up for you."

"What, are you a fucking vampire now? Since when have I had to send an invitation for you to show up at my place? Last I checked, you just wander in at will."

He ignored her and growled, "I promise you will enjoy our night together if you just say the words to me."

The breath rushed out from between her lips before she could stop it. She knew he could hear the small gasp. Knew that he knew he affected her just as much as she affected him. Fuck, it still didn't give him the right to force her will to his. Despite the fact that her nipples tightened against the edge of the tub where she clutched it tightly. That her body begged her to give him the words he wanted, to ask him over.

Wait, punishments? What punishments? Fuck him!

"Fuck you, Soloman!" she snapped. "You don't get to tell me what to do. Ever! You don't get to fucking send me gifts and dictate what I wear or where I'm going to wear it. And you don't get to demand dates with me, asshole. I'm so over this shit!"

She could feel his anger rising through the phone as though it were a living thing. She stood in the tub and reached for a towel, suddenly feeling too vulnerable. Wrapping it around herself as best she could with one hand, she hurried dripping through her apartment to the front window. It was next to the door. She peeked through the curtain, down to the street. Sure enough, she could see Roman standing next to Soloman's S7 looking bored while he waited for her.

"We haven't even begun yet, little girl, and we will *never* be over," Soloman's voice whipped through the phone. "Go get dressed right now or Roman will come through that door in two minutes and drag your ass down to my club, naked or not. I'm partial to the second option, although if you force my man to put his hands on your bare body, you better believe I will beat your ass when I get my hands on it."

Her breath came out in short, gasping pants. She could see Roman check his phone, then look up toward her condo. He turned and started striding toward the building, his long legs eating up the distance to her place. She whirled on the spot, letting the curtain drop and ran full tilt down the hall toward her bedroom.

"And Riley?"

"What?" she asked in a panicked gasp.

"Wear my gift."

Soloman had never been a patient man. He was used to getting what he wanted and killing the things that stood in the way. The dance he had decided to engage in with Riley Bancroft was one of the most enjoyable things he could remember doing in recent memory. All of his pursuits thus far had been for power, money and stability. This was for him. He was amazed at the patience he was cultivating for this woman. Though his dick was begging him to get on with things. Every time he saw her, touched her, was like fresh torture.

He took a long drink of A.H. Hirsch Reserve bourbon, neat, and watched the ebb and flow of a busy Tuesday night in his underground casino from the privacy of his screened office. Setting the glass down, he took a draw of his cigarillo, allowing the smoke to linger in his mouth. It was a habit he had picked up years ago to replace cigarettes. His dark and lushly decorated office was set on the floor above the casino, so he could see everything, including the beautiful, if somewhat oddly dressed, brunette being hustled in through the side door by a grim-faced Roman.

Soloman assumed the grim face was due to whatever sharp tirade she was treating his bodyguard to. His lips quirked as Roman's fingers tightened noticeably and he gave the woman a little shake before dragging her up the stairs toward Soloman's office. He would have to speak to Roman about manhandling Riley. Though he sympathized, as the woman would have tried the patience of Mother Teresa herself, she was not to be touched unless absolutely necessary.

Roman knocked, waited for Soloman's sharp command to enter, then punched in the code to his office. Soloman remained by the window while Roman ushered Riley into his private sanctum. She looked pissed and was doing nothing to hide her anger.

"Thank you, Roman," Soloman nodded toward his man, dismissing him.

Roman grunted, shot Riley a look that clearly said it didn't matter how hot she was, he'd rather put a bullet in her. He turned on his heel and left the room, slamming the door shut behind him. Soloman arched an eyebrow in curiosity. What had she said to him? Roman wasn't usually so hostile toward women.

"Your fucking dog has no manners, Soloman," Riley snapped, crossing her arms over her chest and glaring at him.

His eyes travelled down her body, taking in her ratty grey sweatpants and black T-shirt with a giant set of red lips emblazoned across the chest. He could see a hole in the side of the shirt showing glimpses of her creamy skin when she turned. Her hair was piled precariously on top of her head with long wisps framing her oval face. She wore no make-up.

"What happened?" he asked, pretty certain anything Roman had done to her was at least partially a result of self-defence. Riley was turning out to be a bit of a hellcat.

"He broke my taser!" she threw up her hands and stomped her foot, swinging her black purse with pink and white skulls wildly.

Soloman frowned. "You tried to taser my man after I told you he was coming to collect you? That was a bad choice, Riley. You're goddamned lucky he didn't put you down, little girl."

"No, asshole," she growled. "I tried to taser him after he admitted to me he kissed Katie, *against her will*, and then tried to make me leave my condo. Also against my will."

Soloman closed his eyes for a moment, torn between amusement and annoyance. This woman really didn't do anything easy. And he wasn't used to having to work for the things he wanted. She smelled like vanilla spice and lavender.

He wanted to fuck her more than he'd wanted anything in his life.

He found himself asking one of the least badass questions he thought he would ever have to ask in his career. "And how exactly do you know Roman kissed Katie," he sighed and rubbed the bridge of his nose, "against her will?"

"Because the fucker bragged about it!" she snapped, rolling her eyes. "And *obviously* she wouldn't have kissed him willingly. So, I *obviously* had to respond by tasering the shit out of him. For the sake of the sisterhood."

"Obviously," he repeated dryly. "How did Roman respond when you tried to shoot him?"

"I told you!" she snarled, tossing her bag down on the table and causing his drink to jump. "He grabbed my taser and broke it like it was some kind of child's toy. Then he tossed me over his shoulder like the caveman he is and shoved me in your shitty, pretentious car. The Neanderthal fucker."

"Watch your language, Riley. I've allowed a lot of leeway where you're concerned, but it is time for you to start acting with a little more dignity. As is befitting my woman," he said coolly.

She stared at him for a moment, her eyebrow slowly rising. Then she burst out laughing. "That is some kind of My Fair Lady bullshit," she said in a crude cockney accent, pointing her finger at him. "Good luck with that, professor."

Ignoring her, he continued. "And watch how you treat my bodyguard. He isn't a man used to taking insults lightly. Your actions toward him are only tolerated because of my interest in you."

"Oh yeah," she said haughtily, her lip curling, "and I'm only in danger from your damn dog because of your interest in me. So maybe you should back the fuck off!"

He stalked toward her, reaching for her arm before she had a chance to back away from him. Her eyes widened in alarm, but he wrapped his fingers around her resilient, smooth bicep before she could move. He yanked her into the hardness of his body, exactly where she should be and growled into her face, "No fucking chance."

Her breath whooshed out in a gasp as she stared up at him with wide, melted chocolate eyes. Though she sounded like a bitchy, world-weary siren, those eyes belied her nervousness every time. Her tongue poked out from between gorgeous plush lips to moisten them. His body begged him to drag her loose sweatpants down her hips and shove his fingers deep into her body, then shove her to the floor and fuck that begging mouth.

"You're not wearing my gift," he said, his voice holding an edge he couldn't contain.

His body was so wound up he knew he would have to find some kind of release, even if he couldn't fuck her yet. He fingered the length of her delicate throat. She tried to flinch away from him, but he held her by the back of the neck. He didn't care if it made him a sick bastard, he loved the size difference between them. He loved that she could try to flutter against him, beat her wings like a bird trying to escape. She would fail every time and he would be right there waiting to cage her.

With a huff, she unzipped her purse, reached inside and pulled out the choker he had bought for her. She dropped it on the table, supremely uncaring of the value as they hit the marble. Soloman felt his blood pressure rise and had to remind himself that it was her fiery nature he was attempting to cultivate for himself.

Still, he was not gentle when he took her jaw in his hand and jerked her around to look at him. "When I purchase a gift for you, I expect you to accept it and wear it when I tell you to wear it," he said with quiet menace.

"I don't like it and I won't wear it," she said simply, glaring up at him, every line of her body set in stubbornness.

Her pupils dilated until her eyes were nearly black. She was afraid of him and what he could do to her, but she wasn't so afraid of him that she was willing to back down. He had threatened Katie and that had turned out fine, except for a little unwilling kissing. Apparently.

Soloman rolled his shoulders and cracked his neck. Closing his eyes, he nodded his head. Fine. If this was how she wanted to play it, he would set his cards on the table. She would hate him for what he was about to do, but he was reaching the end of his patience with her continued resistance. Maintaining his grip on her arm, he dragged her toward the wide, one-way window of his office. She stumbled against him a little at the sudden movement and reached out to grab hold of his other arm for balance.

She frowned as he swept the heavy curtain aside and pushed her forward with a heavy hand at the small of her back. Knowing how she would react, he stepped up behind her, caging her against the window. She glanced back at him in confusion. He took her chin in one hand and pointed down at one of the poker tables with his other. He knew the moment she saw her mother.

Riley's entire body stiffened and a cry like a wounded animal tore from her lips. She jerked against him with more strength than he would have thought possible, lunging sideways in an attempt to break free and run toward the door. He knew that she was instinctively trying to get to her mother so she could tear her away from the poker game. Riley fought an angry, silent battle with Soloman for long minutes.

He wrapped his arms around her, holding her tightly as she cried out, kicking and thrashing against him. Her arms were pinned at her sides so she couldn't scratch him, but she managed to get a few good kicks in. He was forced to haul them away from the window when she managed to get her feet up in a good kick that shook the entire thing. She fought wildly against him, until he was forced to take her down to the hard floor and pin her body beneath his.

She lay curled on her side with her arms wrenched behind her in his strong grip. She panted and heaved against him while he crouched over top of her. She managed to twist her head around and sink her teeth into his wrist before he could reposition her arms further back.

"Little bitch!" he snapped, taking her jaw in one hand and restraining her wrists in the other. He pinned her kicking legs beneath his own. He knew he could have ended their fight a lot quicker if he'd been willing to hurt her. She was damn lucky she was the only goddamned person in the world that would get away with the shit she'd been throwing at him.

"You need to calm the fuck down right fucking now, Riley. Or I will be forced to hurt you," he growled in her ear, tightening his fingers around her wrists to the point of pain.

"You've fucked with my family, you bastard!" she hissed up at him, "You've already done your worst."

He laughed cruelly and shook her with his grip on her jaw, bumping her head against the floor. "Pay attention, little girl, because I won't say this again. I have wanted you from the moment I laid eyes on you. And I have been *very* patient compared to my usual expectations. Cilia Bancroft is out there counting cards in my casino, we both know this. You managed to keep her secret well hidden, my gorgeous girl. No one on this town knows what she's capable of, but I have found her out."

The breath whooshed out of her lungs and she froze beneath him. He leaned in and whispered in her ear. "Now what should I do about this information? Do you want to know what I would normally do to someone counting cards in my casino? Even with someone as beautiful and intelligent as Cilia."

A tear trickled from the corner of Riley's eye, running across her nose and then down her plush lips. He ran his thumb over her lip, capturing the sign of her surrender. For the first time since his youth, Soloman felt something close to remorse. Had he gone too far in threatening the woman's mother? His Riley was fierce, but also vulnerable and possibly breakable. He was a monster with a black soul. He hadn't had to be tender with anyone. Ever. He didn't know if he was even capable of such an action.

He turned her so she was laying on her back underneath him. She looked up at him with such hatred that he knew she was ready to give him what he wanted. He felt both satisfaction and concern. First, he would continue to play their game, then he would figure out a way to force her forgiveness.

"What do you want from me?" she whispered.

That was more like it. She was starting to ask the right questions. "I want you to wear my gift."

She nodded her head. "And… and if I wear your gift, you won't hurt my mom?" she asked, anxiety lacing her voice.

Fuck. He had played this hand a little too well. He'd wanted to make her more biddable, he hadn't wanted her to worry that he was about to murder her mother at any moment. But it was too late for him to reassure her. He pulled her to her feet, careful to watch for signs that she might attack him again. She merely stood stiffly, watching him warily.

He strode toward the window and dropped the black, velvet curtain back into place. She didn't need the distraction. The next little while would be about them. "If you do as I say, then Mrs. Bancroft will be fine."

Panic flashed across her beautiful face and her hands clenched into fists at her side. "Fuck, Soloman. I'm just not so good at listening. What if… what if I accidentally piss you off? Will you… oh god?" Tears filled her eyes and she stared at him helplessly.

He chuckled darkly. "I'm well aware of your ability to piss me off. How about you do your best to listen to me and we'll go from there. Sound good?"

She nodded, her eyes still wide and wet with worry. She chewed on her full lower lip. He had the urge to shove his thumb into her mouth while ravaging her pussy with his cock. His body responded quickly to the thought and he nearly groaned out loud. Running a hand down his face, he said, "Why don't we start with the choker? Bring it here."

She picked up the expensive piece of jewelry and approached him, trepidation in each step she took. She clearly wanted nothing to do with him now that she'd seen exactly what kind of ruthless machinations he was capable of. Not that she wanted anything to do with him before, but there had been *some* flirting. Now he saw only fear in her beautiful velvet eyes. He was going to have to distract her. Refocus her terror and train her body so it responded to him, despite what her brain screamed at her.

He took the choker from her cold fingers and, placing a hand on her delicate shoulder, turned her so she faced away from him. Reaching around her, he slipped the necklace around the base of her long, beautiful neck and latched it at the back. He turned her around and looked down at it, possession blazing sharply in his dark, almost black eyes.

He took her hand and pulled her to the mirror next to his bar. He stood her in front of it and forced her to look at herself wearing his property. It was a black and silver entwined choker with a black diamond encrusted 'S' in the front surrounded by silver vines. It was very beautiful and very pagan. The flowing lines gave it a fluidity, but the letter with his initial made it feel barbaric.

Bending, he whispered in her ear, "I believe I told you to wear something appropriate with it."

"What?" she said, her confused gaze clashing with his in the mirror.

His hands went to the waistband of her sweatpants and bit into the flesh of her hips. "Since you chose not to dress appropriately for the occasion, then you can wear the next best thing with your new necklace."

Riley's breath caught in her throat and she stared at him. His fingers slid further into her waistband, caressing her hipbones and pressing further into her flesh as if testing the resiliency. His thumbs pressed into the generous flesh of her ass as his hands spanned her from front to back.

"Wh-what do you want me to wear?" she asked, finally managing to find her voice.

"Nothing."

CHAPTER TEN

He was sitting behind his desk, watching her as she slowly stripped her T-shirt over her head. She had already kicked off her Sketchers. Riley closed her eyes, trying to block him out. How had life gotten so fucked up and out of control that she was doing a striptease for the most dangerous mafia boss in town, right in the office of his underground casino? She could feel the heat of his eyes on her and knew he was tracing every inch of creamy flesh she revealed. Her mind frantically scrambled over the problem of which piece of clothing to take off next.

"The sweats," his deep voice instructed, reading her mind.

Her eyes flew open to meet his. When she saw amusement written on his face in the curl of his lip and glint in his eye, she wanted nothing more than to stalk over to his bar and start hurling expensive liquor bottles at his arrogant head. She would have done it too, if her mom weren't right downstairs within easy reach of a dozen knee-breakers.

Narrowing her eyes, Riley reached for the waistband of her oldest pair of grey sweatpants and shoved them as unsexily as she could down her legs. She kicked them off and then turned to glare at him, her temper rising with each lost item of clothing. Next, she reached behind her and unsnapped the hooks on her C-cup bra. She shrugged it off and let it fall to the floor, while simultaneously bringing her arms up to cover her breasts from his view.

Soloman stood, his hot, demanding gaze sweeping over her. He unbuttoned his suit jacket and shrugged out of it, tossing it over the back of his chair. Then he removed his cufflinks and dropped them onto his desk. A quick glimpse showed her that they were silver with a black diamond S on them. Her heart jumped as she realized he had marked her with the same jewelry he wore. Her wary gaze remained glued to his every movement. He rolled up the sleeves of his fine white dress shirt, pulled his tie off and unbuttoned the top few buttons. The tattoo on the back of his hand showed stark on his skin. Others flowed up arms to the edge of his shirt and then continued on his chest and neck.

The scar on his lip looked more sinister than ever when he turned to look at her. His cold dark eyes, touching her exposed skin, made her feel both hot and cold. She shivered under the onslaught of emotion. "Drop your hands, Riley. I want to see what's mine."

A whimper broke free from her lips. She raised her chin and glared at him, but thrust her hands down to her side, exposing her breasts. She forced herself to watch him as his gaze roved over her pale, full, pink-tipped breasts. She wondered what he thought of the quote tattoo scrawled along her ribcage just under her left breast: "Life ain't always beautiful, but it's a beautiful ride." It was something her dad used to say. She'd gotten the tattoo done shortly after his death.

Soloman stepped forward, reaching for her. Riley stumbled back, but he took hold of her and forced her to stand still. He brought his other hand up and brushed it across the tip of her breast, causing the nipple to stand even stiffer. She gasped and tried to jerk back, but his fingers tightened in warning. She bit her lip and looked up at him, begging him with her eyes. She wasn't prepared for this, she couldn't do this!

She saw no mercy in his eyes. She saw nothing but raw lust and blazing possession. He had no intention of letting her leave until he was done exacting whatever he had brought her there for.

"Now the rest," he said, his deep voice sending shivers cascading down her spine.

She tilted her head back and whispered with every ounce of loathing she felt for him, "I hate you."

He nodded his head and replied, "It doesn't matter. Take it off." He removed his hand so she could take her underwear off, but he didn't step away from her, forcing her to bend over with him in her space.

Glaring up at him, she hooked her fingers into the edge of her soft, blue cotton panties and dragged them down her legs. Her face came within inches of his incredibly hard cock as she bent over. She felt his body stiffen as her breath fanned across his crotch. She could almost feel the fight within him to not grab her by the neck and shove her to the floor. She wondered why he fought his baser instincts. She was just another pussy to a guy like this, right? Even through her loathing, she could recognize the rare delicacy in which he treated her. Fuck, anyone that pulled a quarter of the shit she had done or said with this man would be in pieces at the bottom of the ocean.

She straightened, totally nude except for the choker he had placed around her neck with his initial on it. He reached out and wrapped his hand around her throat over top of the expensive necklace. He dragged her forward into his fully clothed body. His voice was hoarse when he spoke, telling her exactly how much she affected him.

"I am going to bend you over this desk and punish you for your constant defiance. Then I'm going to make you come, because you need to see how much your body can crave what

I can give you, Riley. After that I will mark you as mine before I send you home."

She stiffened against him and opened her mouth to protest. He squeezed her throat, biting the precious metal of the necklace into her tender skin just enough to quiet her. "Do not forget what I am capable of, little girl."

Her mouth closed as she was reminded sharply that her mother was at that very moment counting cards in his casino. He nodded his head, his thumb shifting to caress the delicate skin above the choker. "I am describing what I intend to do to you so you will understand that you can always trust what I say to you."

She stared up at him with wide eyes. He meant that she could trust what he said, whether it was good or bad. He would always tell her the truth. Which meant, when he said he intended to take her and keep her, he wasn't lying. He meant every word. Suddenly, her future seemed much more uncertain than it did just a few hours ago.

"Bend over my desk."

She shook her head, refusing to move. It wasn't like she planned on defying him. She just couldn't do it. She simply couldn't force her feet to move. She didn't want to be punished. She'd never been punished before. Not this way. She didn't know what to expect, but considering Soloman's reputation, it probably wasn't going to be good. Although the punishment wasn't the worst part. Her problem was his second promise. He said he was going to make her come. *What the fuck was up with that?* Not fucking possible. She was way too scared to be even a little aroused right now.

He didn't take her minor defiance badly. Instead, he took her arm and turned her to face the desk. Then he gently applied pressure to her lower back. At first, she didn't move, too petrified to obey. He moved up behind her and shoved his knee into hers, sending her forward into the desk. When she automatically bent forward, he pressed a large hand between her shoulder blades until she was laying completely flat on his desk. Her breath came out in panicked gasps. She lay her head down on the hard surface and stared at the contents of his tidy desk with unseeing eyes.

He leaned across her, pressing his broad, muscular chest into her back and whispered, "You need to relax, Riley, or this will hurt."

"No!" she gasped and tried to rear up.

He held her down as she struggled against him. He took a fistful of her hair and pressed the side of her face against the desk. She flailed out until he was forced to grab her wrists and hold them pinned against the small of her back. After a minute, she realized fighting was useless and likely to just get her and her mom hurt. She relaxed against the desk with a whimper.

"You done?" he growled, finally sounding like he was losing patience.

"Yes," she whispered.

"Fuck, you try my patience," he said coldly, leaning back. He still held her wrists tightly in one hand. "I'm done with this shit, Riley. You've really earned this."

She didn't get a chance to ask what she earned before his hand came down on her ass in a sharp slap. She cried out in pain as the blow rocked her against the desk. Her brain barely managed to register the slap before another blow landed on her other ass cheek, and then another and another. He beat her relentlessly, without mercy until her ass felt as though it were on fire. She barely had time to process the pain and the aftermath of each hit when another landed.

Finally, after several long moments, the beating ended. She panted and moaned helplessly against his desk. Her ass was on fire. She flinched when his hand touched her again, this time curving over the heated skin and rubbing. She tried to move her hips to get away from him, but his hand tightened on her wrists, threatening pain if she protested.

He moved his hand back and forth across her ass cheeks, exploring them, soothing the heat and gently kneading. After his rough treatment, the tender touch felt amplified, tingles of pleasure skittering down her legs and up her back. He used his foot to pull her leg apart, opening her up to his exploration. She cried out in protest as his hand dipped down between her ass cheeks, circling her tight anus for just a second before moving down to her wet pussy.

She jerked her hips forward to get away from his long fingers as he touched her plump pussy lips, dragging his fingers through the soaked folds, before thrusting two of them into her tight passage without warning. She cried out and arched her back up to relieve the pressure. He released her hands to push her back down with a hand between her shoulder blades. He spread his hand over the angel tattoo on her back and shoved her sprawling across his desk, just the way he'd imagined her, and fucked her from behind with his fingers until she was mewling underneath him.

She bucked her hips and screamed out in pleasure as she soaked his fingers, reaching for the orgasm he knew he could give her. He fucked his fingers in and out of her while strumming his thumb across her clit, causing her to buck and bow beneath him uncontrollably. Her reaction beautiful and completely unsimulated. He leaned across her, still holding her down and driving her toward an explosive orgasm she never wanted to experience with a man like him.

"You still hate me, Riley?" he growled in her ear, pressing his thumb against her clit while thrusting his fingers hard against her g-spot. She came with a long wail, soaking his hand and filling his head with her sweet music.

Before she could completely come down from the sweet high of her orgasm he lifted her limp body off the desk and allowed her to collapse at his feet. He took a fistful of her soft, gorgeous hair in one large hand and unzipped his pants with the other. Taking his hard, veined cock out, he watched the half-confused dreamy look on her face and the jiggle of her perfect, bare breasts as she fought to get her breath back. He imagined her insanely gorgeous lips wrapped around his thick cock while he fucked her mouth and throat.

He had been so wound up from the first moment he laid eyes on this woman that it took him minutes to finish jacking off. The dark, greedy bastard in him enjoyed the look of surprise on her face as his hot semen hit her lips, chin and breasts, marking her as his.

CHAPTER ELEVEN

Riley was pretty sure Soloman wasn't planning on letting her go home that night, despite his assurance that he meant everything he said. Except someone set fire to his car. The wild look in his eyes as he stared down at her freaked her out. No one had ever wanted to possess her the way this man did. Sure, she had been lusted after, but this guy took the whole 'me Tarzan, you Jane' thing to a new level.

He was in the process of reaching for her when someone had banged on his door, yelling that there was a fire in the parking lot. With a growl of frustration, he told her to get dressed and wait for him, then stalked out of his office. Riley didn't need to be told twice. She'd run immediately toward the private washroom in his office to clean herself up.

"Fuck," she whispered, taking in the vulnerable look on her face as she wet his hand towel and used it to clean the evidence of his release from her skin. Her heart thundered in painful reminder of the erotic scene that had played out moments before. Of how close she had come to begging him to fuck her on the floor of his office.

With a moan of distress, she tossed the towel down and frantically began pulling on her clothes. Knowing he would be back any moment to check on her, she shoved her bra into her purse and flew to the door, praying she hadn't been locked inside. It opened easily, swinging inward. Without a second thought for how furious Soloman was going to be to find his prize toy gone, she flew down the stairs and made a beeline for Cilia.

Clearly, most of the bouncers were busy with whatever was happening in the parking lot, because no one stopped her from getting near one of the medium stakes poker tables. She slapped her hand down on the table in front of Cilia and snapped, "Time to go."

Cilia's head jerked up in surprise. Her honey blond hair was piled in a chic twist at the back of her head with curls framing her high cheekbones. Her wide, plump lips, similar to her daughters, formed an 'oh' as she took in Riley's sudden appearance. Several others at the table, including the dealer were also eyeing Riley.

"You aren't wearing a bra, Riley. I can see your nipples outlined clear as day in this lighting. A girl with your assets should really always wear a bra in public," Cilia announced, carefully placing her cards facedown on the table.

Riley blushed and crossed her arms over her chest as interested gazes began to check out the truth of Cilia's state-ment. "It's in my purse. Now, let's go," she growled.

Cilia raised an eyebrow and gave Riley a disappointed once over. "Well I guess that's better than nothing, although your entire ensemble isn't really appropriate. If I had known you were going to join me, I would have sent something over for you to wear."

Riley shook her head and glared at her mother. She leaned over and spoke in Cilia's ear, "Mr. Hart knows your secret, mother. It's time for us to leave before he comes back."

Cilia sat back in her chair and looked up at her daughter. Though she resented Riley's interference in her life, she did trust the girl implicitly. Reaching for her chips, she gave the table a gracious smile and stood. "I suppose I will have to concede this game to you gentlemen. I must go and help my daughter dress more appropriately."

Geez, what was up with everyone hating on her outfit?

With chin held high, Cilia headed for the front door. Riley grabbed her arm and swung her around toward the side exit Roman had dragged her through earlier. She had been way too angry at the burly bodyguard to notice her mother gambling a few yards away. Cilia nearly tripped over her long, black velvet skirt as Riley rushed her through the thankfully unguarded door and into the parking lot.

The two women took a brief moment to gape in awe at the inferno created by Soloman's Audi S7 turned into a fireball. Cilia looked at her daughter, awe and respect reflected on her face. "Did you set a fire just to get me out of there?"

Riley laughed and pulled her mom toward her blue Subaru WRX sport. "I wish!" she giggled, amusement shining in her eyes. "Keys," she demanded, sticking out her hand.

Cilia handed over the keys without further comment and went around to the passenger side. Like her father, Riley always drove. She'd been driving since before she was old enough for a license. Cilia was long past complaining about who drove her car, as long as she got to where she was going. She relaxed into her seat as Riley reversed out of the parking spot and pulled sharply onto the road. Riley made a point of ignoring the men surrounding the flaming Audi.

"I'm going to have to take another vacation, aren't I?" Cilia sighed, watching the play of streetlights on Riley's face as they sped through the dark city streets.

Riley rolled her eyes toward her mother. "Unless you'd like to hang around and see what Soloman Hart does to people who count cards in his illegal casino? Maybe he needs a new accountant. Want to go ask him?"

Cilia's delicate brow crinkled in thought as though she were actually considering Riley's suggestion. "No," she finally said. "I've done the math and I don't think it's worth the risk. What if he actually likes his current accountant? We both know that I would be much better than anyone he has on his payroll, but he doesn't know that and he may not take our word. I could give him references, but that would require him not murdering me long enough to do the correct reference checks first. I don't know that I'm willing to take that risk. He would also have to forgive my 'infraction,' though I maintain it's not really counting cards if everyone else is just too stupid to remember the numbers that are right in front of them. I think there are probably too many bodies in Mr. Hart's past for me to just trust that he would see things my way."

Riley wanted to bang her head on the steering wheel. There really was no getting through to this woman. She pulled the car up to a cheap, run-down looking garage she rented in case of emergencies. Sliding out of the driver's side, she ran up to the key pad on the wall next to the door and punched in the code that would open the big garage door. She pulled the car into the dimly lit garage and secured the concrete building once more.

Cilia stepped out of the Subaru with a sigh and rubbed her bare arms. She'd been in the garage a few times and wasn't surprised Riley had brought her here. She trusted her daughter to know what was best for her when it came to disappearing for a while. She sat on the low cot next to the concrete wall and dumped her purse on the ground. It clattered with poker chips.

Riley was on her knees pulling a safe out from a hole in the wall. She looked up sharply when she heard the poker chips. Her lips twitched.

"How much?"

Cilia grinned despite the abrupt end to her evening. "I won $16,279.67, but I had to leave $1,203.21 behind on the table. That was really bad timing, Riley."

Riley laughed and began pulling cash, a passport and a phone out of the safe. "Sorry, mother. I didn't have much choice in the timing. I'll make it up to you by cashing your chips in and transferring you the money. Now what would you rather spend the next month doing? Hanging out on the Canadian side of Niagara Falls or cruising around Alaska?"

Cilia tilted her head to the side, studying Riley for a moment before answering. "Can't I cruise the Mediterranean? I really enjoyed that the last time we had to send me away. The beaches of Mykonos were spectacular!"

Riley sighed and plugged in the burner phone. "I want you closer than that in case I need to bring you home. Besides, these are my fake credit cards and Greece is expensive."

Cilia huffed. "Fine, then I want the cruise."

Riley sat quietly for a few minutes connecting the phone to the garage's internet service then searching for plane and cruise tickets. Fifteen minutes later she had her mother booked on a flight to Seattle leaving from a nearby airport in six hours. After that, Cilia's first-class passage was booked for four weeks on board an Alaskan cruise ship that would leave Seattle in four days, giving her plenty of time to shop for an appropriate wardrobe.

Riley stood and handed her mother the phone, a passport, a stack of cash and a credit card. "Your name is Lilith Abernathy. You're fifty-two years old and you were born in Fresno, California. Take the Eclipse and leave it at the airport. Put it in short-term parking, I'll have one of my mechanics pick it up tomorrow afternoon."

Cilia stood and accepted the proffered goods from her daughter. Shoving them in her purse, she handed over her legitimate identification for safe-keeping and picked up the keys for her new vehicle.

"You don't think Mr. Hart will find me, do you?" she asked anxiously.

"No, mother," Riley said softly, holding the car door open while Cilia slid into the driver's seat. "He's not after you. I think he was just using you to get what he really wants. Once you're safely away, he'll forget all about you."

"Oh," Cilia said, looking at Riley speculatively. Riley wondered what was going on behind those crystal clear blue eyes. Sometimes Cilia saw so much more than everyone else, but then other times she couldn't see the things that were directly in front of her. "Riley, do you think sea turtles migrate to Alaska? I just don't know about this. I think I'm having second thoughts."

Riley almost laughed out loud, but she managed to suppress it. She knew her mother wasn't really worried about sea turtles. Well, not exactly. "No, Cilia, I think it's probably too cold for them up there."

"Okay..." she sighed. "Well, I can do more research when I arrive in Seattle. If they were really so smart they would have conquered the North. That's where the resources are. All the fresh water is up there, you know?"

"Sure," Riley agreed. "Stay away from the gaming tables. I don't want to have to bail you off a cruise ship."

"Uh huh," Cilia said, still deep in thought over sea turtles conquering Alaska. She turned the ignition on while Riley opened the garage door. Finally, she turned and focused on her daughter. "Hey, can you go back to my place and release Scuttles? I'm done with him now and it would be a shame for him to just die."

She rolled up the window and pulled out of the garage, leaving Riley with the ethical dilemma of whether or not she should go save Scuttles' life or just let him die and never find out who or what he was. Shit! What if Scuttles was a human and Riley became complicit in kidnapping and murder? This is why Riley had followed in her father's shady footsteps instead of her mother's.

CHAPTER TWELVE

Soloman sat back in his leather chair, staring at the exact spot that she had stripped off her clothes and stood gloriously naked in front of him. His eyes moved from that spot to the edge of his desk where she had come for him, responding even more beautifully than he could have hoped for. But she had left. Despite knowing he would be back for her.

Rage burned in him. He glanced down at his phone. She had yet to respond to any one of his calls or text messages. He had first tried calling her over an hour ago, after the fire had been brought under control. He knew the moment he reentered the club and realized that Cilia was missing that Riley would also be gone.

His fist crashed into the desk. Fuck. He just wanted to know that she was safe. He was done playing her fucking games. He picked up the glass of whiskey and downed the contents before slamming it back down. He had men waiting for her at the shop, her condo and her mother's place. So far, she had shown up to none of her usual haunts. He even had Roman swing by Katie's parents' place and then over to Wendell's place. No one had seen her and now an irate Wendell was out searching for her as well, also worried that something had happened to his boss and friend. Soloman wanted to tell the asshole to mind his own fucking business. He probably would have followed it up with his fists except the man was happily married with two children.

Soloman was damn concerned and that made him fucking angry. What if she was hurt? What if someone had set the fire to distract him so they could grab Riley. He hadn't been easy or subtle in his pursuit of the woman. Fuck, he wanted the entire damn city to know who she belonged to. He didn't want any other motherfuckers sniffing around during his pursuit of the beautiful mechanic. But he had enemies that could make use of a weakness. He didn't think anyone would be stupid enough to have a go at him or anyone close to him, but he was beginning to realize Riley meant enough to him that he couldn't be casual in his assumptions.

Just the fact that she wasn't texting him back was killing him. He wanted to put his fist through the wall and whip her ass red until she understood her place. She would not be allowed to misstep like this again. Once he had eyes on her, he was locking her down. She'd have bodyguards at all times. She belonged to him and she was about to learn what that meant.

His phone buzzed in his hand. Glancing down, he saw an unknown number flash on the screen. Something told him it was her. He had no idea why he would make such an assumption, because he would ordinarily never take a call from an unknown number. But he knew Riley well enough to know that she was careful. She would assume he would trace her regular number and she would be right. He'd put a tracker on her phone the moment he found out who Riley Bancroft really was.

"Riley." His voice was like a whip when he spoke.

He listened to her breath for a moment and then she said his name, "Soloman." It was the sweetest thing she could have said to him. The word was like a ribbon of silk wrapping around his cock. He could see her lips forming each syllable. While rage still ran hot in his veins, relief eased the tight band of worry around his chest.

"Where are you?" he demanded, trying with difficulty to temper the anger in his voice so she might give up a location. His girl was smarter than that.

She laughed huskily. "I don't think so. You have this nasty habit of collecting me and forcing me to go places I don't want to be."

He gritted his teeth and breathed hard through his nose, picturing the ways in which he would punish her when he got his hands on her. "Tell me you're safe."

She didn't speak for a moment as though she were taking in his words and wondering what to do with them. Finally, she whispered, "I'm safe."

"I want you to come to me *right fucking now*, woman," he growled into the phone, fisting his hand on top of the desk. His knuckles popped from the pressure, his tattoo standing out stark against his skin. He willed his stubborn woman to listen to him, knowing she wouldn't. She had gone to ground and wouldn't show herself until she was good and ready. Or made a mistake.

She laughed, her husky voice wrapping warmly around him. "Well that's very convincing. You know, I can barely sit down, asshole? Why the fuck would I come crawling back to you? So you can spank me some more, or worse?"

He stuck a fresh cigarillo between his lips and lit it, wishing it were a cigarette. The woman was wearing him down and pissing him off. "If you come to me now, I'll forgive your trespasses and we'll start clean. No punishments this time. We do things in your time," he lied.

"I think that's the first time you've said something to me I didn't believe," she said coldly, her voice revealing a hint of betrayal. She was upset at him for lying to her. He didn't know if he should be fucking livid that this little girl was getting under his skin so much or pleased as shit that she was beginning to read him so well.

He sighed. "You're right, Riley. I'm going to beat the shit out of you the first chance I get my hands on you. But I promise, I'll make you learn to crave my every touch, even the ones that hurt."

She gasped so loud his dick twitched in response. "I'm good where I am, actually. Thanks, but no thanks. You can keep your oh-so-tempting offer."

"Not an offer, little girl. This is a promise," he growled into the phone, sitting up straight in his chair and blowing out a stream of smoke. "Soon as I get my hands on you, you will be coming home with me. No more dancing around. I'm fucking keeping you, Riley Bancroft."

Her breath caught and he could envision her teeth sinking into her plump lip as she worried over his words. Her breath came out in a rush and she said, "I'm not your damn plaything, Soloman. You don't get to fucking decide shit like that. I have a life!"

"You forget about Cilia's little transgression in my club this evening. Should I have my man go collect her?" he asked, taking another long smoke. It disgusted him to use such a low threat, but he wanted to bring Riley to him. The more expedient the better.

"Go ahead," she replied, supremely unconcerned.

He understood right away and chuckled at her cleverness. He should have realized what she had been busy doing for the past hour. "You sent her into hiding, didn't you?"

"Of course I did," she said scathingly, showing him she wasn't as unconcerned as she'd sounded a second ago. "How could I possibly leave my mother unprotected when someone like *you* is willing to use her to get to me?"

He sighed heavily and ran a hand over his short hair. Finally, he admitted, "I wouldn't have done it, Riley. I wouldn't have actually hurt your mother because it would have hurt you. I needed something to bring you under control. You've been denying me at every turn. I don't know any way to play but dirty."

She didn't say anything for a moment and he wondered what she was thinking. He could hear rustling, like she was laying down on a bed. Then she whispered, "Even if you didn't intend to, you *did* hurt me by using my mom."

Her confession was so unexpected it felt like a punch in the gut. He wasn't used to feeling things like this. His mother had died when he was two and his dad had been a brutal man. An underground boxer, caught up in illegal fighting and gambling until one of his debts finally ended both his career and his life. Any kind of tenderness Soloman had once known had died with his mom. Yet this woman was drawing emotions other than sexual from him. He didn't understand how it was possible.

"I'm sorry," he said quietly.

"Jus… just don't do it again."

He pressed his knuckles into his eye and thought for a moment. Could he give her this promise and be truthful? He was a cruel bastard. He was willing to do just about anything to get what he wanted. But truthfully, he couldn't picture himself hurting the mother of his woman.

He nodded his head. "Yes, you have my word. I won't touch Cilia again."

"Thank you," Riley said softly, her voice tired.

"You need sleep, woman," he stated, stubbing his cigarillo out in an ashtray he kept in a drawer. "If you won't come to me, then at least stay safe where you are until I can flush you out of hiding and back under my influence."

She laughed, the sweet sound wrapping around his body causing his muscles to tighten in response. "I still have things to do before you drag me off to your lair. I'm not going to make it easy for you to find me, Soloman," she said with a yawn.

"I don't think you know the meaning of the word easy," he growled.

"That's not what my high school boyfriend said," she giggled.

He slammed his fist against the side of the desk, angry despite knowing she was just making a silly joke. "You just signed his death warrant," he snarled.

"Okay, okay, I'm sorry Soloman, that was a stupid thing to say! Please don't kill anyone!" she begged.

He groaned into the phone and gave her all the ammunition she would need to bring him to his knees. "I don't think you get how fucking on edge you make me. I spend half my time wanting to beat the shit out of anyone that looks at you, which is every damn guy with eyes, and the other half nearly coming in my pants just from hearing your voice. You're ruining me, gorgeous."

She didn't say anything for a moment. He could hear her breathing lightly and rustling around. Then she said quietly, "I'm going to bed now. Sweet dreams, Soloman."

He stared at the phone after she hung up on him. No one had ever said anything like that to him before. Fuck, it sounded good coming from her lips. He still badly wanted to get his hands on her, but now he was picturing her curled on her side in a bed somewhere, sleeping safely, waiting for him to find her.

CHAPTER THIRTEEN

"Okay Scuttles, I don't particularly like seafood, but I'm willing to make an exception if you don't calm the fuck down and just get in the damn bucket," Riley growled at the angry, snapping creature she'd managed to corner in her mother's kitchen.

If she didn't already know Cilia had serious issues she would consider having the woman committed for allowing a crab of this size and ugliness to free roam in her house while she went off to count cards at an underground casino. Riley swallowed a scream as Scuttles lunged at her, snapping at her shoelaces in an attempt to drive her away from his prized corner. She drove him back with the BBQ tongs she'd snatched from the counter and swung her bucket at the claw the little bastard was waving at her.

She quickly glanced over her shoulder at the shadowy doorway of the cottage-like bungalow and held her breath. There had been a guy watching the front of the house. She'd seen the flare of his smoke as he sat in his car. She guessed he wasn't bothering to be too stealthy because she had told his boss that Cilia had left town. There wasn't any point in Riley coming back to the house. He was probably just a precaution.

Riley had gone through the neighbour's yard to get to her mom's house. The dog had greeted her silently. Apparently, Cilia's barking experiment had done one good thing. Giving the dog toys back had made her a non-barking friend for life. The boxer-cross had greeted her excitedly, jumping all around and dragging her into the flower bed with kisses of joy. She'd hugged him around the neck and glanced up at the silent house to make sure their enthusiastic greeting hadn't woken anyone up, then proceeded over the fence and through the side door.

"Oh god, oh god," Riley mumbled, "please don't take a finger, Scuttles!"

She lunged forward and slammed the bucket over the smelly, angry creature. He smashed his body against the side of the plastic bucket in violent protest to his captivity. She personally thought he should have taken it up with Cilia.

Riley's phone chose that moment to buzz an incoming text message. She rolled her eyes, but grinned. It had been 24 hours since Soloman 'lost' his prize and he'd called and texted her pretty much consistently after giving her a solid eight hours of sleep. She ignored the calls, but occasionally responded to the texts when they didn't piss her off. Each one was becoming progressively more demanding. This one wasn't from Soloman, though. She maneuvered herself so she was sitting on top of the bucket.

Wendell: UR in Reaper

Riley's jaw dropped and she could barely type the words.

Riley: Sparrow Hawk Cup???!!!

Wendell: Got the invite at the shop. Had to sneak it by your stalker tho. Don't think he saw anything.

It was everything Riley could do to contain the scream of pure excitement that bubbled up inside her. She stomped her feet on the ground and flailed her arms instead, causing her crabby friend to react angrily. She knocked on the side of the bucket. He knocked back. She stifled a laugh. Maybe she should keep the little bastard. He had serious attitude.

Riley: Want details buddy!

Wendell: U get them when I C U for practice. Babe U got work to do if U gonna win this.

Riley sighed. He was right, she'd been too busy with work lately to practice as much as she should be. Some of the guys she was going up against were damn good. Rich dudes that spent their entire lives racing expensive cars. She was a natural talent and she had a trick up her sleeve, but she needed to spend a few days preparing. Honing her timing and working with Wendell on their partnership. He would be in her ear while she raced.

Riley: We're on lockdown thanks to my not-so-secret admirer. How R we supposed to practice?

Wendell: I'll think of something. Just be ready to go when I say. K?

Riley: Yeah, NP. Sparrow Hawk, bitch!!!!

Wendell: UR going, Reaper baby!

Riley: No, we're going!!!

She grinned and looked down at the bucket between her legs. "You ready to go swimming, guy?"

Riley pulled her car in for a tire change, glancing surreptitiously around as she climbed out the window of Wendell's Acura. Wendell had assured her repeatedly that no one had followed them to the track. He'd also purposely chosen a rough, little used, little known track two counties over in a place called Blackbird for Riley to practice on. She still felt exposed. Like Soloman was going to swoop in any second and snatch her away.

Riley had been holed up in her dingy little garage for nearly two days, hiding from Soloman and his men. Wendell had assured her that Soloman had eyes on the shop at all times so she absolutely could not go into work for any reason. The boss man himself had actually gone down to the garage and insisted on the *full* tour, which Wendell was smart enough to give him. Luckily for Wendell and his acting abilities, Soloman seemed to believe he had no clue where Riley was. Either that, or Soloman was having Wendell followed and waiting to dismember him until after Riley was found.

Wendell had managed to dislodge his tail through a clever exchange of cars and dumb luck. Someone had set fire to another one of Soloman's vehicles while it was parked outside of Riley's shop. Wendell had rushed out to help stop the fire, negating the need to keep eyes on him, which is when he'd managed to slip away and meet Riley. He'd driven to Riley's hidden garage to pick her up in a tow truck with his car and several sets of tires. Now they were holed up in a cheap motel in a small town paying only cash and practicing from dawn until dusk. It'd been nearly two days since their arrival in Blackbird. A total of five since she'd escaped Soloman's club.

Instead of switching out the tires, Wendell was deep in conversation on his phone, wandering toward the edge of the overgrown track. Riley watched him curiously for a moment and then went to work on the first tire. She hated changing tires. It was her least favourite chore as an auto mechanic, which is why she preferred Wendell do it for her. She wouldn't get a chance to switch tires during the big race, which is one of the things she and Wendell had been working on. How to preserve tire integrity. Not something she usually cared a lot about when she raced, but the Sparrow Hawk Cup was a much longer race than she was used to.

Just as she finished tightening the last bolt on the first tire, Wendell slammed his hand down on the hood of the car making Riley jump and drop the tire iron. She stared up at him in surprise. Wendell rarely got angry, but he looked absolutely livid. His pale face was flushed red and his blond eyebrows were shoved down over flashing blue eyes.

"What's going on?" Riley asked in concern, pushing herself off the ground.

"It's Treena," he snapped. His wife.

She figured he'd been talking to his wife. Wendell didn't actually talk to anyone else over the phone, not even his own mother. He was a text only kind of guy. Riley touched his arm soothingly and asked, "What's up, Wendell? Is she okay?"

"Yeah, for now she is," he growled, shoving a hand through his sweat-streaked mop of hair. "Your fucking boyfriend showed up at the house."

"No!" Riley gasped, covering her mouth and stepping back. Her eyes widened and filled with tears. She shook her head. She should have realized this would happen when Wendell disappeared. She had been so stupid! How could she put Treena and the kids in danger like that?

Riley turned on the spot and headed toward the tow truck, then turned back around and reached for the car, then changed her mind again. "Shit, I should have known! I'm so sorry, Wendell. I have to go back. I'll do it right now. I'll go to him, I'll call off his hunt. I won't let him near your family again."

Wendell reached out and grabbed her arm, pulling her around gently to face him. "Riley, stop."

She shook her head and tried to pull away, but he didn't let her go. "Wendell, I've put your family in danger. I have to go back to him!"

He shook her arm, drawing her attention to him. "No, Riley. Treena's fine. He didn't threaten her or anything. Just wanted to know where I was. Treena couldn't tell him anything because I didn't tell her. Hell, if anything she feels sorry for the guy. You know how she is, an incurable romantic. She thinks anyone that looks like him, with a past like his must be some kind of tragic soul."

A bubble of laughter burst out of Riley as she pictured Wendell's tiny, round wife fawning over the big, bad mob boss, forcing baked goods and sympathy on the man while he grilled her for information. He wouldn't know what hit him. The kids, aged fourteen months and three years would be all over him along with the two cats and two dogs. There was not a shy creature in that household.

"Besides," Wendell continued, "Treena is first and foremost a huge fan of the Reaper. She would never forgive either of us if you didn't compete in this race. She has all her splurge money riding on you, babe."

Riley nodded her head, tears filling her eyes. She grinned up at her best friend. "I don't know how you convinced that woman to marry you, Wendell, but you are the luckiest guy in the world."

"Fuck, don't I know it," he said, grinning back. "She's about the only wife in the world that would believe I could share a motel room with a woman that looks like you and keep it business only."

"Yeah," Riley agreed. "Let's keep that little fact on the DL because I don't think a certain Mr. Hart is going to see our sharing a room the same way."

A look of sheer horror crossed Wendell's ruddy features as though the thought had never crossed his mind before now. "I'm a dead man," he groaned.

"Yeah, you are," she laughed. "Can you finish changing the tires before it happens though? I'm so over this."

CHAPTER FOURTEEN

"Is the Reaper actually wringing her hands at the sacred Sparrow Hawk?" Katie asked with a laugh, hugging Riley around the neck with one arm and hanging onto her popcorn for dear life with her other hand. "Don't let the other participants see that crap or they'll think you're some kind of candy ass wuss."

Riley glared at her best friend and reached for a hand full of popcorn. It was a weird quirk that Katie had to have popcorn for all of Riley's races. She adored popcorn more than the average person. She would actually go to a movie theatre just to purchase a bag of popcorn and then leave without watching a movie. She pulled a face and snatched the bag away when it looked like Riley would eat more than a few bites. Katie was also viciously protective of her buttery treats.

"I'm not wussing out over here," Riley defended herself. "I'm wondering where the hell your brother got to with my car. He better be parking it up at the starting line."

Katie shot her a mischievous look and said, "Not your car though, is it?"

"Hey, bitch," Riley snatched the popcorn and backed

away from her friend. "I earned it! Possession is nine tenths of the law, right?"

"Oh, you want to play it like that?" Katie growled, launching herself at the popcorn. "It's on!"

"Draw a little more attention to yourselves, ladies," Wendell snapped, striding toward the two woman as they fake pummeled each other and laughed. "I'm pretty sure only a few of Soloman Hart's guys haven't noticed you yet."

"Fuck!" Riley gasped, springing behind Katie and scanning the immediate area as if expecting Soloman to come stalking toward her out of the bushes.

Wendell pretended to cuff her in the side of the head. "I'm kidding. Haven't seen any of those guys yet. But that doesn't mean they aren't lurking. Your boyfriend has a pretty long reach. He may not be in the actual circuit, but he had enough influence to get the information he needs. I guarantee either he or one of his people shows up here looking for you."

"Yeah, I had that thought too," Riley sighed, scanning the crowd.

She and Katie had been attempting to keep a low profile near one of the beer tents. Riley was wearing a baseball cap over her ponytail and Wendell's big leather coat over her T-shirt and denim-clad curves. Katie hadn't gotten the incognito memo. The gorgeous blond was wearing four-inch wedge heels, a red leather mini skirt and a black corset top. So far not a single heterosexual male on the mountain hadn't checked her out.

"Where's my car at?" Riley asked Wendell anxiously.

He'd driven it to the race overnight, while Katie and Riley had driven a separate vehicle. The people in charge of the Sparrow Hawk Cup had sent them the coordinates for the illegal race exactly twenty-four hours before the start time. Considering some people had to fly in, she had no idea how they were expected to get their cars there in time. Maybe some participants were given more time? She knew a South

Korean competitor actually flew his car in. She guessed he must have brought his car into the US ahead of time and then rushed it to the start line when he got his message.

"I parked it at the top of the mountain," he told her. "It's being babysat by at least a dozen admirers. Next time pick something flashier won't you?"

She grinned up at him. "Hey, at least I got in some mountain practice back home."

"Uh huh," he grumbled, picking up a beer and downing half of it. Now that he'd completed his job of getting Riley's car to the starting point, he needed to relax a bit before the race started. "Some of the guys out there are going to try to drop you off the side of one of these cliffs. They won't play nice like Roadkill."

Riley snorted, keeping her opinion of Roadkill's ability to play nice to herself. They spent the next hour chatting nervously with circuit acquaintances while Riley psyched herself up for the race. She nodded to one of the other competitors, but for the most part they stayed out of each other's way. This wasn't a friendly race like she was used to. There was a lot of money and prestige riding on this one. She knew some of the guys thought she only got in because of her dad's reputation and her gender. It looked good for the sponsors to have the daughter of a racing legend in the Sparrow Hawk.

The guys were wrong and she was about to prove it. She was every bit as good as Alan Bancroft had been. Better, even. God rest his soul. An air horn sounded, indicating the drivers were expected at the top of the mountain. Katie lurched into Riley's arms, spilling popcorn between them.

"Stay safe, bestie!" she sniffed, squeezing Riley tight before releasing her. She turned and hugged Wendell too, then punched him lightly in the arm. "Keep her safe!"

They parted from Katie who headed toward a caravan of race watchers. Wendell led Riley toward a line-up of vehicles headed to the top. A flash of tattoos that looked vaguely familiar caught Riley's eye. She turned her head and scanned the crowd, but didn't see the face she was looking for. Strange, but she could swear she saw Shank. Why would he be there?

Wendell gave Riley a leg up into the back of a pickup truck with the South Korean contestant and a few other supports heading up to help their drivers. Everyone else was grabbing rides down to various vantage points picked out along the mountainside. Riley caught a glimpse of Katie being lifted into a raised Jeep with a group of other fans. Her precious popcorn was still tucked under an arm.

"Hey, I'm Riley," Riley yelled over the sound of vehicles taking off up and down the mountain. "How'd you get your car here in time for the race? Wendell and I've been wondering."

The South Korean lifted his lip in a half smile and reached out to shake her hand. "Jun-young," he replied, moving to sit next to her in the bed of the truck, bracing his back against the bouncing metal rim. "I flew the car out a month ago and kept it in a friend's garage in L.A. Lucky for me it was within driving distance and we didn't have to figure out how to fly it again when they sent the directions. You?"

"Same," she said with a grin. "So fucking glad it's not raining either. Luck seems to be with us."

He nodded and studied her face under the shade of her baseball cap. "No shit. You ready for this?"

She was about to respond with her usual show of blasé arrogance when one of the other competitors pulled up along-side and started shouting something stupid about Asian drivers. Riley immediately stood up and gave him the finger. She recognized the guy as one of the circuit jocks with more money than brains. He'd practically been born in a race car.

"Shut the fuck up, Digger, you racist piece of shit. He wouldn't be here if he didn't qualify," she yelled angrily.

The big blond asshole grinned and gave Riley a once over. "Whose dick did you suck to get in, Reaper? We all know you didn't race your way into Sparrow. This is for the big boys."

"I'm going to fucking kill him," she growled, preparing to launch herself off the side of the truck and into the open window of his Humvee.

Jun-young stood up behind her and grabbed her around the waist, pulling her back down until they were sitting in the bed of the truck again. Wendell put a restraining hand on her shoulder and gave her a stern shake of his head. Finally, she settled down and crossed her arms.

Turning to Jun-young who had settled back down beside her, she shot him a grimace with some teeth. "I've never been more ready for anything in my life. Going to shove my car up that fucker's ass!"

He laughed and put a loose arm around her shoulders. "Good girl. You show these assholes."

The group in the back of the truck relaxed and talked cars for the rest of the ride to the top, doing their best to ignore the tension and shit talk surrounding them. They arrived at the top a few minutes later. Riley jumped out of the truck, wished her new friend luck and made her way over to her car with Wendell.

The Koenigsegg Regera gleamed gorgeous red in the sunlight, waiting patiently for her new mistress to race her to the bottom of the mountain. Another air horn sounded, indicating five minutes to race time. Riley unzipped the leather jacket and handed the coat and cap to Wendell. He took them and set her up with an earpiece, which they immediately tested.

Her heart began pounding as she watched the other race teams prepping. Most cars had more than two people, except for her and Jun-young who caught her eye and winked at her across the hood of his shiny blue and silver Nissan GT-R. He stood with a tall and lanky clean-cut kid that was talking a mile a minute and giving his driver instructions.

Wendell was doing the same for Riley, but seemed to be obsessing over just one thing. "Just promise me you'll stay the fuck away from cliff edges. I don't even care where you place in this damn race. I just want you to survive it. I mean look at the way Digger keeps giving you the stink-eye. Fucker has it in for you. And this damn car is dangerous, never mind where you got it from. It's death on wheels, babe."

She nodded, absently scanning the area for Digger. She didn't really care about him. He kept most of his worth in his pants. Or so he thought. She could work with that kind of idiocy. Then her eyes landed on the second to last person she wanted to see at the race. Roman Valdez. He was looking around like he was ready to spit nails. He must have spotted the car by now, which meant he was looking for someone. With a gasp, she grabbed hold of Wendell and shoved him away from her.

"What the f...!" Wendell began, but she cut him off.

"Go, Wendell!" Riley gasped. "Roman is here! You need to hide, now! I can't hide the fucking car, but I can lock myself in until the race starts."

She didn't have to say it twice, Wendell took off at a run, putting as much distance between himself and a woman who, at that particular moment, posed a whole lot of danger to his health. Riley unlocked the car and lifted the handle, taking a moment to marvel at the smooth opening of the door, before sliding into the driver's seat. She slammed the door shut and locked it.

She waited breathlessly for Roman to make his way over. There was absolutely no missing the incredibly beautiful car she had stolen from his boss two weeks ago. She was absolutely fucked. The air horn blew for a third time, indicating the drivers should take their prearranged places at the starting line.

Turning the ignition, Riley enjoyed the aggressively refined bark of the unparalleled engine before putting the vehicle in gear and pulling it around to her place in the starting lineup. She didn't see Roman anywhere now in the crowd of people lining up to wave the seven drivers off the starting line. She rolled her shoulders in an attempt to loosen the tension and closed her eyes, counting down the seconds until the race started.

She grinned and ran her hands over the warm, smooth steering wheel. *She made it*. She was actually there. One of only three women to compete in the Sparrow Hawk Cup in its entire twenty-two-year history. A legacy competitor; the daughter of a champion. She hadn't been stopped by the dark mafia kingpin who dogged her every footstep, trying to chain her to his side. Hell, not only had she escaped from beneath his shadow, she'd taken his car with her.

She opened her eyes, still smiling and glanced out the driver's side window. The sun blinded her for a moment, before the shadow of a man stepped into the window, blocking it out. She shaded her eyes and looked up. She gasped, the smile melting from her lips. Soloman Hart stood staring down at her through the window, his dark eyes as icy cold as she had ever seen them. There was not a spark of warmth for the woman he professed to want with every fibre of his being.

She. Was. *So*. Fucked.

Riley stealthily double-checked to make sure the car was locked. About two seconds later he checked the handle to see if it would open. It did not. His eyes grew harder, never releasing hers. He lifted his hand and pointed at her, then at the door. She bit her lip and shook her head. She expected him to speak, but he didn't. There was no point. He must have understood that she intended to race his car in the Sparrow Hawk, regardless of his commands. Just as she understood there would be consequences once he got his hands on her.

For once in her life Riley wished she was a praying type of girl. Because the Lord's Prayer seemed appropriate right about now, if only she knew the words. She was pretty sure what she was seeing in his eyes was something similar to what people saw right before he killed their asses. She had stolen his extremely rare 2.5-million-dollar car, lied about it and now intended to race it in a dangerous, illegal race he had expressly forbidden her from attending.

Yup, totally fucked.

She swallowed hard and turned her eyes straight ahead. A tall, black-haired woman wearing fuck-me heels, tight jeans and a bikini-top was holding a green starting flag high in the air. Engines revved all around her. Riley glanced toward Soloman and pumped the accelerator with her foot, feeling the raw power of the Koenigsegg rumble beneath her. He stepped away from the car, his eyes still on her. She couldn't help herself, the moment the flag dropped, she blew him a kiss and then floored his Koenigsegg off the line, leaving him in her dust.

CHAPTER FIFTEEN

Riley had about three minutes to enjoy her very decisive victory before all hell broke loose. One moment she was being tossed up in Wendell's arms, showered in champagne, being offered sponsorship by a prestigious car manufacturer, praised on her hairpin turns by Jun-young, who came in third, and the next moment, she was torn rudely away from Wendell. She gasped as Wendell was thrown across the hood of the burning hot car, with Soloman's hand tight around his neck.

"You let her race my fucking car," Soloman growled down at the other man. "You *know* how much danger she put herself in and you let her fucking race."

Riley realized right away Soloman meant to actually kill him when Wendell started choking and turning red. She wedged herself between the two men, pressing herself into Soloman as close as she could. He didn't take his eyes off Wendell.

"Soloman, no!" she yelled, but he refused to take his eyes off Wendell.

She could see his powerful biceps flexing against his T-shirt and the tattoos rippling down his arm. Tears gathered in her eyes and she felt real fear as she maneuvered herself even closer against him, moulding her body against his and wrapping her arms around his throat. Her eyes met Roman's cold gaze over Soloman's shoulder.

"Help me!" she called out to Roman.

He ignored her and turned his head to bark at someone else to stay back when they would have intervened. Riley could feel the fight draining from Wendell's body as the oxygen left him. She reached up and grabbed Soloman's face, pulling it down to hers and forcing him to meet her frantic gaze.

"Please, Soloman," she begged, tears bright in her chocolate eyes. "Don't hurt him."

His face was set in hard, ruthless lines. His scarred lips an unrelenting slash of cold fury. She was positive he couldn't hear her when, after a moment, he dropped his forehead to hers. She felt a subtle relaxation in his body and knew he had loosened his fingers when she heard Wendell choke and wheeze behind her. She reached back and gripped her friend's hand to assure herself he was still alive. His fingers twitched around hers.

Out of the corner of her eye she saw Katie flying toward them, running as fast as she could on her four inch wedges, screaming her brother's name. Since Dexter Pullman's death, Katie and Wendell had become extremely family oriented and protective of each other. Roman caught her around the middle and held her tight against his chest while she kicked and screamed.

"Look at me," Soloman commanded, drawing Riley's attention back to her own drama. She could feel the seething fury still surrounding his large frame, but he was attempting to put a leash on it. "Get in the fucking car now and I won't kill your friend."

"Don't... go..." Wendell rasped from behind her, his voice a harsh gasp.

Soloman wrapped a thick arm around Riley's waist, hauled her off Wendell's body and into the heat of his own. Then he kicked Wendell off the car and into the dirt. When Wendell looked as though he would rise, Soloman kicked him in the stomach, sending him sprawling back into the dirt. Riley lunged forward, intent on getting to her friend, but Soloman held her so tight she knew there would be bruises on her arms.

He lifted her up against his chest and spoke in her ear, "Get in the car and he lives."

Holding her by the waist with one strong arm, he took her hand in a hard grip with his other hand and guided it around his back. He forced her to feel the gun that was at his back. She gasped and went rigid against him, her eyes wide on Wendell who was rolling in the dirt choking.

"Give me a reason to end him," Soloman breathed in her ear, his jaw scraping against her ear and his breath brushing against her cheek. "I'll do it right here in front of everyone. In front of his baby sister."

Riley's eyes flickered to Katie who was sobbing in Roman's arms, tears streaming down her cheeks. Her knees had buckled and he was clearly holding her up in one strong arm while keeping an eye on the crowd of curious onlookers. Jun-young caught Riley's eye and raised an eyebrow in question. She gave him a tiny shake of her head. She so didn't need anyone else to get involved in this mess.

She turned to look at Soloman, her lips barely brushing his as she whispered, "I'll go with you."

He nodded and pushed her away from the hood of the car with a hard hand at her waist. She stumbled back. He opened the passenger side door and pushed her down into the seat. Riley stared up at his cold, implacable face and shivered. As the door slammed down she knew it was closing on her independence. She defied Soloman Hart, despite his many warnings, and now she was about to pay the consequences.

He got into the Koenigsegg with her and fired the engine. Someone pulled Wendell out of the way, thank god, because she was certain Soloman would've run over him if he was still laying in the dirt. She stared helplessly out the window as they sped away from what should have been her shining moment of victory. She wondered if she would even see the prize money or if Soloman would lock her up so tight she would never even hear the words Sparrow Hawk Cup again, let alone speak to the race organizers. She glanced sideways at his terrifyingly sinister visage and decided she would wait until later to ask him.

After four solid hours of ignoring him, exhaustion from a long, adrenaline-fueled day finally won and Riley fell asleep. She sat slumped in her seat with her arm curled against the door and her head tucked in the curve. Her chestnut ponytail cascaded across the side of her face and over her chest, frustrating his efforts to watch her sleep as he drove. Her other hand was curled innocently in her lap, her black chipped nail polish facing him.

He reached across the space separating them and, as gently as possible, pulled the long curls of her hair aside so he could see her face as she slept. He smoothed the soft hair against her shoulder where it stayed, obedient to his wishes. Her plump lips were slightly parted against the curve of her slender fingers, where her head rested against the window.

Fuck. The things he wanted to do to that mouth were so far from innocent. It was everything he could do not to pull the car over and give into the urge. Especially now that she had willingly handed herself over to him. He didn't even care that he'd coerced her into getting into the car. As far as he was concerned, she gave herself to him. In his world, he could now do whatever he wanted to with her. She belonged to him. And the savage in him wanted to fucking tear her to pieces in the best possible way.

The rage he'd felt when he saw her in his car was indescribable. It was not something he'd *ever* felt before. When he did business, it was always with a cool head. When he killed, it was with icy calm. He did not make decisions without deliberation. But what he felt when he saw Riley take off down the side of the mountain in such a powerful, dangerous car, racing against men that would try to kill her on every curve, was complete and utter blackout rage.

He couldn't kill the woman that put herself in the damn car, so he was going to fucking murder the next best person. The man that helped put her there. Wendell Pullman, her mechanic and wingman. He would have done it, too, without a moment's remorse, if she hadn't stood between them and begged him not to. Riley Bancroft now had the pleasure of being the only person on the damn planet to pull him back from a kill once he made up his mind.

He glanced at her again, taking in the shadowy sweep of her long, dark lashes against her cheekbones. The smattering of freckles on her cheeks and nose were beginning to show from time spent outdoors over the past several days. She also had more of a tan now. Soon they would arrive home and he would no longer have to deny himself access to this woman. He would fuck away the fury and bury the rage in that delicious body. She would finally belong to him in every way he'd imagined since first setting eyes on her.

CHAPTER SIXTEEN

A chill breeze from the ocean played with the tendrils of hair that had escaped her ponytail. Had she forgotten to close her bedroom window? Her seatbelt released and arms closed around her. She was lifted from comfortable warmth into the hardness of someone's arms. A familiar and somewhat alarming masculine scent enveloped her. With a sigh and a frown, she forced herself to open her eyes and look at the person that dared interrupt her deep sleep. Soloman Hart looked down at her like the dark criminal overlord he was, desire clashing with triumph in his eyes.

She wanted to punch him in the eye and show him exactly what she thought of his near kidnapping. But she chose to yawn instead. Maybe he would be less attracted to her if he saw the gaping inside of her mouth? He chuckled and shifted her in his arms, holding her against the side of his body with one arm while closing her door with the other. She took a moment to both marvel and despair at his easy strength. He was a large man and he filled those sleek, expensive suits out very nicely. But they definitely hid a musculature most people didn't get to experience up close.

Riley liked to think she was fit. Enough. Her favourite

food groups were ice cream, bacon and orange juice. At least one of those was a fruit! Sort of. She hated working out with a passion and liked to tell people she would save them in case of zombie apocalypse by being the fastest speed walker in the group. Riley also had a bad tendency to forget to eat. She got that from her dad. A beautiful car wanders into the shop and bam! She's in love, half-starved after two days of working on the babe and turning a tidy profit. The only thing that probably saved her from modern day scurvy was that shopping for Cilia forced her to shop for herself.

She wasn't going to be beating off Soloman with her unused muscles and nonexistent running skills any time soon. She was going to have to rely on her wits and the fact that he seemed to want to kill her a lot less than most other people that entered into his orbit. Riley tilted her head back and smiled shyly up at Soloman, gaining his surprised attention. Clearly, he'd been expecting some kind of fight from her since they were most definitely not in front of Riley's apartment building. It was dark out, but she could see enough to recognize he was striding toward the front doors of a massive house.

"I'm hungry," she announced, fluttering her lashes at him and trying to look weak.

She *was* actually hungry. But she also figured the kitchen wasn't the bedroom and since he wasn't looking at her any less lustfully after her gigantic yawn, she needed a new tactic. He nodded his head absently and shifted her once again to dig in his pocket for keys to the house. She crossed her arms awkwardly against his muscular chest and rolled her eyes.

"Or you could put me down?" she suggested sarcastically.

He ignored her, unlocked the door and carried her over the threshold. He quickly tapped in a ten-digit code to the alarm, disarming it. She gasped as the cold air conditioning hit her and all humour left her for the moment. It felt significant, entering his home in the middle of the night in his arms.

As though he were a conquerer returning to the castle with his captured prize held tightly against him. She turned her face against him and shivered. His arms tightened around her.

He didn't bother turning on any lights as he strode with her toward the back of the house. Light from the moon shone through the windows as they passed, his shoes tapping against the dark marble flooring. He stopped abruptly and she realized they were in the kitchen. Gently, he set her on the counter next to a huge refrigerator. Without a word, he opened the door and started rifling through the contents.

Riley glanced surreptitiously around, taking immediate stock of a back door to her left. Soloman was to her right with the fridge door open between them. She would have at least a tiny head start if she decided to make a break for it. She curled her fingers around the edge of the countertop and shifted her butt just a little further forward, her entire body tensing for flight.

"You don't want to do that," his voice rumbled from the fridge.

Riley's head snapped to the right and her mouth fell open. How did he know? Was she that predictable? She jumped when he slammed the door shut cutting the light off. He set containers down one at a time on the counter next to her. She couldn't tell what was in them since there was so little light. She really hoped he knew, because she detested liver, asparagus and marmalade. She didn't care how badass he was. No way, no how, was she eating any of those three things.

He went to the sink and washed his hands. Drying them off on a hand towel, he came back to where she was sitting. She'd pulled one of the containers into her lap and was toying with it when he took it from her hands. He removed the lid and pulled something out. She reached for it, but he pulled it away.

"Open your mouth," he said gruffly.

"I can feed myself," she complained, giving him a suspicious look and reaching for another container.

He captured her wrist in his other hand and trapped it against her thigh. He took a step closer, swamping her with his large presence. Even sitting on the counter, he was still taller than her. His narrow hips and stomach pressed against her legs, keeping her immobile while he attempted to feed her. Her breath caught in her throat and she wished she could see his face in the shadows of the kitchen, but she could only see his silhouette.

"I will take care of you from now on, including feeding you." His voice rumbled through her.

"That's pretty creepy, dude," she replied, flexing her hand under his. He responded by tightening his knuckles over hers.

He sighed, the breath fanning across her face, and she found herself breathing in his subtle masculine scent as he leaned toward her. She *really* didn't want to find him even remotely sexy, especially since she had been coerced into coming to his house in the middle of the night. And she knew exactly where he intended for this night to end. She wasn't ready for that outcome yet. Not with someone like him. He was too intense and he wanted too much from her.

"You said you were hungry, Riley. Now eat or we go straight to bed," he told her with a clear edge of impatience to his voice.

Well that was blunt, she thought, blinking at her lack of options.

Hoping the food was liberally laced with garlic, onions and whatever else might turn him off, she leaned forward the few inches that would bring her mouth to his fingers and tentatively took the offering. As soon as her lips touched his skin, the fingers of his other hand clenched, biting into her thigh. She felt the electric tension swirling around them and almost spat the food out. She brought her hand up to cover her mouth where his touch still burned against her lips.

He had fed her a piece of chicken and it was delicious. She moaned slightly as she chewed and swallowed. With a sigh of satisfaction, she smiled and said, "More, please."

He was standing frozen against her, staring hard at her face. His long fingers continued to hold hers, wrapped around her thigh possessively. She frowned up at him and tossed her ponytail over her shoulder.

"That one bite didn't really do it," she told him slowly, as though she were explaining the obvious to a child. "I'm still hungry. Pretty sure even kidnappers have to feed their victims. Don't make me go to the Human Rights Watch, buddy. I don't think you'll like what they have to say to the likes of you."

He snapped out of his momentary trance and snorted down at her. Reaching for another piece of chicken he held it up. She opened her mouth expectantly, but before he placed it on her tongue, he said darkly, "Watch that sassy little mouth or I'll turn you over and fuck you right here against the counter before we even make it to the bedroom. And I promise, if you piss me off to that point, only one of us will enjoy it. You're treading a slippery slope, gorgeous. I haven't forgotten about my car. Or that you took off from my club and ignored all of my summons. I simply bide my time."

Riley gasped and straightened against the counter so quickly she knocked the back of her head against a cupboard. She could feel the colour draining from her face. She had become so used to his pursuit and their banter over the past few weeks that she'd nearly forgotten who she was dealing with.

He tapped the chicken against her lips. She opened automatically and allowed him to slide the meat into her mouth. She wasn't hungry anymore. He had effectively scared the hunger away, but she ate anyway. It was better than the alternative.

He continued to feed her chicken and then pieces of chopped up mango and pineapple until she pushed his hand away and quietly announced that she was full. He ate a few bites of everything in between feeding her, though his main focus seemed to be on caring for her. After his chilling declaration, they didn't speak again until after he finished putting the containers away and washed his hands again.

"Time for bed," he announced.

He reached for her and lifted her easily off the counter. She was grateful when he set her on her feet instead of carrying her once again through the massive house. He took her hand and once more, without turning on any lights, began leading her. They arrived at a set of stairs leading down. He placed her hand on a railing and helped her glide down the wide staircase.

She frowned. "You sleep in the basement? That seems like an odd choice for a guy with tons of money. Why don't you buy a house with upstairs bedrooms? Or get a condo like me. Well, not exactly like me. My place is pretty small for a big-time guy like you. Something bigger, like a penthouse, with a pool or something."

She knew she was babbling, but she couldn't seem to help herself. She was becoming more and more nervous as they descended further into the darkness of the house. She was beginning to feel like Persephone being swept off into the underworld by Hades. That had always been one of her favourite Greek myths because of the dark romance involved. Now that she found herself in virtually the same situation as the virgin goddess, she was rethinking what she considered romantic.

"I have a pool," he grunted in response to her question, amusement lacing his deep tones.

As she stepped off the last stair and the bottom floor

spread out in front of her she saw why his bedroom was down there. She gasped in surprise and, momentarily forgetting both her fear and his hold on her, she stepped toward the panoramic windows. He followed her. The windows faced a massive lawn that stretched out toward the inky black ocean where waves crashed against the beach. The moon flooded the entire area with light, including the interior of the room they were standing in. She could see a free-standing fireplace and a leather sofa set.

His estate home must be set on a slope where the front half of the house was level with the front lawn and the back half of the house was at the bottom of a hill. It was both modern and beautiful. She quickly calculated how much an ocean front property like that would cost and realized she was way further out of her depth than she had originally thought with this mafia boss. Like, maybe a few dozen of her little chop shops could buy a place like this.

Soloman curved a hand around her waist and urged her down another dark hallway. Her heart crashed in her chest the further he escorted her into his home. She began to feel as though there would be no escape. She knew she wouldn't make it five steps if she tried and not just because of her dislike of running. He finally had his prize and he was not letting her go.

He lead her through another doorway at the end of the hall. She blinked in an attempt to bring something into focus. Did this guy have something against lights? She licked her suddenly dry lips and quickly stepped away from the arm that was curved around her waist. Surprisingly, he let her go. She guessed now that he had her where he wanted her, he didn't need to pin her to his side.

The windows in this room were covered in blinds, she supposed so he could sleep in darkness once the sun rose. Glancing at the clock she realized sunrise was only an hour away. It was 4:22am. They had driven all night. After leaving her Sparrow Hawk victory behind, they had only stopped once for gas and to stretch their legs. Ironically, Soloman had chosen to stop in Blackbird. The seething look he'd given her as he'd pumped gas told her that his choice hadn't been accidental. He had traced her there. He knew about the track. He probably knew she shared a room with Wendell. It was a fucking miracle that guy was still alive.

Riley carefully made her way to the window and touched the cord on the blinds covering the sliding glass doors. "May I?" she asked quietly.

"Of course," he murmured, coming to stand behind her.

She pulled, opening the blinds and revealing the magnificent view. A sigh escaped her lips as her eyes traced over his immaculate lawn and the dark ocean beyond. The faint beginnings of dawn were starting to crest over the water, creating a blue glow. He ran a hand over her shoulder and curved her into the strength of his arms. She brought her hands up against his stomach to push him away, but as soon as her fingers brushed the fabric of his shirt she felt the heat of his body. She gasped and dropped her hands. Her fingers brushed the rigid length of his cock, pressed hard against the fabric of his jeans.

Oh god! She couldn't do this! She thought dizzily.

She pressed her hands back against the door behind her and reached for the latch. It opened beneath her fingers. Without thinking, she shoved the door open. She turned to run, but he was on her in seconds. His growl turned feral as he wrapped long fingers around her arms and dragged her back through the door. The kiss of ocean breeze barely touched her before she was turned around and slammed into his hard chest.

CHAPTER SEVENTEEN

"No more games, Riley," he said in a hard voice, shaking her hard. "Trust me, you do not want to come to my bed this way. I will hurt you, woman."

She opened her mouth to deny him, but nothing came out. She realized she was both desperately frightened and aroused. They had been dancing around each other for weeks. And if there was one thing Riley loved it was the adrenaline rush of a good chase scene, but somewhere along the way things had changed. He had changed. Things became real. She sensed this was no longer just a fuck to him. He intended to keep her. To chain her to him. And she so wasn't ready for that.

"Please," she whispered, her lips shaking as she gazed up at him, hoping he could see the fear in her eyes. Hoping it wouldn't call to the predator in him.

"We passed please when you took my car, little girl," he growled, his fingers biting into her biceps. He pulled her closer until her breasts brushed against his chest.

"I'm sorry," she offered, biting her lip and trying to look contrite. She really wasn't sorry at all. She'd won the fucking

Sparrow Hawk Cup! She'd shown the world what the Regera was built to do.

He sighed angrily and shook her. She brought her hands up to brace herself against his chest. "Don't lie to me," he snapped. "You're sorry you got caught. And believe me, Riley. I'm about to make you very sorry."

She opened her mouth to snap back at him, but he brought his head down, closing the space between them. Crushing her lips with his, he took her mouth in a brutal kiss that told her exactly how their time together would be. Desire fled as fear set in when he continued to ravish her mouth with no thought for her comfort. When she tried to turn her head away, he took her ponytail in his fist and pulled it back in a brutal hold, twisting her head beneath his until her face was tilted exactly where he wanted it.

He fucked her mouth with his tongue until she was helpless to deny him what he wanted. The fight drained from her and she opened her lips with each invasion of his tongue. The hands that had been shoving uselessly against the immoveable muscles of his chest now clutched his shirt so she wouldn't fall at his feet. Not that he would allow that. He had her pinned with her back against the window.

He wrapped an arm around her waist and lifted her until only the toes of her Sketchers grazed the floor. He crushed her against his body, forcing her to feel the length of his erection against the cradle of her thighs. She whimpered into his mouth as he moved to kiss down her throat, his mouth hot and demanding against her tender skin.

"Soloman!" she cried out, when he bit into the skin of her shoulder blade through her T-shirt.

His head snapped up and he immediately swooped down for another intense, dizzying kiss. She cried out in pain as the day old growth on his cheeks and chin scratched against the ravaged skin around her mouth where he had brutalized her. He jerked back and looked down at her with a frown. It was clear he couldn't see what was wrong in the shadows surrounding him. Taking her by the arm, he dragged her roughly to the side of the bed and switched on a nightstand lamp.

Riley gasped and turned her head away from the sudden light. So he *did* pay his electricity bill, she noted bitterly. He took her ponytail in his hand once more and, before she could jerk it away, used it to turn her face to the light. His frown turned fierce and he swore so viciously Riley wondered if she was about to die. Instinctively, she tried to yank her arm away from him, but he held her tight. She flinched back when he brought his other hand up, but all he did was run his fingertips over the swollen, reddened skin around her lips.

He growled in annoyance and thrust a tattooed hand through his hair before dropping it to his side. Did he care that he'd hurt her? But she thought he intended to punish her for her constant defiance and denials. She was confused. Was the mafia kingpin about to fuck her or take pity on her? She glanced down to see if she was still in danger. Yup, still fucked. Or about to be.

"It doesn't matter," he growled quietly, almost to himself.

He pulled her in more closely and continued to watch her face. His was set in stone, his scarred mouth a relentless slash. He swung her around and began lowering her onto the bed. She brought her hands up in a panic and clutched his arms as though he might stop if she clung onto him hard enough. She suddenly understood what he meant. He wanted her bad enough to take her using whatever means necessary. He was a bad man, used to doing very bad things. Yet it bothered him that he had hurt her. But he didn't understand why, because nothing in life had taught him to be soft. Her heart melted just a little.

She was still terrified though. Far too frightened to give him what he was about to ruthlessly take from her. She just wasn't ready. She stiffened as he lowered his hard body against her, crushing her into the soft mattress.

"Soloman!" she gasped. "Please can I take a shower?"

He stiffened over top of her, clearly not expecting that kind of a request from her. But he *did* stop. She pressed her advantage by wiggling a little, trying to get out from under him. He groaned and thrust his hips hard against her, forcing a sharp gasp from her throat when his erection pressed intimately into her. She stopped moving, looked up at him pleadingly and begged, "Please, Soloman, I feel so dusty from driving all day yesterday and this morning."

He thought for a moment and then finally grunted his assent and rolled off of her. She shot off the bed as though it were on fire. They both knew she was buying time, but it didn't matter. She would take *anything* he gave her. He grabbed her by the arm and dragged her against him.

"Ow!" she snapped. She was getting *really* sick of all the arm grabbing.

He hauled her into an ensuite and smashed his fist against a light switch, flooding a gorgeous, marble washroom in yellow light. Someone was clearly getting grumpy at being constantly denied his sexy time prize. She pressed her fingers against her lips and shuddered. His patience was running out as fast as her time.

She glanced around the washroom and quickly assessed her ability to squeeze through the window over top of the whirlpool bathtub. Yeah, no problem. She dropped her eyes so he wouldn't divine her thoughts. Too late. His annoyed gaze met hers.

"Clothes off," he said coldly, leaning a hip against the vanity and holding a large hand out.

Her jaw dropped. "Not with you in here!" she gasped, horrified.

"Do it now, or I'll do it for you," he snapped. "And I promise, little girl, if I get my hands on you right now, I will fuck you right here and now. I'm just about done waiting. Don't want you jumping out that window and running."

She continued to glare at him angrily until he took a step toward her. She gasped and jumped back until her elbow touched the immaculate glass of the huge shower stall. "Fine!" she snapped back at him. "It's not like you haven't seen it all before, asshole!"

His scar quivered and his lips thinned for just a moment before he spoke. "Watch that mouth, Riley."

She glared fireballs at him, but kept her lips sealed. There was a whole lot she would love to say to him, but kept her peace for the moment. She could tell he was rapidly reaching the edge of his patience. She wasn't used to playing with men like him. Fuck, she didn't think anyone survived long enough to play with him. He deserved it though. He was a dick through and through. She would make him regret fucking around with her. Yeah, she'd burn his house down or something. Not his garage though. She bet he had some sweet deals in there. She'd boost those babies and sell them. *Then* she'd burn the garage.

She threw her T-shirt in his face, ignored his growl of annoyance and reached for her jeans. She did her best to pretend he wasn't there, but knew her face had gone cherry red as she pulled her jeans and panties down her hips. She didn't bother taking her time. There was no point. She wanted him out of there as fast as possible. She reached around behind her and unsnapped her bra, allowing it to fall into her other hand. She was about to fling it at him when his hand closed over hers in a crushing grip.

His eyes burned into hers like glowing coals. She felt his desire to own every inch of her like a physical presence filling up the space in between and all around them. She didn't understand how he could want her so bad. He barely knew her. Yet he had maneuvered her to this point. She was now in his power. She swallowed and dropped her eyes, submitting under the heavy heat of his arousal. He pulled the bra from her fingers and released her hand.

"You have five minutes, Riley."

Soloman stood outside the patio door next to his bedroom listening to the shower run. He took a long draw of his cigarillo and allowed the smoke to linger in his mouth, hoping the subtle scent would calm the blood that sizzled through his veins. The blood that raged through his cock and demanded he stalk into his washroom, drag Riley wet and dripping out of the shower and make her his woman.

He pressed the heel of his hand against his painfully engorged erection and tried not to picture the woman naked beneath the spray of his shower head. It had been a mistake to force her to undress in front of him. He knew she wouldn't be able to go through the ensuite window. The damn thing was welded shut. Every window in his home was shatter proof and only certain windows and doors opened. No, he had wanted her to strip for him, the way she had in his office. And something about having her strip naked while angry was even better. He wondered how she would fuck angry?

She had been in the shower for seven minutes. Of course, she would push her time limit. Goddamn woman never did anything easy. Would he want her as much if she did? She had been a challenge right from the word go. Glaring up at him with those beautiful melted chocolate eyes and refusing to tell him her name. Even after admitting she knew who he was. That made her reckless and brave. A combination guaran-fucking-teed to get him and his dick's attention.

What she didn't know was he noticed a whole lot more than that. She was strong, with a backbone of steel. But gorgeous and soft in all the right places. She was loyal to a woman that was never the mother Riley needed. A woman that was batshit crazy one moment and fucking brilliant the next. She was loyal as fuck to the people she called friends. She ran her legitimate garage and her chop shop like a fucking pro, despite her relative youth and inexperience. She was a woman willing to give the world the finger and do whatever it took to make the people around her happy and proud.

He needed a woman like her by his side. A loyal wife.

He stubbed the cigarillo out and dropped it into the ashtray on the patio table next to the door. He turned and reentered the bedroom. She was standing hesitantly next to the bedroom door as though she had been about to run upstairs and out the front door despite her lack of clothes. She wore only a fluffy white towel over her curves with another one wrapped around her long, dark hair.

Her wide eyes met his and she edged toward the door a little more. The glow of the rising sun coming in from the door behind him caressed her features. She looked so vulnerable, standing there with her arms wrapped around her waist. As though she would break apart if he reached for her now.

"Don't run," he said softly.

Her eyes jerked to his and he saw genuine fear. He wanted to soothe her, but this wasn't the time or place. He knew she wanted to beg for more time. It wouldn't be granted. Every step he took had driven them to this point. He would impress his domination on her, no matter what she wanted. He watched her carefully, expecting her to fly at any moment.

"Do you trust me not to hurt you?"

She narrowed her eyes at him. "You've already hurt me. You nearly killed one of my best friends, you sicced your guard dog on Katie, you drove my mother out of town. You're a dirty, ruthless son-of-a-bitch. You've clearly never heard of honour among thieves."

His eyes became glacial as he continued to watch her every move like a hunter about to make his kill. "If you believe that, then I have no need to be gentle with you. I might as well take you and fuck you the way I crave."

She shivered and took another step away from him toward the open door behind her. Her gaze darted frantically toward escape, before her long lashes swept down in an attempt to conceal her thoughts from him. He took another step closer to her, stalking her.

"You know, that night I went to the shop looking for Riley Bancroft? The night we met?" his deep voice drew her in, commanded her to look at him.

"Yes?" she whispered, her lashes sweeping up. Dark eyes clashed with darker. How could she forget that night? It was the night he decided to stomp all over her life and steal her independence forever.

"I knew you took my car," he told her, his dark eyes cold. She froze, pinned to the spot by his words. "How could it be anyone else? I knew of only one man capable of stealing a car of that rarity and quality. Your father, Alan Bancroft. It only made sense, since the man was dead, that his illusive progeny would follow in his footsteps. I had heard rumblings that the 'son' was most likely going to qualify for the prestigious Sparrow Hawk Cup and needed a car. I put two and two together. Unfortunately, I didn't get quite the right answer, did I?"

She froze, pinned to the spot by his words. He stepped closer to her, his gaze taking in every nuance of her features as she worked out what he was saying.

Reading the growing horror on her face, he nodded. "I was going to end you that night, Riley. Put a bullet in your head," he admitted, his deep voice caressing her, despite the chilling content of his words. "I had to send a message to anyone else interested in touching my property."

"Only... I wasn't what you thought," she whispered, her velvet eyes wide with apprehension. She had come so close to death in her single-minded pursuit of racing glory. What if Solomon hadn't become fascinated by her that night?

He reached her side but he didn't touch her. He didn't need to. His eyes and his voice were powerful enough to capture and hold her. He watched as a drop of water escaped from beneath the towel, fell from her temple and dripped onto her breast. Her chest rose and fell with her rapid breathing. He brought his fingertips up to touch the water drop, catching it on his knuckle and sliding his finger up the soft curve of her breast. She flinched and stared at him wide-eyed as he brought the water to his mouth.

"No, you weren't what I thought," he admitted. "You can now claim the privilege of being the only person to change my mind once I set my course. And Riley?"

She moistened her lips. "Yes?" she whispered.

"I don't change my mind," he told her, his words holding deep significance.

Her chest lifted and dropped with the effort it took to just breath. He pinned her in place without touching her, watching closely as she struggled to breath. He hoped she wasn't having a panic attack. He was going to fuck her. No matter what she threw at him in the next few minutes. He didn't care if it made him a monster, he would fuck a hysterical woman. He couldn't go one more minute without sinking into Riley's delicious body.

"What now?" she asked him.

He didn't answer. Instead he brought both hands up and gently unwrapped the towel from her hair so he wouldn't tug the wet strands. He let the damp towel drop to the floor and reached for the one knotted against her breasts. She brought her hands up and took a quick step back. He snagged her wrist in one hand and wrenched the towel away with the other, baring her once more.

"Soloman, please!" she gasped out.

He didn't fucking care that she was saying his name in protest. That she was afraid and half-heartedly trying to stop him. He loved the way she said his name and then "please" after. It sounded like she was begging him and, fuck yeah, he liked the sound of that on her lips. He wanted her to beg him. They would get there. Soon. Once he'd slaked his lust on her body a few times and brought the raging hunger under control. He would be calm enough to show her exactly what he was capable of giving her in bed. She would never want him to stop. She would wonder why she was so afraid to begin with. Then she would say his name and beg him for more, forming those words with those too sexy lips in something other than fear.

But now… now… as she struggled against him, her naked body wiggling in all the right places, he only saw a green light. He picked her up, took the necessary step to the bed and threw her into the mattress. She let out a yell and rolled onto her belly. She tried to climb onto her hands and knees and crawl away from him, but the view of her ass and pussy from behind only inflamed him further.

He shook his head, trying to remind himself that he wasn't a beast. That he usually had enough finesse to ensure his sexual partners enjoyed themselves. He took hold of her waist in a bruising grip and jerked her back toward him. Her arms flew out from under her and she landed on her chest in the bedding. He buried his face in her ass from behind, inhaling the scent of her pussy.

Heaven.

She froze at the first stroke of his tongue. Probably because she had been expecting a brutal assault, not the ravaging but pleasurable touch of a tongue against her clit. He explored each fold of her pussy while she whimpered and squirmed underneath him, until he finally sat back and spanked her ass cheek with enough force to draw a scream from her.

"Stop trying to get away from me or I will tie you down."

He flipped her over, pinned her arms over her head and glared down at her. Her wide luminous eyes stared back at him, begging him for something. His lust fogged brain tried to understand what she wanted. More time? Slow down? Impossible. His body was on fire for her.

"Stop fighting. Just feel." He tapped the side of her head with two fingers. "Stop thinking so much. Stop thinking about my reputation."

"The things you can do to people..." she whispered up at him. "I've heard things."

"I won't do that to you," he promised fiercely. "I will never touch you that way."

"But you might hurt me." She arched her body underneath him as though to get away, but only managed to press her naked body further into him. He grimaced and tensed, trying to hold himself back from savagely ripping into her.

He didn't want to lie to her. It was inevitable that he would hurt her. She was willful, head strong and loved to throw herself into dangerous situations. "Hurt, yes, probably," he said as softly as he could. She shivered underneath him. "But break, never. I want you whole, gorgeous girl."

"I'm scared of you," she admitted.

He nodded. It was what he thought he wanted. Now he wasn't sure. He ran his fingers down her cheek. "Just feel, Riley. I can make this good for you. Will you let me?"

Her eyes shimmered luminous in the early morning light. She didn't have a choice. He was giving her a reprieve from the anger and punishment he had felt when she ran from him with his damn car. He was willing to make their first time together good for her if she stopped fighting him.

Finally, she nodded and forced her body to relax. Something inside his chest, something he didn't know existed, loosened and melted for the woman underneath him. He would make it good for her if it killed him.

CHAPTER EIGHTEEN

She didn't want him to hurt her and if she didn't let him fuck her he would tear her apart. He wasn't going to let her go and he wasn't going to stop. Her choices had narrowed down to this moment. She either submitted or faced his wrath for the infractions she had committed.

He sat up, his powerful legs on either side of her naked thighs, trapping her in the soft bedding. His possessive heat raking her breasts as he unbuttoned his shirt and slid it over his powerful shoulders. Her wide eyes traced over the tattoos mapped across his chest and up his neck. She reached out hesitantly to touch one on his pectoral muscle, but dropped her hand quickly.

"Touch me," he demanded, capturing her fingers in a tight grip.

He covered her much smaller hand and forced it to his hair roughened chest. He held her hand tightly for a moment until he was certain she wouldn't take her fingers away when he loosened his hold. Her eyes stayed on his tattoo as she traced the pattern. It was some kind of pagan tattoo – almost Celtic, but in the shape of a four-sided, bladed weapon. It protected his heart. She traced her fingertips over the intricate

knots, fascinated by the depth of the work. Her nail accidentally scraped against his flat nipple, drawing a hiss from him.
Her eyes flew to his and she nearly snatched her hand back.

"Don't stop," he growled from between gritted teeth.

She nodded and continued her exploration, touching his
tattoos each in turn and tracing them over his torso and arms.
Once in a while his muscles would go rigid under her delicate
touch until he forced himself to relax. Much to her astonish-
ment, she found herself growing bolder as she explored his
hard body. She wanted to understand the story behind each
tattoo. And she knew there must be one. They were each
unique in their own way and flowed from one to the other.
She leaned up on her elbows and reached for the waist of his
jeans, tracing her fingers around the edge, blocked from
exploring what she suspected was a blade on his hip.

Her eyes met his as her hesitant, trembling fingers reached
for his heavy belt buckle. This was going to happen anyway,
she may as well control the speed. His eyes burned into hers
as she fumbled with the metal. He brushed her fingers aside
and unbuckled the belt for her, then undid the button and
drew the zipper down. Peeling the material of the jeans back
for her, he captured her hand once more and pressed it
against his hip to encourage her to complete her exploration.

Riley's face flushed as she realized he wasn't wearing
underwear. Her eyes dropped down his body, skittering
down the tattoos once more until she reached the blade she'd
been trying to discover. It was clutched tightly in the upraised
bony hand of a hooded grim reaper. She gasped and her jaw
dropped. What were the odds of the man, whose terrifying
pursuit had brought them to this moment, having a tattoo of
her racing handle? She moved further up on her elbow to
better see the artwork. It was both horrifying and beautiful,
frightening and lonely. Just like his owner. Her breath shivered across the skin of his hip, caressing the top of his erection
still trapped in the material of his jeans.

Soloman's hand landed on the back of her head, threading through her damp hair. He tilted her face up to his, devouring her gorgeous features with his scorching gaze. "Fuck, I need you so bad."

He swooped down to capture her lips. Though his kiss was fierce, his lips and tongue insistent, he was careful not to hurt her this time, drawing back each time his control threatened to snap. He coaxed her tongue out to play with his until she was moaning into his mouth and clutching his naked shoulders, holding him tight against her naked chest, driving him crazy with each brush of her engorged nipples against his body.

Crouching over top of her, he broke their kiss for only as long as it took to shove his jeans down his thighs and kick them off the bed. He settled between her perfect, curvy thighs and spread them wide with his knees. She moaned and reached between their bodies, intent on feeling for herself what he had thrust against her so many times. He captured her wrists and held them over her head. Her eyes flew open and met his in question.

He shook his head. "No, gorgeous. If you touch me, it'll be game over. I refuse to come anywhere but inside that beautiful cunt."

She flushed at his blatant words and squirmed against him, her body arching involuntarily into him. She bit her lip and tried to hold his gaze as she whispered, "What about condoms?"

He shook his head sharply, dropping his face into her neck and biting her collarbone, causing her to gasp and jump against him. He licked the small bite of pain away until she was moaning, her pussy dripping for him once more. How could this man make her crave both pleasure and pain in so short a time? What was he doing to her?

He took her jaw in a firm grip and forced her to look into his dark, stern eyes. "Nothing will come between us, Riley.

You understand? I know you're on the pill. We're both clean. We fuck without protection."

Her eyes widened as she digested his words. How the hell did he know she was on the pill and had a clean bill of health? And it wasn't like he knew for sure she took it regularly. With his caveman idiocy, he was damn lucky she happened to have them in her purse and had taken one the evening before. She opened her mouth to tell him to fuck off and put a condom on, when he captured her lips once more and distracted her with another zero to sixty kiss.

He hooked her leg around his arm and pulled it up the bed, opening her wide. She gasped, giving him the opportunity to fuck his tongue deep into her mouth, taking advantage of her momentary shock. He lined his thick cock up against her soaking entrance and pushed forward, forcing his way through tight, unused tissues. Riley cried out into his mouth and arched her back against the mattress in an attempt to relieve the pressure. His cock felt so good, but it was tearing her apart!

He pulled away from her mouth and dropped his forehead to hers, gritting his teeth as though in pain. "Feels so fucking good, Riley. Can't fucking hold on!"

Riley knew she would be sore later, but she also knew he would take her on a ride she would never forget. She wrapped her arms around his neck and arched her body up into his, driving his cock further into her silken depths. She bit back a scream as pleasure and pain crashed through her, tipping her head back into the mattress. He grabbed her neck and forced her head up into the curve of his neck. She flicked her tongue out and licked him, tasting the masculine saltiness of his sweat slicked skin.

He groaned and crushed her into the mattress. He lifted her legs and wrapped them around his hips before driving completely into her. Unable to hold back her screams, Riley rocked the room around them with her hoarse cries as he took her hips in a bruising hold and slammed into her over and over until they were both flying over the edge together. Riley reached her peak first, her clitoris stimulated unbearably by the rough mauling of his hair-roughened body slamming into her. She arched backwards in his arms, flying apart in beautiful abandon.

Unable to hold on once he watched Riley throw her arms over her head and scream out her ecstasy in his bed, in his home, Soloman quickly followed her, his dick gliding through her incredibly tight pussy as though knowing it had found the only home it ever wanted. He slammed himself deep within her, pressing tight against her cervix and flooding her with semen while watching the shock on her gorgeous face as heat penetrated her lower belly.

After a few moments of just watching her flushed face relax into sleepy confusion, he finally pulled out. Her tight pussy spasmed around him, reluctant to release him. He could feel himself growing hard all over again. At his age that should be damn near impossible, but this woman made him feel fucking inhuman. Looking down into her exhausted face, he knew he would have to give her time to rest before taking her again.

He rolled off the bed and strolled toward the washroom, dick in hand. He made quick work of cleaning them both up with a warm washcloth. Riley tried to roll away from him with a moan of embarrassment, but he caught her by the ankle and flipped her on her back. He wedged her knees open and gave her a stern look that she didn't dare ignore. Her breathing grew raspy as he ran the cloth roughly over her sensitive clitoris.

"Soloman!" she cried out, reaching for his wrist and tugging on it uselessly.

God, he fucking loved the way she said his name like that and the way her angel-like hands fluttered against his tattooed hand where it touched between her spread thighs.

Soon she was moaning instead of protesting and her hips were moving restlessly with the maneuvering of his strong fingers against her flesh.

"Oh god, oh fuck, I'm coming again!" she cried out, throwing her head back into the bed.

"Fuck, yes," he growled, watching every part of her move in beautiful supplication on his dark bedspread. He was going to keep this woman forever and make her come every day of her life so she couldn't think about leaving him.

She grabbed a fistful of her own hair as a keening cry left her full lips. A shudder rippled through her body and her hips stiffened against the washcloth as she came once more. He felt the gush of fluid as her body forced his semen from her tight channel. Fuck, he was going to come all over the bed just watching her. Instead, he quickly finished cleaning her up while she shuddered and moaned, turning her hot face into the pillows and closing her eyes in exhaustion.

By the time he returned from the washroom she was sound asleep, emitting the sweetest snores he'd ever heard. His cock was so hard he doubted he would get any sleep, but he crawled in next to her and pulled her limp body into the curve of his arm, cradling her head against his shoulder. Though it pained him to cover her nudity, he reached behind her and pulled a blanket over her body. He frowned. It was one of the first unselfish things he'd done in his life without expecting something in return. A simple act of kindness so she wouldn't be cold. And she wasn't even awake to appreciate it. He barely knew her and already Riley Bancroft was changing him.

CHAPTER NINETEEN

She was gone.

He should've known, the first fucking chance she had, his little bird had flown the coop. Fuck. As soon as he got his hands on her he was going to beat her senseless, fuck her until she couldn't walk, then he was going to lock her in a cage and teach her the meaning of staying where she was put. He couldn't believe he had slept so hard that he'd missed her slipping out of bed and sneaking out of the bedroom. He never slept like that.

Soloman didn't bother with a shirt or underwear. He pulled on the same pair of jeans he wore the day before, tugged them up his thighs and zipped them. He took the stairs two at a time, pulling his phone out, intent on calling in backup. Roman knew how to find people. The guy was a hunter with razor sharp instincts. It was eerie. The last thing he needed was Riley going to ground again.

He was just about to hit dial when the smell of burnt bacon hit his nostrils.

"What the fuck?" he growled as he strode into the kitchen. He stopped and took a moment to just gawk at his usually pristine marble setup.

It. Was. Destroyed.

There were five pans of varying shapes and sizes in complete disarray spread all across his counters. One of the lids was on the floor. There was a bag of flour, also on the floor, but half dumped out, as though someone had tried to lift it onto the counter and realized they couldn't so just tilted it and missed the bowl. He was starting to suspect who that someone was. There were at least half a dozen eggs in various stages of cracking spread from the fridge to the sink. A carton of orange juice was laying on its side, with some of the contents dribbling lazily out.

Well that explained why she had someone in twice a week to clean her tiny condo. He had wondered when he looked into her financials. He thought she was just a total neat freak, like him. Now he saw that it was likely the opposite. Fuck. Now he knew he was in love. Instead of feeling disgust, he only thought this new quirk was adorable. He'd have to see if Richard, his housekeeper, was willing to come in more often. Or hire an assistant.

Deciding he needed to put industrial sized locks on the cupboards, Soloman headed straight for the garage. The only place that would hold Riley's interest once her stomach was filled. His dick came immediately to life the closer he got to discovering her whereabouts. He entered the garage quietly, determined to observe her unnoticed for a few minutes.

He wasn't surprised to find her under the hood of one of his cars, messing around with the engine of his BMW, a plate stacked high with pancakes and semi-burnt bacon perched on the battery next to her elbow. Her dark hair was loosely knotted on top of her head with tendrils floating down around her face. She wore only her Sketchers and one of his white dress shirts with the sleeves rolled up so she could reach deep into the car. The shirt landed about mid-thigh on her until she leaned forward. Then it rode up to the top of her thighs, high enough that he could see the shadowy cleft of her cunt. She wasn't wearing underwear.

Which would have been fine by him except his bodyguard and best friend was leaning negligently against the vehicle right next to her. A growl of anger and jealousy rose up in Soloman's throat and he was preparing to launch himself toward the pair when he realized that the animosity that usually existed between the two was completely missing. In fact, their tones as they spoke were platonic and borderline friendly. Soloman forced his muscles to relax.

He knew if Riley and Roman were both to be part of his future then they would have to develop a rapport. His insane jealousy couldn't get in the way. Roman was obsessed with Katie, not Riley. Taking a deep breath, he stepped back into the shadows and listened to their low-voiced conversation.

"Why'd she leave him?" Roman's voice rumbled. Luckily, though he spoke quietly, his deep voice carried.

Riley went up onto her toes as she reached forward, tinkering with something deep in the BMW's engine compartment. She held some kind of tool in her delicate hand. Soloman couldn't tell what from his position. It was a damn good thing he'd done his research on her or he'd never trust this woman with the guts of his fleet. She turned her face toward Roman and blew some hair off her face.

"She didn't leave him, it's the other way around. He kicked her to the curb. Damn good thing though. That douchebag was as poison as poison can get," she announced angrily. "Hey, how much do you charge for a hit? I'd love to pay someone to take that rotten fucker out. I'd do it myself, but, you know… squeamish."

Roman snorted his laughter and reached out to snag a pancake off her plate. Soloman raised an eyebrow. They had gone from her wanting to scratch out Roman's eyes to sharing food in a matter of days. Apparently hating Katie's ex was an excellent common goal.

"I'll do the bastard for free, just give me a name."

"Colin Schell," she said instantly.

Roman stood up straighter. "You're serious."

"As a fucking heart attack," she mumbled back, still buried in the engine. "That asshole did a number on our sweet Katie. She hasn't been the same in years. I know you haven't really had a chance to hang out with her lately... but she's different now. She *looks* like sex and confidence."

Roman growled, his body tensing. Soloman felt certain he was going to have to intervene. Roman kept his distance though, forcing himself to just listen to what Riley was saying, even if he didn't like it.

"She's not, though. Confident, I mean. She might look like she sleeps around," Riley cocked a brow at him when Roman made a choking, snarling sound. "Okay big guy, we both know it's not true. You're the stalker. You don't see guys coming and going from her place when she's in town, do you?"

"Fuck, I don't know what she's doing when I don't have eyes on her. That's the problem," Roman snarled, looking as though he were going to punch something. Soloman sincerely hoped it wasn't his girlfriend. Because then he'd have to murder his best friend. He sort of hoped the big man wouldn't punch one of his cars either.

Riley straightened and looked up at Roman. "She hates herself, Roman. She only flirts to feel a little bit of self worth. She's broken inside. That fucker broke her and I can't fix it."

Soloman vowed right then and there that if Roman didn't go hunting, he would. Just to take care of the haunted look in Riley's eyes when she thought of what her best friend had gone through. He felt a twinge of guilt that he'd almost killed Katie's brother in front of her. It sounded like the poor girl had been through enough.

"I should've kept a better eye on her over the years,"

Roman rumbled as Riley turned back to the car, stuffing a piece of bacon in her mouth.

She shrugged her shoulders and climbed onto the fender to get a better look at something in the back. Soloman winced as his car dipped and the shirt she was wearing rode dangerously high in the back. Woman probably had zero respect *because* it was a newer model BMW. Probably thought she was too good for his snooty ass car. She loved her classics. With the exception of the Regera, of course.

"Katie told you to leave her alone years ago. Said she couldn't be happy with you breathing down her neck all the time. I know it hurt her to do it, but she pushed you away and married what she thought was a safe man."

He grunted. "I watched from afar. Not close enough, it seems."

Riley shrugged again. "If there's one thing that woman can do, it's make things look good from the outside."

"No shit," Roman agreed.

Riley reached deeper into the darkness of Soloman's engine. The back of his shirt slid right up her ass, revealing her smooth, plump pussy lips to him. All the blood rushed from his head to his already engorged cock. Lucky for his friend's life, Roman's focus was entirely on his phone. He was probably already checking in with their information guy and getting everything he could on Katie's ex. Soloman was done watching from the shadows.

Stepping into the garage, he walked toward the pair. Roman's eyes snapped up and then slid sideways, guiltily taking in Riley's lack of proper apparel. Soloman raised an eyebrow, but didn't say anything. They both knew Roman should've sent her back into the house the moment she showed her gorgeous half-naked self out of doors. Instead, Roman had chosen to pump her for information on his favourite obsession.

Roman straightened as if expecting Soloman to land a

punch somewhere. It spoke to the depth of their friendship that Roman didn't raise him arms to defend himself. He just stood there waiting for a fist to the jaw, his eyes hard, but expectant. With a grunt, Soloman reached into the car, snatched the plate from the battery block and handed it to Roman who took it wordlessly and headed into the house.

Oblivious to Soloman's presence, Riley continued to work on the engine, her small hands flashing in and out of the greasy interior. Smudges marred the previously pristine whiteness of his shirt and showed dark against the light skin of her arms. He never knew oil stains could look so sexy before.

"You know," she murmured thoughtfully, "I bet I could convince her to meet you. I mean we'd have to be sneaky about it, but I could ask her to meet me somewhere first, then…"

"You're not going anywhere, gorgeous, but straight back to my bed," Soloman said from behind her.

Riley gasped and whipped her head around, the tip of her ponytail trailing over her shoulder. She blushed at the smouldering look he gave her. Her eyes quickly flickered down his bared chest, interest flaring bright in their velvet depths. She tried to climb down off the bumper, but he wrapped a strong, tattooed arm around her waist before she could extract herself.

He lifted her by the waist and held her away from the car while he slammed the hood down. Then he lifted her up onto the hood of the car on her knees facing away from him. She glanced uncertainly over her shoulder. He gave her a wicked grin, reached around, took hold of his dress shirt and tore it from her body. She gasped loudly as buttons flew in every direction, some of them pinging off the hood of the beautiful car.

She was left to crouch naked over the hood of his black BMW. He didn't think he'd ever seen anything more beautiful. He grabbed her by the back of the neck and forced her forward until her palms hit the hood as well, spreading out against the sleek metal to catch herself.

"What if we... dent or... or scratch..." she panted as his intention became clear, her breaths coming out in short gasps. She moaned and began to wiggle backwards with the intention of sliding off the car.

He brought his hand down hard on her ass, making her jump and leaving a gorgeous red imprint on the pale skin. She moaned and stopped trying to get off the car. "Fuck the car," he growled, leaning forward to nip at her ear. "I know a great mechanic. Maybe she can fix it."

She laughed throatily and he swore he felt that laugh sizzle through his veins right down to his fucking dick. "I'm a mechanic, not a body shop. And besides, I wouldn't fix this shit. Come on Soloman, you gotta have better taste than this?"

He slapped her ass again in punishment, causing her to squeal and then moan as heat from the slap quaked through her limbs. "Fine," he growled, in response, "then let's fuck this shit up and buy something you like."

"Ooooh, I like the sound of that, Mr. Moneybags," she moaned, looking back at him, begging him over her shoulder with her beautiful, chocolate eyes. "What if someone comes in?"

"Don't fucking care," he growled, running his fingers down the crease of her ass and sliding one into her tight passage, massaging her from the inside. "You wear sexy shit like that in my garage you're going to get fucked, Riley. Now reach out as far as you can and let me see that sexy angel tattoo or I won't let you come all over my hand before we go for a ride."

She moaned and instantly did as he commanded, reaching up the car and stretching her body across the metal hood of the car as he fucked her with his finger. She rocked back into the rough plunge of his finger through her silken passage. When he added another, her eyes rolled into the back of her head. She flexed her shoulders, tilted her head back and bore down on his fingers as the need to come started rippling through her vaginal passage. He wrapped his fingers around her neck and flexed as he forced her further down until her forehead touched the metal of the car next to her hands.

"Stay," he commanded, taking his hand away.

She whimpered and tensed but did as he told her. He was dominant and sometimes brutal, but so far he had done nothing but brought her body to life. She would trust him to give her more of the same. Just for a little while. He wrapped his long fingers around her legs just above her knees and forced her thighs wider. She could feel the slick lips of her sex open for him from behind. She moaned from both embarrassment and need.

"So fucking gorgeous," he growled, running one large hand over her ass and then cupping her pussy from behind. "All mine, Riley. No one else will ever touch this again."

Embarrassment fled as his words washed over her. She knew she should be horrified by his meaning, but in that moment, she couldn't bring herself to care about his possessive tone. She wanted the orgasm that was rippling through her belly and up her spine toward the angel tattoo with her arms reaching heavenward.

"Please, Solomon!" she gasped, rocking her hips back into his cupped hand.

"That's my good girl," he growled, shoving his fingers back into her dripping hole and massaging her g-spot until she was shrieking with pleasure, filling the garage with her sweet sounds.

He leaned down into her and began eating her out from behind, taking long swipes of his tongue through the folds of her labia. He circled and played with her clit, drawing it from its hood and coaxing it into a hard nub of sensation. She was so slippery the sounds of sucking and wetness filled the garage making him wild for her. He kissed his way up her thigh toward her perfect little ass and began licking around the puckered hole. She froze and tried to lift her head.

He shoved her back down with a feral growl, banging her head against the metal. "Don't fucking move."

She whimpered and bucked her hips involuntarily as his tongue swiped up and down the seam of her ass, playing with the tiny, forbidden rosette. He would leave no part of her untouched. He didn't care if it was too soon. The quicker she learned who she belonged to the better. He planned on fucking every part of her, often and without reservation. She needed to get used to the idea.

Her hands reached up the car as though to escape, but he anchored her to him with the relentless, driving pleasure. Fluid slipped from her delicious cunt to trickle down her thigh and onto the hood of the car.

"I-I'm coming!" she wailed, bucking against him.

He twisted his fingers inside her and used his other hand to strum against her clit. She arched her lower back down toward the car while thrusting the angel tattoo upward. Her lips parted in a scream as she came all over his hands and face. Her knees gave out and she collapsed onto the hood of the car, her belly landing on the fluid that had flowed freely from her.

Solomon stared down at the woman that owned him the moment he laid eyes on her. She was his perfection, his every-thing. He unzipped his jeans and pulled his thick, veined cock out. She moaned and rolled half onto her side. His eyes traced the quote that ran along her narrow ribcage below her beautiful breast. He loved her ink because it was part of his girl, but he didn't want anyone else touching her ever again. No more tats for her.

He took a handful of her hair and pulled her head back sharply. She cried out. "Give me that ass, Riley."

Fear flashed in her eyes as she stared up at him. She chewed on her lip and slowly shook her head. "Please, Solomon, no..."

Lust punched him in the gut at the way she begged him. Then understanding caught up. His eyes softened and he touched her lips, still swollen and ravaged from his early morning kisses.

"I will have that ass, gorgeous. But not today. You aren't ready for me yet. I mean lift that beautiful ass off the car so I can fuck you properly."

She nodded and pushed herself up on shaking limbs. Impatient, he grabbed her by the waist and yanked her to him. As he sank into her delicious, silken heat from behind, he dropped his head back and closed his eyes, breathing hard through flared nostrils so he wouldn't lose control and start savagely fucking her. He wanted it to last longer and she deserved another orgasm. But fuck she felt so good. Being inside her was like coming home. Something he never knew was missing until her.

He began moving in long, hard thrusts that shoved her forward back onto the hood of the car. He brought his leg up onto the chrome bumper for better control and held her tight against his body. She cried out with each crashing thrust, her silken pussy slowly strangling him as she climbed higher and higher toward another orgasm. He reached around her, slid his hand over her belly and glided one long finger over her clitoris until her cries turned to strangled screams. He could feel her spasming around him.

He bent his head into her neck and bit down, sucking on her tender flesh. He growled in her ear, "Come hard for me, Riley."

She shrieked and flew apart in his arms, one hand clutching the forearm that was clamped around her middle and the other spread out and reaching desperately along the hood of his car.

Solomon grunted in satisfaction, his dick flaring wide within her, before he followed her over the edge of his own orgasm. Fire ripped through his belly and balls as he thrust one last time into her vice-like pussy before emptying what felt like a lifetime of pent up semen into the woman that belonged to him.

CHAPTER TWENTY

Riley smiled and swiped a towel over the steamed-up mirror. She looked pretty sexy if she did say so herself. It must be all the fucking she and Soloman had been engaging in. It was good for the blood flow. After the insanely hot garage sex, Soloman had brought her back inside to half-heartedly lecture her on the proper use of his kitchen. She had proceeded to show him how good she was at naked clean-up, which ended in the bedroom (it turned out she was not good at naked clean-up, but she was very good at naked other things...).

Finally, after another round of sex and an in-depth discussion on foreign cars and exactly what type of car Soloman was going to be buying her – because no way was she going to let dude promise her a car and not follow through – they fell asleep wrapped in each other's arms. Once again, Riley had woken before him, but this time she had slipped into the shower instead of the garage.

She decided she would surprise him with a naked wake-up blow job and dropped her towel before reentering the bedroom. He was already awake and dressed though when she stepped through the doorway. He was sitting on the edge of their unmade bed, his eyes on his phone and a deep frown on his face. The scar bisecting his lips looked more prominent.

"What's wrong?" Riley asked, wrapping her arms around her middle and wishing she had held onto her towel.

His eyes flicked up and warmed as soon as they landed on her naked body, taking in the delicious flare of her hips and slope of her breasts. Her hair was piled precariously on top of her head.

"Trouble at Merchant's. Someone managed to bypass security during our few closing hours and graffitied the shit out of my lobby. Several thousand in damages," he growled, irritation obvious throughout the tensed lines of his body. He stood and looked at her. "I have to go deal with it."

"I didn't know you owned that one too," she said, avoiding his eyes. The MO sounded a little too familiar. She really needed to call off her troublemaking dog.

"Yes, that and most others in town," he acknowledged, watching her carefully. "I don't like competition."

She nodded absently. "Will you be gone long?"

"I don't know," he said, rubbing a hand over his short hair. "I'm sorry, you'll have to stay here."

She shrugged. "No problem, it's a big place, I'm sure there's lots to do. I'll go for a swim in the pool or watch TV or something. But I do need to get back to my shop eventually, Soloman. Maybe we can discuss it when you get back... and why are you looking at me like that?"

His frown had turned fierce, his eyes cold in a way she hadn't seen in days. "You won't be going back to the shop any time soon, Riley. And I meant you'll be staying here, in the bedroom."

Her mouth fell open.

"Don't be ridiculous!" she snapped, stepping toward him. "I can't stay in here. As nice as your bedroom is, there's nothing to do. You don't even know how long you'll be. You can't just lock me in the bedroom every time you leave the damn house!"

"Nonetheless," he said, taking her by the arms and swinging her around. He walked her backwards until her ass hit the bed. "You will be a good girl and wait for me here in *our* bedroom, where I know you won't get into trouble."

"Fuck you!" she yelled, losing her temper. She tried to shove him away from her, but he was like a brick wall. He didn't even flinch when her hands slapped against his solid chest.

He picked her up by the waist and tossed her in the middle of the bed, where she landed with a bounce. He grunted in pleasure at the sight of her tits bouncing with her. She rolled onto her hands and knees and glared fireballs at him. Her hair came loose from its messy knot and fell in thick waves around her shoulders.

"I would do exactly that and show you just how much control I have over you right now, Riley. But unfortunately, I don't have time." He turned and strode toward the door.

She called his name just as he reached the threshold. He looked back at her and waited for her to speak. She glared at him and said, "It would seem from this whole 'bang, bang, mine, mine' routine you have going on here with me that you want some kind of relationship, correct?"

He growled at her, clearly not amused by her word choice. But he raised a brow and remained standing in the doorway, waiting with as much patience as she assumed he was capable of. She raised up on the bed on her knees, heedless of her nakedness. His eyes flickered over her bare body, a pained expression entering his eyes. He did not want to leave her to take care of the emergency at his club.

"Locking me up isn't a good way to start building trust, Soloman," she deliberately said his name with a slight purr, the way she knew he liked it. "You want me to want to be here with you, right?"

His gaze pinned her to the bed, licking over her body. He gave her a sharp nod.

"Then you have to start earning that respect from me by giving me a little freedom. You have security around this place I assume? Where am I gonna go? Just give me the run of the house. Please, Soloman."

She thought maybe he was going to listen. Her heart sped up in anticipation. Was it possible that this hard man was willing to grant her a little freedom. If he was, then maybe she could consider a possible future with him. Maybe he wasn't as unyielding as she thought.

"Both doors lock from the outside, Riley. Don't bother trying to leave the bedroom," he said, his voice held no warmth as he spoke.

"Underestimate me again, fucker," she snarled from between gritted teeth as the door closed behind him. She hurled a pillow at it as the lock engaged. "That's how I stole your fucking car in the first place!"

Two hours later she was wearing another one of his shirts and roaring up the beach on a stolen motorcycle. She ginned under the black helmet. She'd never ridden a Ducati XDiavel S before. She'd've pegged Soloman as more of an old school Harley kind of guy. But hey, she wasn't going to complain. She needed the kind speed only a crotch rocket could provide to put some distance between her and the kind of hell that would fall on her head once Soloman found out she was gone.

She knew better than to try to go through the gates of his private estate. Security would stop her in about two heartbeats and then there would be hell to pay when Soloman got home. There was going to be hell to pay anyway, but at least she got out for a joyride and was going to check on her shop.

Thank god for Katie and her supreme patience in teaching Riley everything she knew about breaking out of impossible to escape places. Riley's dad had taught her how to steal cars and Katie had taught her the fine art of breaking and entering. Between her two favourite mentors, Riley was unstoppable. Or unlockupable anyway. She grinned from beneath her helmet and enjoyed the feel of Soloman's fine ass Ducati as it purred like a kitty between her thighs.

Riley decided to go to her hideaway garage instead of her condo in case security had already informed Soloman of her departure. They would likely check her condo first. Once she exited the beach through one of the other private properties, she took as many back roads as she could, avoiding main thoroughfares. Dressed as she was, a half-naked curvaceous chick on a bike, she drew attention.

First thing she did was pull on some underwear, a pair of torn up black skinny jeans and a low-cut camo tank top. Knowing she wouldn't have much time before her badass mafioso boyfriend came looking for her, she went flying back out of the garage, hitting the door code on her way out. She was in the process of lifting her leg over the bike when she found herself seized in a vice-like grip and lifted off the motorcycle.

Riley shrieked and began clawing at the arm around her belly. She swung her head sideways and saw a familiar ghoulish grinning face. The fight drained out of her. The anger did not.

"Shank, you fucking asshole!" she yelled, gasping to catch the breath he had scared out of her while attempting to shove an elbow against his chest and gain some distance. "How the fuck did you find this place?"

"Followed you here a couple weeks back," he said easily, pulling her hips into what could only be an erection.

"Fuck. Off," she snarled. "And take your hands off of me right this instant."

He finally lifted his hands. She whirled around and backed up into the bike. She only got another foot of space, but it was enough to give her some breathing room. God, the guy was such a prick!

His gaze roamed appreciatively over her. "Been doing what you asked me to, angel. You like the results so far? Think I've been pissing off the big man, yeah?"

A flash of guilt shot through her. Both at the trouble she caused Soloman and for dragging Shank into her mess. Something that could be extremely dangerous for his health. It was time to call her crazy dog off.

"Yeah, Shank, you've done great," she agreed with a strained smile.

She reached into her back pocket and pulled out a roll of bills. It was something she intended to put in the float at the shop to keep the guys going when Soloman put her back on lockdown, but this would be a better use for it. She pressed it into his hand. He looked down at it with a frown.

"It's time to stop now, though."

He pushed the bills back at her and shook his head. "No, angel baby, I say when it's time to stop. I don't want your money. Never did. I'll take my payment when I'm ready."

She moistened her lips and tried again. "Please, Shank, I'm afraid it's getting too dangerous for you. What if he finds out? He'll kill you. Fuck, man, he'll probably kill us both. Please, just take the money and head back home."

He looked down into her earnest features. She could see him softening and knew her little lie was working. Solomon would never truly harm a hair on her head, even if he found out she was the cause of his mischief, but she needed Shank to crawl back into the hole he came from.

She studied the two teardrops beneath Shanks eye and wondered who he'd killed to earn those. A shudder rippled through her frame and she turned away from him. How many teardrops would Soloman have? He would probably need a bucket tattooed across his face.

That stark reminder of who she was in the process of

pissing off with her disappearing act sobered her up. Once again she pressed the money into his hand. This time his fingers curled around the money and the fragile bones of her hand, pressing a little too hard for a moment before pulling away with the money.

Finally, he nodded. "If that's what you want, angel."

Relief flooded her and she flashed him a quick grin. She turned around and reached for the bike. Lifting her leg, she swung it over. She turned the key and stepped down on the kick start.

Before she could take off, Shank grabbed her from behind again. She was half expecting it this time, so instead of reacting with anger she just sat stiffly in his arms. He pressed his lips against her ear as he brought a knife up to her face. Her eyes flashed in fear.

"Until next time, my sweet angel," he murmured.

He slid he blade through her hair, taking a section of it with him. She stared around in consternation as he jumped off the back of her bike, kissed the long, dark lock of hair and shoved it into his pocket.

What a freak, she thought, shaking her head. She jammed Soloman's helmet over her head and took off before Shank could do anything else weird.

CHAPTER TWENTY-ONE

Fury and pride ripped through Soloman as he stalked out of the mess that had once been Merchant's beautifully furnished lobby entrance. Now, instead of dealing with this shit, as the boss should, he would have to go find his own personal Houdini woman and explain to her exactly what he meant by stay in the fucking bedroom. Goddamn was she ever a handful. And she'd stolen another fucking vehicle.

He threw his cigarillo into the gutter and flung open the door to Roman's '69 Mustang. Soloman was starting to to run out of his own cars. Without being asked, Roman drove like a demon, running lights to get them to Riley's garage. Their guy had spotted her pulling his bike into the lot thirty minutes earlier. Soloman already had three men sitting on the shop ensuring her safety. And making sure she didn't pull another disappearing act on him before he could get his hands on her.

"Gonna mess her up?" Roman grunted from the driver's seat.

Soloman turned his face slowly to look at his right-hand man. Roman's jaw was knotted with tension, the old gang tattoos rippling down the cords of his throat. He knew he was overstepping with the boss, but he chose to ask the question anyway. Roman had a pretty fucked up moral compass when it came to everyone in the world except one particular blond. And now, apparently, the woman that was fiercely loyal to Katie Pullman had wormed her way into his affections.

Soloman studied him for a moment, wondering if this was going to be a problem. He couldn't have a man unwilling to pull the trigger, no matter who the gun was pointed at. Then again, that gun would never turn on Riley and he knew it would tear her heart out if he ever gave the order to take out her friends. So, he didn't think there would be a problem.

"That woman has disobeyed me at every turn, stolen at least two of my vehicles and I'm guessing is instrumental in turning my Audi to ash," he responded quietly. "Have I harmed her yet?"

Roman's eyes met his for a second before turning back to the road. A flicker of relief had passed through them. "I'm fucking pissed that I have to chase this woman all over a city we both know I own, but I'm not going to mess up my future wife. I want her the way she is," he growled, tapping his fingers impatiently against the windowsill as they pulled up to Riley's garage. He reached for the door. "Maybe just a little less goddamned headstrong."

An uneasy hush fell over the garage when Roman and Soloman stepped through the shadows of the doorway. Something metal hit the concrete floor and an engine being quickly shut off were the only sounds that could be heard throughout the large area. Soloman's eyes narrowed as he scanned the space. He didn't see her. She was either in her office or she was hiding out in the bowels of the building where they kept the stolen vehicles. It wasn't like her to hide.

"Close the doors and get out," he barked.

The harsh words had every man dropping their work and moving for the exit. As loyal as they were to Riley Bancroft, they valued life too much to cross Soloman Hart for the sake of a job. Within seconds, there was no one left but the two tall, sinister men waiting on the owner to show herself. Silence reigned.

Without turning to face his man, Soloman said, "Go and keep an eye on things outside. They won't leave her for long. She inspires loyalty in dickless idiots."

Roman grunted, turned on his heel and slammed out the door. Seconds later, Riley emerged from the depths of the building with a frown on her face. Wendell Pullman was only a few steps behind her. He was scowling in an attempt to cover his fear.

She crossed her arms over breasts chilled by the shadowy interior of the garage. He watched her every movement with a predatory glint. "I thought it might be you causing havoc in my shop," she said, her voice a husky shiver of apprehension.

"And yet you still chose to run from me," he gritted out, anger sizzling through his veins. His dick pressed hard against the front of his suit pants. He did nothing to hide his sizeable erection. He'd discarded his suit jacket and tie in the back of Roman's car already, knowing exactly how he would want Riley once he found her.

She shrugged lightly. "Lock me up like an animal and you better believe I'll find a way to escape my cage."

The negligent way she spoke to him, as though his words, *his fucking orders*, meant nothing to her, made him see red. Worse, she spoke back to him in front of someone. An outsider. That someone was taking a protective step closer to Soloman's woman.

"Next time I use chains, little girl," he snarled, stabbing his middle finger at her. "Let's see if you can turn yourself loose if you're chained to me or my goddamned bed at all times."

"You're a fucking lunatic!" she yelled back at him, finally losing her cool and lunging toward him. Wendell caught her arm as if to remind her of exactly who she was freaking out at.

Soloman's dark gaze zeroed in on Wendell who must have sensed the imminent danger. He dropped his hand as though it were about to be ripped off.

"Get the fuck out. Now." Soloman's deep voice held such quiet menace that only the incredibly brave would've disobeyed.

Wendell's feet immediately shuffled toward the exit, but he glanced desperately at Riley as though he wanted to grab hold of her and drag her out with him. He wouldn't have made it two steps before he died an incredibly quick and gruesome death. She put a soft hand on his arm and gave him a quick, negative shake of her head, urging him to leave quickly.

"Take. Your. Fucking. Hand. Off. Now." Soloman gritted out with incredible patience that he was not known for. He was navigating new territory with this woman and he didn't enjoy it. A small, dark part of him questioned if he would have been better off just killing her all those weeks ago as he'd originally planned. Of course, he now knew it would have be like cutting out his own heart.

Riley dropped her hand and watched with undisguised longing as her last champion left her alone and unprotected with the most evil man in the city. A man determined to own her until she bowed down and broke beneath him. When the door closed behind Wendell, she turned and faced Soloman, glaring at him with flashing velvet eyes. Her hands were fisted angrily at her sides.

"Come here," Soloman commanded quietly.

She ignored him, standing her ground.

He raised an eyebrow. "If I have to come over there, I promise little girl, I will put you on your knees and break that mouth in. And I won't be gentle."

"Fuck you," she spat, "since when have you been gentle?"

He didn't give her any more chances. Stalking toward her, he reached out and took her arm in a brutal hold as she tried to stumble away from him. She cried out when he shook her and snarled into her face, "I have been more lenient with you than any other. No more, Riley."

She brought her hands up, but he shoved them down, heedless of the delicate bones he might be bruising. He took her tank top and bra in one hand and ruthlessly yanked them down below her breasts, stretching the material to accommodate her cleavage. He let go and allowed the underwire and elasticized top to push the gorgeous globes up. She gasped and squirmed in his hold.

"Soloman…" she cried out.

Ignoring her, he bent his head and clamped his teeth over one already hard, succulent rose-coloured nipple. He sucked hard on the peak until she was begging him breathlessly to ease up. He wrapped a thick arm around her waist and clamped her hard against his rock-hard erection before moving to pay attention to her other breast. While sucking and biting it into turgid awareness, he fingered and squeezed the wet nipple of her other breast until she was practically crying in his arms. She alternately begged him to stop while at the same time clamping her arms around his neck and holding him hard against her and arching her back, thrusting her breasts toward his hot, torturous mouth.

"Oh fuck, oh god, I think I'm go… going to come just from this," she moaned in garbled surprise.

He let go of her breasts and pushed her slightly away from him. "No, gorgeous," he said with a cruel smile. "Bad girls don't get to come."

She stared up at him, a cloudy frown on her beautiful face. As the dreaminess began to clear and anger set in, she reached for her bra. He slapped her hand away, catching her nipple in the process. She gasped and flushed at the small bite of pain. She tried reaching for her shirt again and he deliberately slapped her other breast, flicking her nipple. She cried out sharply and thrust her breasts out involuntarily.

Her eyes popped open and she stared up at him in horror. They both knew she had just given him something very special. A piece of herself. Something she shouldn't have given. Something he could and would use against her. She enjoyed pain with her pleasure. Fuck, she was too perfect.

"On your knees," he demanded, steel underlying his words.

She licked her lips and glanced down toward his raging hard on. She was a curious little kitty. She was also headstrong and willful. Which girl was going to win this round? Her chocolate eyes hardened and she shook her head, chin coming up defiantly. His lips pressed together, tightening his scar into a thin line. He had hoped playing first would soften her up a little. Ah well. Her downfall would be so much sweeter for the fight. She would make a magnificent queen.

He reached out and took a firm hold of her ponytail, drawing a startled gasp from her perfect, pouty lips. His balls ached just from that one look. He gave in and brought his tattooed hand up to her face. She flinched, but he held her tight, shoving his thumb into her mouth. She looked surprised for a second and then tried to jerk back. He held her jaw tight and forced his thumb deep into the silken recess of her mouth, enjoying the soft, wet feel of her, knowing he was seconds away from feeling that tongue slide along his dick. She gurgled a little before closing her lips around his thumb and sucking him helplessly.

Fuck, she felt like heaven and her lips hadn't even touched his cock. Unable to wait a moment longer, he used her ponytail to drag her ruthlessly to the floor of the garage. He controlled her fall so her knees wouldn't bang hard against the unyielding concrete. Her hands clutched desperately against his thighs, trying to gain some kind of control as she went down. He jerked her head back for just a second, watching the prick of tears form in her wide, innocent eyes as she took the bite of pain in her scalp with a hiss. He slashed a knowing grin down at her and she glared back. He knew her guilty little secret now. He knew she liked that bite of pain. He tightened his fingers, enjoying the way her hands flexed involuntarily into his thighs as her eyes clouded.

He pressed his thumb against her lips, taking just a moment to savour their plush softness before reaching for his belt. He made quick work of his pants, pulling his thick, engorged cock out. She licked her lips, the breath rushing out of her mouth in quick pants of anticipation and anxiety. She wanted to take him in her mouth, but she knew he was going to control every moment. Her eyes flickered up to him and, fuck, he could tell she was turned on by the prospect.

With one hand on the base of his cock and the other on the back of her head he urged her forward, tapping the purple crown against her mouth. He groaned out loud as precum smeared across the perfect, plump surface of her lips, painting her, claiming her. He pushed against her, forcing her lips to part. He'd intended to go slow, enjoy the view as he went deep the first time, but the primitive sight of her pretty little mouth stretching to take his big cock was too much.

Adjusting his grip on the back of her head, he slammed himself forcefully into her mouth, making her take as much of him as she could. Her eyes flew wide and she gurgled in protest as spit pooled around her lips. She gagged against him, her lips stretched wide. Her hands fisted against his thighs. She rolled her eyes desperately up to his, tears forming and overflowing. Fuck, he couldn't believe how good her throat felt working to accommodate him. He wasn't even all the way in. He could only imagine what that would feel like.

"Just breathe through your nose, baby. You'll be fine," he growled down at her through gritted teeth.

She was moving under him, struggling against his hold.

Finally, he allowed her to move back a little. She took a few deep breaths and wiped at the spit that had gathered on her chin. He swiped his thumb along her chin and stuffed it in her mouth. She looked up at him shocked and then began sucking greedily. Ah fuck, such a good girl. He pulled his thumb out and lined his cock back up with her mouth. She tried to turn her face away instinctively, but he used her hair to guide her back and slammed himself back in.

This time instead of just feeling the squeeze of her throat, he fucked her mouth, feeling the incredible velvet glide of her silken mouth against every inch of his cock as he forced it inside her. She choked and gagged on him, but after a moment, caught onto the rhythm and began enthusiastically sucking as best she could while he brutally used her. She moaned in delight, obliviously caught up in the barbaric act. She was so much better than he'd ever hoped for.

She clutched at his muscular ass with her small spread fingers as he used her face for his own pleasure. Far from fighting him, she was helping to give him the best goddamned blow job of his entire life. He was most definitely in love. His gorgeous woman was sealing her fate more effectively with every lick and squeeze than anything else possibly could. He would never let her go.

With a roar, he clamped her head tightly against him and pumped himself into the wet, silken depths of her throat, coming with such ferocity that he doubted she was prepared. He could feel her trembling against his legs as she gagged and coughed on dick, her body automatically coughing up what he was forcing into her. He wouldn't let her though. She'd just have to take every drop until he was satisfied. After a few seconds, he released her. She collapsed onto her hands and knees on the concrete, gasping for breath.

Her now messed up ponytail fell forward obscuring her eyes from his sight. She brought an arm up to cover her quivering lips and wipe away any leftover spit and come from her now red and swollen mouth. He quickly tucked his semi-hard dick back into his pants, buckled his belt and went down onto one knee next to her. Worried that she was upset or hurt, he took her chin in his hand and turned her face toward him. Gently, he brushed her messy brown hair off her forehead.

Blazing eyes met his. She grinned up at him and gave him a silly laugh. "Holy shit, that was hot!"

He couldn't help himself, he laughed too. He genuinely laughed. For the first time in as long as he could remember. Maybe for the first time ever. This was how he knew Riley was special. She pulled things out of him no one else was capable of. Taking her arm in a gentle grip, he helped her stand up.

He watched her carefully while she attempted to right her clothes, then he reached out and took her hand. "Time to go," he said, tugging her toward the door.

She resisted, digging her feet in. When he glanced at her, she shook her head. "Soloman, can we just talk for a second?"

"No need to talk," he growled, tugging harder on her hand until she stumbled against him. Some of the satisfaction he felt at having her suck him off left to be replaced by annoyance at her constant resistance. "You know where I stand. Now walk out the damn door and get in the fucking car. If I have to carry you, I will make sure you regret it later. I have things to take care of. Things I had to leave unfinished to come down here."

"Please, Soloman!" she said more loudly. The edge of desperation in her voice made him stop and look back at her. Tears shimmered in her dark eyes, making them look bigger, more innocent.

Fuck. He let go of her hand and swung around to face her.

"Speak," he demanded roughly, shoving a tattooed hand over his head. He didn't miss the flash of fear on her face as her eyes followed his hand before falling away. Fuck, he thought she was getting past her fear of him.

She hesitated for a second but the scowl he gave her suggested she better start talking quickly. She took hold of his wrist in both of her hands and squeezed it pleadingly. "I've been away from my garage for several days now, Soloman. It needs me in order to keep running smooth. If I'm not around then invoices don't get done, payments don't get collected and shipments don't get negotiated. This place will fail without me."

The ice didn't leave his eyes as he looked down at her. They both read between the lines. He didn't care about her garage. In fact, it was probably for the best if it failed. Then she wouldn't have something to tie her down. Something to keep running back to. A tear trickled from the corner of her eye and spilled down her smooth cheek. He flicked it with the tip of his finger.

"My father built this garage with nothing but hard work and a few good friends," she told him, her eyes flickering with sadness. "I grew up here. I learned to drive here. I made my best friends here. When he died I made sure that his legacy would continue. No matter what. I've poured everything into this place. If I lose it because of you, I promise you will never hold my heart."

Soloman watched the emotions cross her beautiful face. He wanted to capture each one and cage them for himself. He wanted to be the selfish bastard that he was. She was trying to teach him to be someone else though. He didn't know if he could, but he knew he should try. He gave her a quick nod. Surprise flashed in her eyes.

He chuckled deeply and turned to walk to the door, intent on putting at least two more guys on the garage to keep an eye on his woman. "You can stay for a few hours. I have business at Merchant's anyway. We'll discuss what happens after that. No promises though."

"Soloman..." she called out, guilt and hesitation saturating her voice.

He turned and looked back at her, taking in the way she was biting her lip and refusing to meet his eyes. She definitely had something to tell him that she didn't want to say. He sighed and rubbed a hand over his short hair. Finally, shaking his head, he said with quiet resignation, "Fuck, woman. I figured you were responsible for doing my car, but the club too? You really know how to push a man's buttons."

Her gorgeous eyes snapped up and her mouth popped open into a perfect round 'oh.' If he hadn't just finished using that beautiful little target, she would be back on her knees, with his dick shoved right back in there. He was already stirring at the thought. She nodded guiltily, her messed up ponytail bouncing against her bare shoulders.

"I hired someone to distract you and piss you off in the process," she admitted.

"Well it worked," he grunted. "Must be one crazy motherfucker to mess with me in my town. Jesus, Riley. Were you trying to get someone killed?"

She hung her head a little and twisted the end of her soft ponytail to brush against her full lips. She peeked at him through thick lashes, scraping her doodled-on Sketcher against the concrete. "I wasn't trying to get anyone killed. I was just super pissed at you. And I won't give up his name, so don't even ask," she said defiantly, tilting her chin a little. "I paid him off and told him to leave town again."

His lip curved just a little at her sassiness. He could get the name out of her if he really wanted, but he wouldn't. It was enough that she put a stop to the mischief. Even though it'd cost him his second favourite goddamn car and thousands of dollars in damage to one of his clubs. Fuck, she was worth it though. He'd have to remember her idea of vengeance next time he pissed his beautiful girl off.

"I'll accept that for now," he agreed. "I have the one responsible for all the damage anyway. I can spank her ass until I'm satisfied."

She quit playing with the ends of her hair, allowing them to slither back over her smooth shoulder. She watched him closely with those incredible chocolate eyes as though trying to figure out a puzzle. "You really did know it was me that took out your Audi? And stole the Regera? How the fuck am I still alive after all that, Soloman?"

He stood completely still without speaking, allowing her to work it out on her own. She was a quick woman. Even if she didn't want to understand, she would come to the correct conclusion. He could see the moment her eyes flared wide. Panic and awe mixed in their velvet depths. She looked as though she wanted to run and hide from him. Not something he would ever allow.

"Y-you actually care about me," she said, her voice barely above a whisper. It was a statement, not a question.

Anger at her refusal to truly understand crashed through him. He tensed his muscles so he wouldn't stalk back over to her and shake her until she got it through her thick skull.

"Care? That's a fucking stupid word for what I feel. For what I want from you, Riley," he growled across the space at her. Fear flashed across her face and he knew she was seconds away from begging him to stop talking. He cut her off, ignoring her vulnerability and plowing on. "I fell for you the first fucking moment I saw those idiotic shoes sticking out from under that stolen car you were working on. For the first time in my life I had to pull back from a kill. I was forced to question my entire existence as you sat on this very pavement and looked up at me with those eyes, begging me not to end your life. Something inside me shifted. You took hold of me that night and haven't let go since."

She stared at him, her eyes shimmering with tears, small hand covering her mouth. She dropped her hand and said in a shaky voice, "You haven't let me go either."

"And I never will," he said, releasing a breath from deep in his lungs that he hadn't realized he'd been holding.

He'd been afraid she would reject his words. Throw them in his face and run in the opposite direction. Not that it would matter, but he was man enough to acknowledge it would hurt if she chose that path. Instead, she was looking at him with the first hints of tentative acceptance.

"You love me?" she barely breathed the words.

"What the fuck else could it be?" he groaned, annoyed that she was so slow to come to the correct conclusion. "You're it for me, woman. Forever, mine. Get used to the idea, because I won't be separated from you."

She pressed a hand unconsciously against her chest and blinked at him dazedly. She opened her mouth as though searching for the right words. He shook his head. "I know it's too soon for you, gorgeous," he said, quirking his lips. "You've spent too much time being afraid of me and running in the opposite direction. I'll give you as much time as you need. I'll give you forever if that's what you want. As long as you spend that time with me."

He winked at her and strode toward the door, leaving her to sort out her twisted emotions and run back to the safety of her office. She needed to check the mirror and make sure she didn't look like she'd just been mouth-fucked into oblivion. As she adjusted the stretched straps of her bra and tank top, her fingers drifted to her slightly swollen, full, red lips. A dreamy look clouded her brown eyes.

"Wow," she breathed, leaning her hip against her small desk and covering her face with her hands. "Who knew that man could be so romantic? I am so fucking fucked."

CHAPTER TWENTY-TWO

Six weeks later

Riley was in heaven.

She sat on the beach of *her* sprawling estate home waiting for her super sexy badass boyfriend to come home. Yeah, she was claiming his shit. She figured if he could just up and claim her then she was claiming his house, his pool, his cars (except for the dented BMW), the golf course (who knew he had a golf course!), a few hotels, a yacht, a nightclub and various other businesses she had yet to lay claim to. She didn't want the casinos though. She told him in graphic detail her thoughts on gambling. He thought she was being over-sensitive because of Cilia. She thought he was being an asshole for not getting rid of his casinos. Their fight ended in bed, as usual.

She even gave her new yacht away. Of course, she hadn't exactly told Soloman yet. It was payment to Roman for services rendered. But Soloman *had* told her his stuff was her stuff, so as far as she was concerned she could give away whatever she wanted. And Roman loved the yacht.

She dug her freshly painted black toenails into the cooling sand and sighed in contentment while contemplating what car she was going to buy next with all of Soloman's copious money. She enjoyed the rush of boosting cars, but Soloman preferred she go the old-fashioned 'kept woman' route and just shop for them. She squinted at something moving along the beach toward the gentle crash of the ocean waves.

"Scuttles, is that you, man?" she asked, wondering if their brief but emotional affair was about to enter a second chapter. She stood up and moved toward a crab that was clearly trying to get into the water and away from the crazy woman that was chasing after it. "It's me, your one time saviour. Dude, we can talk about old times. Cilia's kitchen, the neighbour dog, barbecue tongs! You remember? Hey, come back!"

She watched as it scuttled its way beneath the waves as quick as its crabby little legs could carry it, disappearing into the dark blue of the Pacific Ocean. She stood with her hands on the the waist of her short black sundress.

"Wow, those little bastards are fast," she breathed, squinting her eyes against the glare of the sunset. "I don't think that was Scuttles anyway. That guy would've said hey and come up to the house for a beer. We had a thing."

She squealed in alarm as she was seized from behind and lifted off her feet. Soloman's masculine scent surrounded her and she relaxed into his arms, tipping her head back into his solid chest. He set her on her feet in the sand and nuzzled the skin of her neck.

"You talking to yourself, gorgeous?" he said warmly, his deep voice washing over her in a way nothing else could.

"Nope, was talking to my sea creature friends," she said with a grin.

She turned in his arms and gave a little jump. She wanted up in his embrace. He lifted her easily and helped her wrap her long, curvy legs around his waist. He groaned as her hot panty-clad pussy came into contact with his stomach. He slid one broad hand down her back and then up under her dress until he was holding her up by the ass. He wrapped his other arm around her waist and held her tight against his body, caging her against him. He slid his long fingers into her panties and down the bare crack of her ass. She moaned and arched against him.

He could feel her pussy soaking his stomach through his shirt. Fuck, she was so goddamned wet for him already. It amazed him how quick she responded to him every time he got his hands on her. He took hold of the strap of her dress and pulled it down her arm, baring her breast. He moaned when he saw she wasn't wearing a bra. Fuck, he was starting to think half the clothes she wore should be outlawed. That was going to be his next project. Get Riley to dress more conservatively.

"Tell me you didn't wear this dress to work, woman," he demanded, dipping his head to nip along her throat until he reached the supple flesh of her breast before sinking his teeth in. She moaned and squirmed against him.

"God, I don't want to talk about work right now, Soloman!" she yelled, arching in his arms in an attempt to force him to her nipple.

"Answer me, or I'll tear it off and you'll never get to wear it again," he growled, carrying her off the beach toward the house. The setting sun lit the windows of their house in an array of beautiful colours.

"Only for you!" she gasped. "I wore jeans at the shop."

"Good," he grunted.

His intent had been their bedroom, or at least a couch somewhere in the house. He didn't make it. With Riley squirming in his arms, rubbing her hot hot little pussy all over his crotch and stomach, he couldn't wait that long. Knowing security would be watching made the lawn unfuckable. He swung his head around through a haze of gut-wrenching desire and then stalked toward the garage. It was closer than the house.

Riley immediately lifted her head from where she'd been

moaning and licking his neck in abandon. "Stay the fuck away from the garage," she moaned, nipping his ear. "You dent another one of my cars and I'll castrate you."

He ignored her order and stabbed the code in, releasing the side garage door. She began struggling in his arms when she saw his intent. "No, Soloman, you'll wreck one of my beauties!"

He took a fistful of her hair and brought her face up to his for a heated kiss, spearing his tongue into her mouth. She took a moment away from her protest to return his kiss with enthusiasm, wrapping her arms around his neck and rocking her hips against his flat stomach. He reached behind his neck and gently untwined her arms. She moaned in protest as he lifted her away from his body.

Her sexy moan turned to a screech of horror when she saw exactly where he intended to set her down. "Oh no you fucking don't! We'll knock it over! I want to keep this one forever! It purrs like a kitten. This is a very selfish move, Solo-man. Can't we just go fuck over there and finish off the stupid BMW?" she yelled and flailed her limbs.

He ignored her tirade, bent her over the Ducati, flipped up her skirt and spanked her ass until she quit yelling. He helped her stand straight after he'd reddened her ass and stripped the dress over her head. She raised her arms and reached for her panties, shimmying them down her thighs. She groaned in dismay when he picked her up, opened her legs and forced her to straddle the bike. Her groan turned to a strangled, throaty moan as her pussy touched the bare leather seat. She gasped and tilted back on her ass.

"You look so good on my bike, gorgeous," Soloman growled, his voice deep and sexy and he unbuttoned his shirt, his fingers lingering over his stomach, touching the wet spot she had left. He groaned, his dick hardening to an unbearable degree. Finally, he peeled the shirt off and let it drop.

"My bike," she purred, petting the bike possessively.

She kept her eyes glued to his bare chest but leaned forward to hug the bike, protecting it from what she perceived as inevitable destruction. His lips compressed into an evil grin. Fuck, he wanted to take a picture of her so he could look at her doing that whenever he wanted. Her beautiful full breasts were smashed against the black metal curve of the fuel tank. Her feet were up on the pedals and her ass pressed tightly against the seat.

He unbuckled his belt and unzipped his pants. Reaching into his underwear, he pulled out his cock and stroked it a few times. Riley abandoned her protective attitude and sat up straighter to watch him, licking her lips in anticipation.

"Have you been using the toys I bought you?" he asked huskily, his gaze flickering to her ass.

He'd bought her several anal plugs of varying sizes. Sometimes they played together, but he told her when he wanted her to wear one when he wasn't around.

She blushed and bit her lip. Glancing away, she shook her head, some of her hair escaping the knot on top of her head to drift around her flushed cheeks. "I can't wear them when I'm at work, Soloman. Way too uncomfortable when I'm climbing around underneath a car. I need to be focused on the machine not my body."

He gave her a wicked, heated look. "Not my problem, gorgeous. I'm ready for you now. You should have listened to me when I told you what to wear this morning."

She gasped, realizing his intention when he stepped toward her. The intense look on his face, combined with their weeks of play should have told her where he was leading her. She tried to swing her leg off the bike, but he brought one broad hand down on her thigh in a slap that reverberated through the garage. She cried out and then moaned as painful heat morphed into something delicious.

"Soloman, I don't think I can…" she moaned.

"You can and you will," he said, trailing his fingers across the angel tattoo on her back and coursing shivers down her spine. He loved watching the angel dance for him when she was excited. He leaned over her, placing his lips against her ear and murmuring, "you'll take whatever I give you, understand?"

Her breath hitched and she swayed forward, but nodded eagerly. "Yes, Soloman," she moaned as he ran his hand down her back over the curve of her ass. She lifted herself slightly off the seat so he could reach underneath her. He slid two long, rough fingers into her clasping heat.

"Ooooh fuck, that feels so good…," she moaned, dropping her head forward onto the handlebars while he pumped his fingers in and out, her slick passage easing his way. She started to rock with his movements but accidentally turned the front tire of the bike. She moaned in frustration and shot him a glare.

He chuckled, pulled his fingers from her scalding body and brought them to his mouth. He licked her delicious juice from his hand while yanking his pants and underwear down with his other hand. Her eyes had gone dark velvet brown with lust and she was sliding her pussy along the seat in an attempt to get some friction on her clit after he abandoned her pussy. When that didn't work, she reached down the front of her body knowing it would take only seconds for her to arrive at an explosive orgasm.

Naked now, Soloman stepped back up to the bike and brought his hand down hard on her ass in a stinging slap. She jumped and cried out. He took her small hands and wrapped them around the handlebars, stretching her across the bike once more.

"I own your orgasms, gorgeous, not you," he snarled in her ear.

Her breathing came in short gasps and she held onto the bike for dear life while he climbed on behind her. He was so tall he could easily straddle the bike and remain standing on the concrete. She glanced back over her shoulder, eyes wide with a combination of heated desire and apprehension. The intense heat of his eyes burned into every part of her, tattooing "mine" everywhere he looked.

He brought a broad tattooed hand down on her lower back and gently caressed, running his fingers soothingly up her spine. She wasn't expecting the light touch and shivered as goosebumps raised along her flesh. At the same time, he slid his other hand underneath her, found her soaking entrance and roughly thrust his fingers back inside her body, shoving them all the way in. She cried out and arched back-wards but he held her down.

When she settled against the bike once more, allowing him to continue, he began tracing his fingers in delicious circles across her back while simultaneously plunging his fingers inside her body with enough force to shove her up the bike if she hadn't been clinging to it so hard with her knees. The dual sensations of gentle and rough swept through her like a fire, combusting her from the inside out.

"Oh fuck!" she screamed, as an orgasm ripped through her with surprising speed. Fluid gushed from her pussy and onto the leather seat underneath her. She didn't have enough brain power to care at the moment. Later she would give him hell for treating one of her sweethearts so poorly.

She collapsed against the bike, resting her heated cheek against the cool metal of the tank underneath her. She gasped for breath, her body sizzling with aftershocks while he used her own sweet, sticky fluids to coat her tiny asshole. She moaned as he circled and pressed the tiny bud with his finger until he was sliding in with ease. She loved the tiny catch as it pushed through the ring and the breathless feeling in her chest as she wondered if her body could manage. Then the delicious, taboo feeling of something filling her ass.

He took his time preparing her, stretching her, using her own dripping pussy juice until she took two thick fingers. She moaned in a combination of pain and ecstasy as he pumped them in and out of her ass. She writhed underneath him, seeking relief from the fullness while gradually climbing back toward another mind-blowing orgasm. She could feel his cock hot and heavy between them, ready to take a piece of her ass as soon as she was ready. Though she'd never experienced it, she craved the bite of him in her ass. She wanted him to own her. Every part of her. God, he was turning her so damn depraved and she loved it!

She rocked her ass back against him, forcing his fingers further into her impossibly hot, tight clasp. She gasped and quivered at the intense, full sensation. "Please, Soloman," she gasped out in a strangled moan, "fuck my ass now, please!"

She felt him go rigid behind her, then pull his fingers out of her ass. He lifted her hips, lined himself up with her pussy and slammed himself inside her silken heat. He thoroughly coated himself in her slick fluids before pulling out. He didn't wait. He didn't savour the moment. Her desperation and words unleashed the beast that wanted to take every part of this woman for himself.

He pressed the head of his engorged cock against her puckered asshole and steadily drove through her anal passage until he was seated completely in the incredibly tight, heated embrace. She screamed and arched against him, bucking backwards as though trying to throw him off of her. His cock was too big, so much bigger than his fingers or the toys they'd been using. She wasn't ready. He was tearing her apart.

He hooked an arm around her belly and forced her to hold still against him while her body adjusted to the invasion. He leaned forward and, placing his lips against her ear, he growled, "Just breathe, Riley. You're doing fine."

She panted and gasped for air. Gradually, her body began to relax as the insanely tight fullness subsided. He relaxed his hold slightly and slid his arm down her belly toward her pussy. He ran the pads of his fingers across her clit, sparking sensations through her belly and surprisingly through her anal passage. She gasped and rocked her hips a little. Her eyes flew wide.

"That's right, gorgeous, feel how good that is."

He pulled her a little tighter on his dick and began thrusting his hips while rubbing his fingers in small circles over her slick, engorged clit. Her gasps became shorter and more frantic as her orgasm built. She tensed all around him and her ass clenched down hard on his cock, strangling him with her body. It didn't hurt at all anymore, it felt so incredibly good. He slid in and out of her ass with grunts of intense pleasure, making her feel full and sparking tiny fires all along her body until she finally flew over the edge of another orgasm. This one was different, deeper in her body. She screamed her pleasure, filling the garage with her desperate sounds.

Soloman followed soon behind, though he would have loved to keep fucking her ass forever. Her perfect, curvy ass. Instead, he buried himself deep between her cheeks and hugged her around the waist, pulling her tight against his chest while he flooded her ass with jets of hot semen.

He dropped his face into the angel tattoo and licked a bead of sweat from between her shoulder blades. She shivered and smiled, dropping her chin to kiss his tattooed hand. She couldn't believe she once thought his hands were the most terrifying thing about him. Now they felt safe as he held her tight, allowing her to drift gently down from the highs of her multiple orgasms. Protected.

She glanced back over her shoulder, meeting the dark, possessive look he was levelling at her. The same brooding look he always gave her after sex. Or after anything they did together, really.

"So now that we've messed up my new bike, do I get another one?" she asked innocently.

CHAPTER TWENTY-THREE

"Wake up, Riley."

She moaned and tried to role away from the hands gently pulling her onto her back. She was exhausted and a little sore from Soloman's sexual demands throughout the night. The man was fucking insatiable! Not that she was complaining. Her body was aching in a happy way, but she was so not a morning person. Unless he was waking her up tell her the new car had arrived.

"Mmmmm, my new car here?" she mumbled into the bedding, rubbing a fist in her eye before attempting to crack it open.

"No," he chuckled and rolled her over more forcefully so she was facing him. She covered a yawn and shoved an elbow under herself in an attempt to prop herself up and give her a better glaring vantage point.

"Then why're you waking me up so ungodly early?" she complained, glaring past him through the uncovered patio door at the morning sunlit lawn like it was out to personally destroy her life.

He was already wearing one of his incredibly mouth-watering dark suits with a crisp white shirt and tie underneath. As much as she wanted to tear it off his body and continue their nighttime escapades, she frowned, knowing he was getting ready for work. On a Saturday. What the fuck? They agreed not to work weekends.

"What's the deal?" she demanded, not bothering to hide her crankiness. If dude wanted to fall in love with her, then he was going to have to take all the bits, including the cranky.

His sharp eyes crawled over her naked torso, taking in the superb bounty of her naked breasts and the tattoo he loved to trace his tongue over before torturing her nipples with his skilled mouth. She shivered and tugged the blanket over her skin, drawing his predatory gaze up to settle on her face. He seemed to be searching for something and it wasn't good. The look he was giving her promised retribution if he didn't get the right answer. Maybe not pain for her, because she was very firmly his love, but definitely death to others. For the first time in many weeks, she was reminded of exactly who her boyfriend was. For the first time in just as long, she wanted to run from him. A shiver shook her frame and she shifted away from where he sat on the edge of the bed.

"Soloman?" she whispered.

"I need to ask you something and you need to answer truthfully. It would be a mistake to do otherwise, just because you think you have me wrapped around your pretty finger." His deep voice was quiet, but deadly. His eyes took on a cold quality that she decided she hated and never wanted to see turned against her ever again. She bit her lip and nodded, dropping her eyes to the bed. He took her chin in a firm grip and forced her face up. "Are you still making trouble for me? Sending someone out to my clubs to cause damage? I know how much you hate the casinos."

Her lips parted in surprise. "N-no, Soloman. I swear! I asked him to stop weeks ago. Did something happen?"

He frowned at her genuine reaction and released her chin. He rubbed a hand over his head and nodded absently. "There was an explosion in the parking lot of Stealing Sunday. It rocked the entire fucking building. There was no way to keep it contained to just my people. Police are involved. One of my security guys was thrown through a glass door and cut up pretty bad. I have to go back out and talk to his family then go file the report this morning."

Riley realized right away that he must've already been out for half the night and just not woken her up. She had probably been so dead to the world after he fucked her into oblivion the night before. Despite his sinister, don't-fuck-with-me appearance, she struggled up on her knees, shoved the bedding aside and threw her arms around his neck.

"I'm so sorry, baby," she said softly into his neck, squeezing him tight against her. He sat stiff and unmoving for a second before wrapping his arms around her waist and pulling her into his lap.

He breathed in her delicious scent and ran his hand over her bare back and bottom for a minute before gently setting her aside. She had felt very clear evidence of his arousal, but now was not the time for play. He had to go back to work. She dragged the heavy blanket back up her body so she wouldn't distract him again. He stood and looked down at her, his sinister mafia mask firmly back in place. She pitied the person that had exploded his club.

His dark eyes stabbed into her, pinning her to the spot. Her heart sped up in momentary fear as her body began to understand something her head was too slow to pick up. "You need to tell me who you hired to mess with me."

She gasped and immediately shook her head. She wasn't particularly fond of Shank, but she wasn't going to give the guy up for instant death.

The muscles under Soloman's incredibly well-tailored jacket rippled as he held himself back from grabbing her. Even the affection he felt for her didn't stop the darkness from within. When someone denied him what he wanted, he retaliated. He stabbed a finger at her, marking her. "Later we talk, Riley. You will tell me what I want to know."

She moistened her lips and shook her head. "I-I can't, Soloman. You'll kill him."

He growled in frustration because he didn't have time for this conversation, but it bothered him that his woman would withhold anything from him. He wanted to deal with this now. His hands curled into fists as he stared down at the woman that owned his soul.

"You would protect this man from me?" he snarled angrily, finally losing his renowned cool. Only Riley could do this to him. "You've just signed his death warrant. I will get that name from those gorgeous lips. And then, love, he's a dead man."

"Soloman!" she called after him as he stalked to the door.

He didn't turn back, but he did toss over his shoulder, "I'll have men watching the house to make sure you don't leave. We'll talk later and you *will* give me the answers I want this time."

She scrambled out of the bed and started after him, but the door slammed shut behind him. She stood naked in the middle of their bedroom and wondered if her fairytale was over. A tear slid down her cheek. It was so unlike her that she touched it in surprise. She never cried. Then she realized she was hurt. He hurt her heart. The bastard was actually capable of making her cry. Which meant…

Riley loved Soloman.

Fuck.

CHAPTER TWENTY-FOUR

Riley immediately got over her revelation and decided how best to use it to her advantage. She would tell him exactly how she felt about him before he could beat her or do whatever evil thing he planned on doing to get Shank's name out of her. He hadn't pushed for a declaration out of her since admitting his feelings in her garage. Her dark, sinister man had simply waited and watched, giving her time to come to her own conclusion. He wasn't going to let her go. Presumably he had all the time in the world, anyway.

And if that didn't work, she would distract him with mind blowing sex until he forgot what he wanted from her. And if *that* didn't work, she would make up a name and send him on a wild goose chase. Unfortunately, as an avid fan of The Simpsons, the only fake names she could come up with on the spot were Max Powers and Hooter McBoob. Somehow, she didn't think those names would throw him off the trail for long.

She showered, washed her hair, blow dried it straight and pulled it up into her customary ponytail. Then she pulled on a pair of worn sweat pants and a blue tank top without a bra. There was no one in the house anyway to see her boobs bouncing around. Once Soloman got home, she would use them to distract him from his interrogation.

Humming the theme song to The Simpsons, because of course that was in her head now, she jogged up the stairs and into the kitchen where she realized she was on her own for breakfast. Damn. No kitchen staff on weekends. Soloman usually cooked bacon and orange juice for her on weekends, but he was busy. She frowned. She had been expressly forbidden from cooking.

What should she do? She was pretty sure he didn't intend for her to starve, and bacon was essential to life. Settling on the floor, she set about breaking into the locks Soloman had jokingly installed on the cupboards to keep her out. With a glance over her shoulder at the camera facing the kitchen, she sighed. She hadn't wanted to give away her mad breaking and entering skills so soon, but a girl needed her protein if she was going to avoid some heavy-handed discipline later.

The lock fell apart in her hands and with a happy grin, she reached into the cupboard for the pan she would need. She stood and set it on the stove, turned the stove on to heat and twirled toward the fridge, now singing "Bohemian Rhapsody" to herself. She knew she was in way too good of a mood for the black devilry Soloman had waken her to, but it wasn't every day a girl found out she was in love for the first time.

"Is this the real life, or this just fantasy..." she sang, reaching into the fridge after making short work of the shiny new lock. "I'm just a poor boy... easy come, easy go..." Okay she didn't know all the words. "Mama, I just killed a man. Put a gun against his head..."

She was about to take a gulp of orange juice straight out of the container when a loud boom rocked the house. Riley jumped back into the still open fridge door with a scream of startled surprise and dropped the container. Orange juice splashed over her bare feet and onto the marble floor. Riley brought her hands up to cover her ringing ears and crouched between the fridge and the island, clutching her aching head. What the fuck was that?

It took her a few precious seconds to understand that the sound definitely wasn't natural and that it couldn't possibly be anything good. She also realized that the ringing in her ears was the house phone. She shook her head to clear the cobwebs and stood, reaching for the phone. She pressed the talk button and put it against the side of her head.

A voice instantly roared in her ears. "Ms. Bancroft, go to the safe room, now! We're under attack. Arm yourself and get underground into the safe room."

She didn't recognize the voice, but assumed it was one of Soloman's security guards. He kept himself aloof from his employees except for Roman. Though she suggested they get to know his security better, Soloman had refused, not wanting her anywhere near his men. Riley disagreed, believing the better their people knew their employers the more they would *want* to protect them. But she also thought she would have more time to change his mind. Apparently, she was wrong.

A sob of fear escaped her throat as she clutched the phone tighter. "Th-there's been an explosion. I'm in the kitchen. I-I don't know if I can get to the safe room," she told him, glancing around frantically.

"Okay, change of plans. Go out the back door," he told her. "I'll come get you. As far as I can tell there's only one guy. He's taken out half the team though. He's one crazy motherfucker. Drove straight through the gates, tossing explosives and ignoring our bullets like they bounce right off him."

Riley froze as her fingers wrapped around a butcher knife. There was only one motherfucker crazy enough to penetrate Soloman's private estate alone. He had come to collect what he thought was owed him. She wrenched the knife out of the block and whirled around as he stalked into the kitchen, his wild eyes searching for her. A grin stretched his thin lips, pleasure suffusing his tattooed face when he caught sight of her facing him with a weapon.

"Ah, angel baby, it don't gotta be that way between us, you know," he growled, his eyes roving over her, lingering on her braless chest. She tried to edge toward the back door, but seeing her intent, he lunged in that direction.

She cried out and tried running back around the other way, but he was faster. Catching her around the waist, he swung her around and gripped her wrist, squeezing brutally until she dropped the knife. Fuck! She should have kept facing him. Although Shank was stupid enough to run at her, blade or not. She was no good at fighting anyway. She was a car person through and through. She hated weapons. The only fight she ever won was bloodying Duke Badger's nose in 6th grade when he flipped Katie's skirt.

Shank pulled her back into his erection and pressed his gun hand into her stomach, breathing in her clean, feminine scent as though he couldn't believe he finally had her. The woman he'd loved and obsessed over for years. The woman who'd held herself just out of his reach. His hands tightened around her until she whimpered in pain, the butt of his gun bruising her hip. She promised him payment. Now she would pay.

He dragged her backwards around the counter toward the kitchen entrance. Her eyes widened as she caught sight of the security guard coming up to the back door, preparing to enter. Shank reached for his belt, yanking out what looked like a grenade. He pulled the pin. Riley flinched against him, trying to get away from the deadly weapon clutched in his fist. Psychotic fucking man!

"Watch out!" she screamed toward the back door as it was wrenched open. Luckily the guard reacted instantly, throwing himself to the side as Shank threw the grenade.

Shank hurled her backwards out of the kitchen and

followed her through as debris exploded throughout the kitchen. She landed hard on her hands and knees. He was laughing maniacally at the destruction, as though it delighted him to see the gorgeous kitchen go up. Grabbing her arm, he dragged her off the floor and carried her straight through the front door with an arm around her middle.

Riley was too shocked to put up much of a fight as they approached his classic Charger. She was *not* too shocked to flinch at the damage the front fender had sustained when he went through the gate. Okay, the bastard deserved to die for that alone. The next time she saw Soloman she was singing like a canary. He opened the trunk, curved a long arm under her legs and leaned down to place a stinging kiss on her plush mouth.

She gasped and surged up against him, punching his chest and shoulders, but he stuffed her easily in the trunk. "Sorry, angel," he said with a grin just before slamming the lid down on her panicked screams.

Riley braced herself in the cramped space as Shank peeled away from the front of the house and raced up the long driveway. Loud bangs erupted when they approached what she assumed must be the ruined gates. Something pinged off the metal frame of the car. She screamed and flinched further back into the darkness of the trunk, curling in a ball, terrified that she might get shot through the metal. Clearly security had no idea she was in the vehicle.

They roared up the road as fast as Shank's souped-up engine could go. The engine Riley had upgraded for him. She knew exactly how fast his fucking car could go. She also knew these old trunks didn't have a release. She was super fucked. She tried to breath evenly in the hot space as she slid her fingers around searching for anything that might help. Shank was definitely stupid enough to leave a weapon in there with her. He would consider them trading bullets as foreplay.

The only things she found was some kind of fluffy, lacy material that she shoved aside after deeming it useless, and several bottles of water. After determining that the bottles were sealed she twisted the top off one and took several calming sips. The trunk was so hot, she was already beginning to sweat. She could feel the car begin to slow and knew they were now far enough away from the house that Shank was trying not to draw unwanted cop attention. She curled on her side and clutched the water bottle to her chest. Maybe when they stopped she could momentarily blind him with the contents, kick him in the nads and scream bloody murder.

That was assuming they didn't go straight to his club-house. Those fuckers were nearly as psycho as he was. They wouldn't help her. In fact, they might insist on a piece of the action. She shivered and curled tighter into herself, hoping that wasn't the case. She just needed to trust that Soloman would get to her quickly and that this day would end happily. With bacon and declarations of love.

CHAPTER TWENTY-FIVE

It took every ounce of self-control for Soloman to wait the half hour for Roman to get to him before tearing after Riley and the bastard that took her. He knew he had to be patient. Roman was with their information guy, getting what they needed and saving valuable time in the long run. Roman would make the smart decisions where Soloman was incapable at this time.

As he looked down at the debris littering his once immaculate kitchen, rage unlike anything he'd ever known washed over him. It was the orange juice container and the liquid spilling across the floor that felt like a punch in the gut. Each breath he took felt like a vow to the woman he loved. He would find her. He would make the man that took her suffer in ways he couldn't even imagine.

He stepped out the gaping back door and looked across the sandy coloured patio tiles, now splattered in blood. Two security guards dead. Geoff, who had apparently gone to get Riley out of the house, was fighting for his life while several others hunted for the '69 Dodge Charger with a woman in the trunk.

Soloman didn't turn around when he heard the crunch of

shoes approaching through his kitchen. Only one man would brave his presence at the moment. Soloman flicked his cigarette into the pool. He'd gotten a pack as he'd headed out of the police station. He'd deal with quitting again later.

"Got a name," Roman's voice rumbled quietly from behind him.

Soloman nodded. The name of the man that would soon die a very brutal death.

"Manuel Alvarez, known as "Shank" on the street. Nasty, batshit crazy piece of work. Deals on both sides of the border and don't mind killing anyone who gets in his way. Apparently, your girl tried to steal his car several years ago. That pretty face is what saved her life. Don't think she knows the half of what he's capable of or she would not have stayed in touch with him."

Soloman grunted his acknowledgment, fury and stone-cold fear rushing through his veins. It was that pretty face and blasé attitude that was going to get her fucked up by the psycho that was bold enough to cross a known mafia kingpin. A man that no one dared to fuck with. For good reason. Soloman Hart did business with brutal efficiency.

"Where is he taking her?" Soloman finally spoke, his words clipped.

Roman didn't hesitate. "Straight for the border. He's going to bury himself in Mexico."

Soloman turned and strode back through the trashed kitchen with Roman on his heels. He walked right out the front door and reached for the passenger door on Roman's Mustang.

"Let's go."

CHAPTER TWENTY-SIX

Riley didn't know when she fell asleep, or maybe she passed out, but she woke up to the rush of cool air on her overheated skin and blinding light. She moaned and lifted a hand weakly to shield her eyes. She began to realize she might be severely dehydrated when her hand refused to obey and only flopped beside her. She rolled her head and squinted as a shadow fell over her prone body.

"Ah my sweet angel, sorry you had to go through that," Shank said, reaching for her sweat-soaked body. She flinched away from him, but he wrapped one arm easily around her legs and another under her back.

Her head lolled as he hefted her out of the trunk. Her fuzzy brain tried to decipher how long he'd driven with her in the trunk, but she couldn't seem to think straight. He cradled her against his chest, nuzzling his lips against her sweaty hairline. She wanted to shove him away, but her body just refused to obey.

"So fucking pretty, Reaper," he groaned in her ear, licking the sweat from her skin. She shuddered and moaned in distress. "So small and helpless. You need me to take care of you now, don't you, angel?"

She could barely understand what he was saying, her head was swimming and her limbs felt so heavy. She'd baked in his goddamned trunk for probably hours. She was lucky to be alive! What she did understand was that he seemed to be lowering her back into the trunk. She struggled as much as she could in his arms and croaked, forcing her parched throat to make sounds.

"Sh-Shank... p... please..." she begged, fighting weakly against him. He already had a wiry strength she could never hope to match. But in her dehydrated, weakened state, it was like a kitten trying to fight off a lion.

"Hush, baby, I won't close you in again," he said adoringly into her panic-stricken face. "Just need to set you down so I can give you some water and some medicine."

She so didn't trust him not to close the trunk, but the tiny bit of fight drained right out of her and she flopped weakly back into the trunk, landing on the cushiony softness of lacy fabric. He cracked one of the water bottles, looped an arm around her neck and brought it to her lips. Riley sucked on the bottle greedily, her eyes glued to the gang tattoos inked over every inch of his skin. She decided she hated his tattoos. They were evil and disgusting, not beautiful like Soloman's.

"Now for your pills," Shank told her, pulling something out of his pocket.

Her eyes widened and she shook her head. "No," she whispered, her voice slightly less croaky now that she'd had some water. "Please, I don't want to take anything. I don't take drugs, Shank."

"I know, angel," he said sympathetically, reaching for her jaw. "But I gotta cross the border with you and you can't go in the trunk. It's not good for you. Can't have you fighting me either. It's better with these until you get the idea that you want to stay with Shank."

She shook her head frantically in his grip and brought her hands up to push him away, but she was still too weak to be effective. She did not want to cross the border with him. She especially did not want to cross the border in a drugged-out haze. She needed to be able to tell someone she was being kidnapped.

He squeezed her jaw until she was forced to open her mouth and then shoved something down her throat until she gagged on his fingers. When he pulled his fingers out, she coughed, feeling something small wedged drily in her throat. He poured the remainder of the water into her mouth and then pressed his hand against her lips and nose as she struggled not to swallow. She didn't have a choice. Her eyes flared wide and watered before she finally swallowed the huge mouthful of water along with the pills.

He took his hand away. She immediately rolled away from him and tried to shove her fingers down her throat, intent on forcing the contents back up.

"Don't you fucking dare, Riles," he snapped, grabbing her by the ponytail and dragging her backwards until she was kneeling at the edge of the trunk with her back against his chest. He kept his fist wrapped around her hair while his other arm clamped around her middle, holding her arms down so she couldn't force herself to throw up.

"What did you give me?" she cried out in fear, her voice hoarse.

"Doesn't matter," he growled against her ear, nuzzling his face into her neck. "I'm'a take care of you from now on. I'll tell you what's good for you."

He lifted her out of the trunk and set her on wobbling legs. Holding her up with a bruising grip around her waist, he reached into the trunk and pulled out the bunch of white, lacy material. Her eyes widened when he shook it out and she finally saw what it was. A wedding dress.

Her eyes met his. Disbelief written all over her face. This was not fucking happening. Dude was taking her to Mexico to… what? Marry her?

"Put it on," he demanded.

Her mouth fell open and she finally looked around. Where the fuck were they? She saw nothing but desert and scrub brush in both directions. He'd clearly pulled off the main highway and parked on some back road. And if he was intent on taking her across the border, then they must still be in the United States. Before she had a chance to ask he reached for the hem of her tank top and jerked it up.

"No!" she croaked, pulling back. The material ripped in his hands and without waiting for her to react, he tore the shirt right off her body, heedless of her struggles.

Riley whimpered in protest, a new kind of panic welling up within her. Fuck, fuck, fuck! Was he about to rape her in the fucking dirt on the side of the road? She wasn't even wearing a damn bra. Her arms instantly clamped down across her breasts and she glared at him, her shoulders hunching protectively.

He didn't seem intent on checking out her naked skin though, he was reaching for the dress and trying to figure out best how to unzip it, his bony fingers awkwardly flipping the material around. Okay, so he didn't plan on raping her in the dirt. Yet. She could put the dress on if it meant covering more of her skin and keeping herself out of the trunk.

"Here, give it to me," she snapped, keeping her breasts covered with one arm and reaching for the dress. She gasped and waved her arm in front of her face. It looked blurry, like more than one arm moving at the same time. Weird. What the fuck did he give her?

He handed over the dress, but clamped a hand over her wrist. "Be careful with it," he said seriously, his eyes boring into her. "It's your wedding dress, angel. Gotta be pretty for our big day."

Her mouth fell open. Both because of the idiotic flow of words coming out of his mouth and because his head was bobbing around big time while he spoke, as though there were some kind of song going on that only he could hear. Or maybe only she could hear? She wanted to sway with him and maybe touch his head and see if the tiny shaved hairs would feel as soft as she thought they might.

Holy shit! Get it together Riley! No touching the kidnapping asshole who you intend to let Soloman kill at the first opportunity. She turned her back on Shank, drew the zipper down the side of the dress and stepped into it. Yanking it up, because she didn't particularly give a shit about being careful with the fabric, despite what the eager groom said, she pulled it on. It was a scoop-necked, sleeveless dress that fit a little tight in the bust when she pulled the zipper up the side. It had a satin underlay with a jagged, lacy overlay that landed in different lengths between her knees and her calves. She might have thought it was cool if she wasn't massively pissed off at the situation and on her way to being high on ecstasy or whatever Shank had given her.

"Pants off," Shank grunted, taking her arm and turning her roughly around to inspect her.

"Fuck you!" she snapped hoarsely, losing her temper and stomping her bare foot in the hot dirt beside the car.

His face swam in front of her. The grinning skull tattooed over his mouth looked more frightening than the first time she met him when he cornered her in the dark as she was leaving work. He'd threatened to slit her throat if she didn't immediately take him to her garage and hand over his car.

Shank bent down in front of her, reached under her skirt, took hold of the loose waist of her sweatpants and wrenched them down her legs. She stumbled and would have fallen, but he leaned her against his warm, broad shoulder. She braced her hand against his back while he forced her to step out of her pants. He looked up at her and slid his hand back up her leg, curving it around her bare thigh. His fingers bit deep into the smooth, round globe of her ass. She froze against him, desperately hoping his exploration would go no further.

"Fuck," he grunted. "No panties."

She deeply regretted her choice not to wear underwear that morning. If she got out of this alive, she was never again skipping underwear in case she got kidnapped out of her own home again. Holy crap, was that a tattoo of a sea turtle on his shoulder? Did Cilia know? Cilia would probably kill Shank for her before Soloman could do the job. Riley reached out to smack the offensive little jerk, but it started running around Shank's body. She chased after it with her fingers.

"Okay, angel-face, I think those pills are working," Shank said with a grin when she crawled over his shoulder and shoved her arm down his back, mumbling about a tattoo, while threatening to send her mother after him.

He stood with her over his shoulder and smoothed the floating material of the dress over her thighs. Leaving the scraps of her discarded clothes in the dirt, he opened the passenger side of his car and dumped her in the back seat. They took off toward the border with an extremely high Riley in the backseat. One moment she couldn't keep her hands to herself and would run them over his head and shoulders, drawing groans of appreciation from him, and then she'd remember where she was and that she was a victim and start freaking out.

They made it across the border with very little difficulty. Shank had bribed his usual border guard and given him a heads up. Riley slumped sleepily in her seat during the extremely brief interview. She didn't have to say a word. Then they were in Tijuana, Mexico and Shank pulled up to the first church he saw.

Riley's eyes went wide and met Shank's in the rearview mirror. His shone with a maniacal, possessive fever. She shrank back into the leather seat.

CHAPTER TWENTY-SEVEN

His.

She finally belonged to him.

Riley Anne Alvarez.

It was too bad she had fought so hard. Even after he shoved more angel dust down his angel's throat in the church parking lot. He'd had to slap her a little until she was able to focus and answer the priest's questions at the correct time. The old man had looked concerned, until Shank'd shoved a gun in his face. Then he'd been happy enough to finish the ceremony, take the wad of bills from the groom and usher the couple quickly out.

Riley lolled in his arms. He sat with her on the curb next to the church. She was in his lap with her head hanging off his elbow. He loved watching her sleep. No one could touch his angel in terms of beauty. Those lips and cheeks. She was one of a kind and she was all his.

He wanted to fuck her bad. His dick was poking up at her where he sat on the pavement. But he wanted her awake and in a bed. It would be easy enough to put her in the backseat of the car, flip up her dress and fuck her raw. She wasn't even wearing panties. And he could tell from the way she touched him earlier that she wanted him too. But his Angel deserved better than that. And she would get better. As soon as he got them out of this hot as fuck city where Soloman fucking Hart could still possibly find them.

He hefted her up in his arms and carried her back to the Charger. Draping her over one arm, he opened the trunk. Unfortunately, she'd have to go back in. He needed his full focus on the road if he was going to get them to safety where they could start off their marriage properly. He had to think and she distracted him. She had from the moment she'd put her pretty, sticky little fingers on his car.

He grinned as he slammed the trunk down on his sleeping beauty, tucking her safely away. He would unwrap her later in the safety of a hotel room, far away from the border.

CHAPTER TWENTY-EIGHT

"Help!" Riley screamed into the stifling blackness, tears streaming down her cheeks.

She knew she should preserve the precious fluid, but it wouldn't matter if she was going to die anyway. She'd been hallucinating and cooking for what felt like ages in the hot, dark trunk. She banged on the lid and yelled until she was exhausted and weak once more. She took another desperate gulp of water and pinched herself in an attempt to keep her eyes open. She knew she couldn't pass out again. She might not wake up.

Her moronic *husband* (did Shank really force her to marry him?!) was going to accidentally murder her before he got them to where they were going. She moaned and clutched her aching stomach. She hadn't eaten since the day before. Maybe longer. Fuck, she had no idea how much time had passed since Shank had blown the shit out of her and Soloman's kitchen and stolen her right out of the house. She didn't know how much more punishment her body could withstand.

"Please… Soloman… find me," she sobbed into the darkness trying to ignore the streaks of colour dancing before her eyes and the terrible stabs of pain that attacked her lungs with every breath she took.

Then she saw him. Reaching for her through the fog of red and black and pain. The tattoos on his hands stood out stark against his swarthy skin, safe and true as he cradled her against his chest. Her breathing eased as his masculine scent enveloped her, washing away the hot, sweaty trunk smell.

"Soloman," she cried, tears leaking from her lashes. She rolled onto her back, with her arms outstretched and drifted into the sweet chaos of her drug fuelled mind.

CHAPTER TWENTY-NINE

Soloman checked his phone for what felt like the thousandth time. Hell, it probably *was* the thousandth time. He knew there was nothing. He had the volume turned high. He would've heard immediately if info guy had sent another satellite image of the speeding Charger or a text with directions. He glanced over at Roman's phone. Nothing.

He clenched his fist and checked the urge to punch the dashboard. It wasn't the Mustang's fault they were an hour behind Manuel. He fucking refused to imagine the things a man like that could do to his woman in that time. It made his guts burn with an unholy, vengeful fire.

He'd nearly murdered the priest in Tijuana when he'd described the fucked-up wedding ceremony Manuel had forced on Riley. It was everything Roman could do to peel Soloman off the man and away from the church before he burned a holy place to its sacred ground. How could a man of the cloth let his beautiful, sweet girl be treated in such an evil way?

She's been drugged.

Pain cut through him as he wondered what she'd been forced to take. The priest tried to describe her symptoms but he wasn't an expert on drugs and he was terrified of Soloman's chilling fury. He prayed that whatever the fucker had forced on his gorgeous girl would not cause permanent damage. Or, god forbid, kill her.

His phone buzzed in his hand. He glanced down.

Xsource: Checked into a motel in Rancho el Coyote. 1 hour SE of your position.

A map and satellite image of what looked like a run down log cabin style motel came through via text immediately after. There was a Charger parked out front of one of the rooms. Soloman handed the phone to Roman wordlessly who grunted his acknowledgment and nosed the speedometer higher. Manuel could do a lot of damage in one hour.

Xsource: **Careful boss. He has contacts in the area. If they know you coming in hot, they be gunning.**

Soloman's eyes shifted to the passing scenery, taking in the relentless desert as it flew by. Roman's car ate up the worn road as though it meant nothing. Their information guy didn't need to worry about the person that signed his paycheck. He would set this desert on fire of that's what it took to get her back.

Hang on, gorgeous girl, I'm coming for you.

CHAPTER THIRTY

She slept like an angel.

Her body was spread out in the trunk like an angel with her arms stretched wide like wings. Even her chest barely moved with her breaths. So ethereal. So beautiful.

Shank reached in and lifted her easily from the trunk. She remained limp in his arms. He was sorry to see tear tracks down her cheeks. She must have been sad to wake up in the trunk. He had heard her screams, which is how he knew she was better off in there. He couldn't have her distracting him while he was driving.

She just needed more angel dust. Then she could belong to him like she was always meant to. He should have taken her years ago, before that fucking mobster came sniffing around. Instead, he'd gone back to his gang and given them the years they'd demanded. Bided his time until he was free. Until his angel called him home.

He watched the swell of her breasts as they moved slowly and pressed against the frayed fabric of her wedding dress. He frowned. The fabric was torn along the edge, as though she had clawed at it. He would have to teach her to take better care of her things.

He planned on giving her the world. They would honey-moon in Mexico. He would take her to his boyhood home and introduce her to his family. They would eat good food, party and make love. They would drive to the ocean and have sex on the beach in the hot sand, like couples did in movies.

He just needed to settle his girl down. Show her how good things would be between them. He lifted her head with his elbow and kissed her lips. He frowned. They were dry and hot against his. But fuck, they felt good. He wanted more. He would get her inside and wake her up. Then they could start their life together.

Just him and his angel.

CHAPTER THIRTY-ONE

"Wake up, Riley."

She knew those words. That was what Soloman had said to her before he left for the club to deal with a problem. Right before the explosion. Right before Shank dragged her out of the house, across the sunbaked land, across the border and into a church. Or maybe that stuff didn't happen? Maybe it was a bad dream and her lover was calling her back to reality so he could demand she acquiesce to another bout of lovemaking.

She needed to wake up and tell him to fuck off. She was too sore. He'd ridden her too hard the night before. Everything ached. He loved to impress his dominance on every part of her. But it wasn't like him to push her this much, to drive her to the brink of exhaustion.

She moaned helplessly and tried to open her eyes. It was so hard. Alarm filled her. The sound that emerged from her lips was barely a frail imitation of the vibrant voice she was used to. He shifted her in his arms and pressed something against her mouth, encouraging her to drink. She swallowed willingly. She loved Soloman, she would do as he asked.

Cool, sweet liquid filled her swollen, torn throat. She

moaned in satisfaction and quickly took more sips of what she now recognized as fresh water. Then it hit her stomach. All at once it went from cool to burning, twisting heat. She struggled to rise in his arms, but was too weak. She moaned in distress as her stomach heaved and the water bubbled up her throat. It spilled from her lips and soaked into the front of her dress. She supposed she should be happy the only thing in her stomach was water. Her eyes finally opened as tears of pain leaked out.

The face hovering over hers was not Soloman's. It was pockmarked and tattooed with a skull that gave him a permanent grin. She shuddered, the tears flowing freely from her eyes. She knew she was unbearably weak and getting weaker with each mile that passed. She knew that she was probably going to die. Not because Shank wanted her dead. He was staring down at her with a mixture of lust and psychotic adoration. No. In his driving need to keep her, he was going to accidentally kill her.

"More water," he mumbled. "You'll be fine, my angel."

She tried to shake her head, but he lifted the glass to her lips and tipped it, forcing more water into her mouth. Her stomach cramped instantly, before the water even went down her throat. She tried to spit it out. He clamped his hand hard over her mouth and nose, smashing her lips against her teeth. Her eyes widened in fearful surprise.

"Swallow it," he said gently, rocking her in his lap, despite his vicious actions. She struggled to breath but was too weak to do anything except swallow the water. He continued to hold his hand clamped over her face, watching her dark velvet eyes grow wide with panic. Once he was certain she wouldn't immediately spit up the water he eased his hand away.

Riley sucked air in and sobbed weakly against his chest while he rocked her back and forth and brushed hair back from her face. She wanted to scream at him and shove him away. Tell him he was the most disgusting human being she'd ever met. She wanted to scratch his eyes out and punch him in the dick. She wanted to steal his car and then fuck it up beyond all repair. Even though it was a beautiful car, there were too many bad memories in that fucking trunk for it to be salvageable now. She was going to throw the wedding dress in what was left of that bitch when she was done fucking it up and then she was lighting the whole thing on fire.

"More pills, Angel mine," he commanded, leaning back with her still in his lap. He dug around in his pocket and pulled a couple of tablets out.

"No… no…" she cried weakly against him, her voice barely registering. She tried to push him away, but her hand only landed limply against his T-shirt and slid down his chest.

"Yes, baby. It's time for us to be man and wife. This'll help you feel better," he said gently, pressing his lips against her cheek and then licking her.

She shuddered and turned her face away. He took advantage by licking her ear and then her neck. She wanted so badly to fight him, but her limbs would not obey the vicious thoughts floating through her mind. Maybe she should just accept the pills? If this was going to happen anyway, maybe it would be easier to just float into oblivion. She couldn't accept his touch any other way.

He placed the pills in her mouth. She let him. He trickled water past her lips, washing them down her throat. She let him. She closed her eyes, shutting out the look of burning possession in his eyes. It was never a look that should be his. It belonged on another. She understood that now.

Riley was never a prize to be won, she was her own woman. She knew what she wanted in life and went after it. That was why she never allowed herself to fall in love before. Until she stole the Koenigsegg. And went for a ride with a man that knew what he wanted. She finally allowed her heart to get swept away. She was no man's possession. But she was in possession of his heart, as he held hers. She smiled happily as she remembered their dance. Sometimes brutal, always exciting.

She felt the soft touch of a finger on her lips, tracing her smile. She knew it wasn't Soloman. She knew it was a man intent on stealing her smiles for himself. She didn't care. She was going to float away in the arms of her lover and hopefully never return. She felt something shift underneath her. Her head dropped back and her arms and legs dangled as she sailed slowly through the air.

Riley laughed. The sensation was so similar to floating she almost thought maybe she had died and was in the process of drifting away in the arms of the Reaper. She forced her eyes open and saw that Shank was carrying her around the side of the bed. They must have been sitting on the end. The room spun dizzily around her, lights flashing in a crazy kaleidoscope of colours before her eyes. She reached out to touch one of the fuzzy lights, but it danced away from her.

Then she was being lowered. Panic consumed her. Was she being put back into the trunk? She would almost certainly die this time! Strength she didn't know she had surged through her and she pushed herself up on the bed, crying out in fear.

"No, angel, lay back down," Shank insisted, pushing her forcefully down by the shoulders. He kneeled on the bed between her legs.

"P-please... don't... make me..." she begged breathlessly, trying to force the words out of oxygen starved lungs and past parched lips.

She fought against him with everything she had, but her body was just too weak. Her fingers scrambled helplessly along his tanned arms and her limbs flailed sluggishly against the mattress. The room whirled in her vision, stopped, and then whirled off in another direction while flashes of lights sparked and streaked, sometimes sharp, sometimes fuzzy. She knew it was the drugs.

She called for Soloman. And then he was there. Standing at the end of the bed. Watching her fight with her kidnapper. Why wasn't he helping her? He just stood there watching, his dark eyes as cold as they had ever been. Then he disappeared. Turned and walked through the open door. Except it wasn't open.

Crack.

Riley froze in shock as Shank's hand connected hard with the side of her face, rocking her sideways on the bed. The dress tore where his knee had been holding it down. She curled onto her side and cupped her palm against her hot cheek. She squeezed her eyes shut and tried not to vomit as pain saturated the numbness that had been spreading through her body before. Her stomach heaved in protest and she worried that she might throw up once more.

Shank leaned over her, took a fistful of her loose hair and wrenched her head back violently. She gasped and tried to bring her arms up to grasp at his cruel hold, but her hands dropped to the bed. Her exertions had drained the last vestiges of energy from her. He shook her by the head and leaned against her back to hiss angrily in her ear.

"Don't you dare say his name in our wedding bed."

Her eyes flared open wide. Had she said Soloman's name out loud? She hadn't realized. Tears trickled once more and her chest heaved in reaction. Though Shank had been horribly brutal in his treatment of her, he hadn't been deliberately violent until now. What had she unleashed? Should she apologize?

She closed her eyes, wishing the oblivion would float back to her. She could feel the drug in her system, but adrenaline was also coursing through her bloodstream forcing her to awareness. Shank shoved her torn dress out of the way and ran his hand up her bare thigh toward her panty-less pussy.

She flinched back and closed her knees, only to curve her spine further against the sweaty hardness of his chest.

She whimpered and opened her eyes. A gun lay on the night table next to the bed. If she leaned forward on her hands and knees, it would be within reach. Was it real? Or was it a drug induced hallucination, like the Soloman that had left her in Shank's greedy hands. She could feel Shank's hand glide up and down her bare leg. He murmured lover-like Spanish phrases in her ears in an attempt to sooth and seduce her. Vomit rushed up her throat and she had to force it back. She squeezed her eyes closed and then opened them again.

The gun was still there. Shimmering in a pool of fuzzy light. It might still be a figment of her imagination, but it gave her some hope. Eyes flickering down to the hand squeezing her thighs, she forced her exhausted brain to put in an effort. Shank groaned behind her and rocked his hips, thrusting his erection into her fluffy, dress-clad ass. Grimacing in disgust, she moaned back and pushed her ass into the cradle of his thighs.

He stiffened in surprise for a moment. Unwilling to let him overthink her enthusiasm, she continued to moan as much as her torn, parched throat would allow and wiggled her butt against him. She willed herself not to throw up as she felt his penis rise up again the back of her dress. He reached around her and clamped an eager arm against her stomach, dragging her further into the disgusting heat of his body and a few precious inches away from the gun.

"Knew you fucking wanted me as bad as I wanted you, Riles, my sweet, sweet angel," he moaned in her ear, his breath hot against her throat.

"Yes, Sh-Shank, I've wanted you for years..." she forced herself to say through stiff, swollen lips. The effort of speaking and moving her body against him was quickly draining her meagre strength.

"Call me Manuel," he growled against her.

"M-Manuel," she whispered.

He groaned and let loose a litany of Spanish that was too fast for her to follow. She'd taken Spanish in high school and lived close enough to the border to understand a fair amount of his language, but not when he spoke like this. She continued to wiggle her ass against him and run her fingers over his arms. Gradually, she started rocking forward and backward, pushing her ass into his erection until he was groaning and thrusting against her.

Finally, he did exactly what she hoped he would, he gripped her around the waist and pushed her forward on her hands and knees. She was so wobbly from ill treatment and lack of food that she immediately collapsed into the bed on her front. With an enormous force of will, she shoved herself back up, arching her back in the process and thrusting her ass out. She knew she had his full attention from the sharp exhale behind her.

He went up onto his knees and looped an arm under her waist, holding her up. He pulled her back against him, slamming her ass into his crotch with a grunt of satisfaction. He ran a hand up her thigh, searching under her dress. She bit her lip to keep herself from screaming a denial at him. He flipped her dress up and onto her back, baring her to him.

"So fucking perfect. My angel," he moaned.

She felt him fumbling with his pants and knew she only had seconds while he was distracted. She reached out as far as she could. Her fingers grazed the handle of the gun. She tilted forward just a little more, the arm holding her weight up shook with the effort. The room spun in circles around her. Her palm closed around the handle and she yanked it toward her at the same time as her body collapsed into the mattress.

"Riley, what is it?" Shank asked from behind her.

She moaned, as sexily as she could manage under the circumstances and tilted her head to look at him longingly from beneath her dark lashes. She licked her lips. "I'm just so w-weak, Manuel," she whispered. "I… need my big… strong man to help me."

"Of course, anything for you," he said instantly, crawling over her body, covering her from behind. She shuddered as she felt his bare, excited dick touch her thigh. He clutched her shoulders and hugged her against him, kissing her angel tattoo.

Terrified that he would see the gun, she kept her arm bent over the side of the bed at an awkward angle. "I w-want to… face you for the first… time… please," she whispered, feeling the energy drain from her and hoping she had just enough to do what was necessary.

"Yes, we have to make it perfect!" he said in her ear.

Rearing back, he clasped her in his arms and rolled her over. Riley felt the dress slip to her waist, baring her completely. She felt exposed, but there was nothing she could do about that now. She brought the gun up as she rolled onto her back and pressed it under his chin.

He froze and his eyes went wide with shock. He leaned back, crouching over her hips. Slowly, he raised his hands until they were level with his shoulders. A speculative gleam entered his eyes as they flickered over her prone body, taking in her shaking arms, sweeping down until they landed on her bared pussy. His gaze returned to her face and she saw the same psycho Shank in his eyes that she'd known for years but never really saw. He intended to fuck his wife whether she shot him or not. Tears filled her eyes as realization hit. She would either have to let him have his way or shoot him.

He leaned over her, placing a firm hand near her shoulder. He used his knee to kick her legs further apart and reached down between them. His face was grim. He understood now that his angel didn't want him at all. That she'd played him. And if she didn't shoot him he was going to make her pay. Then he would do whatever it took to force her to love him.

"P-please don't," Riley begged as he touched her pussy. He would hurt her bad. She wasn't even remotely wet. He ignored her. She closed her eyes and turned her face away. He guided his cock to her entrance.

She shot him.

CHAPTER THIRTY-TWO

"Something's fucked," Soloman growled, tensing, ready to jump out as soon as the car got near enough to the motel entrance.

They were just pulling into the entrance of the motel. The door to the room his information guy had indicated belonged to Manuel was open. The Charger was out front along with another car parked behind it, blocking the vehicle in. Fuck. Something was going down in that hotel room. He needed to get Riley the fuck out of there.

Roman stopped the Mustang behind both vehicles. Before Soloman could open the door, Roman's hand fell on his arm, stopping him. Soloman raised an eyebrow in surprise and anger. Roman never voluntarily touched anyone. He used his bulk and deadly intensity to intimidate. He only touched when absolutely necessary. He turned dark eyes toward his boss and friend. They spoke without words.

Be smart. Don't get her killed.

Soloman took a deep breath, reached around his back and pulled his gun. He'd discarded his suit jacket and rolled up the sleeves on his white dress shirt hours ago. He nodded sharply. He could be calm if it meant getting Riley out alive.

Then he would go fucking ballistic on her kidnapper in a way even he didn't think he was capable of. He wanted to see that fucker suffer.

Roman pulled his hand back and reached for his door, pulling his own weapon at the same time. They left their doors ajar so as not to draw attention from whoever was inside. They didn't hear anything until they approached close to the open hotel room, then they heard low-voiced murmurs and masculine moans of pain.

"Let me do the girl man, she ain't worth it. She fucking shot you!"

"Don't you fucking touch her!" someone snapped and then groaned in obvious distress. "She didn't know what she was doing. Look at her! She's my angel, she needs me."

There was a thump followed by a grunt of pain.

"I am looking at her, moron. She's fucking dying anyway man. I'd be putting her out of her misery."

The rage that suffused Soloman was unlike anything he'd felt up to this point. He saw Roman twitch next to him. He shook his head. He needed a moment to control the black that was leaking through his brain and staining his soul. They were discussing the murder of his woman, *his fucking woman*, like it was as simple as breathing. They were dead men as soon as they'd entered the same room as her, but now they'd ensured the death would be slow and fucking painful as he and Roman could make it.

After about a minute he managed to pull himself under control. He'd tuned out the idiotic conversation happening in the room. He glanced at Roman. Once more they spoke without words. This was why Roman was his right hand. He knew what his boss wanted. The two men in the room. Alive. Bloody retribution for Riley's pain.

They entered the room swiftly after a glance around to ensure the men were sufficiently distracted. Whoever had left the door open had made an extremely stupid mistake. Probably thought he was giving them a quick exit. Instead, he'd given Soloman and Roman an easy in. Shank was laid out on the bed with a stomach wound while another man was leaning over him doing a shit job of patching him up.

"Fuck!" Shank snarled, reaching for a gun at his side.

"Don't you fucking dare," Roman snarled, stalking toward the bed, his own weapon steady on the gangbanger, ready to take him out if he even thought about twitching toward the weapon.

The other man immediately stepped back from the bed, his hands up in a conciliatory gesture. "Hey man, I'm not really involved. Just passing through."

"You wanted to kill her," Soloman said, the chill in his voice uncompromising. His eyes scanned the room. Panic began to crack the ice around his heart when he didn't immediately see her. Where the fuck was she? He'd heard the fuckers talking about her.

Then his eyes fell on a pile of dirty white lace tossed in the corner of the room. Was it his imagination or did it just twitch? He took a hesitant step toward it, unwilling to believe his gorgeous girl could possibly be the human that was collapsed against the wall of the dirty hotel room. He didn't even hear the bellow of rage rip through him until the other men in the room flinched and looked at each other. The pile of lace whimpered and brought a frail hand up to touch her ear.

"Riley," he whispered and strode to the corner, now certain it could be no other.

She was so lost in her own world she didn't respond to him. He crouched in front of her and gently took her by the shoulders, lifting her into a sitting position. She jerked violently away from him with a hoarse cry, flying backward into the corner of the wall. She brought a shaking hand up. There was a gun clutched in her slim fingers. She looked so terrified that, even though he knew he could easily disarm her, he couldn't bring himself to take that piece of comfort away from her.

"Riley, my gorgeous girl, it's me, Soloman," he said quietly, for her ears alone.

He took in her pale, bruised features. The terrified, frantic and searching eyes. Faint, blue marks were beginning to litter her poor body along her arms, legs, neck and face. Her dress was covered in blood and hiked up nearly to her waist. Fuck, he hoped to god the blood wasn't hers. He could see that she wore no underwear. Every muscle in his body thrummed with tension. He wanted to put his fists in the man that had done this and not stop until he was a bloody, unrecognizable mess. But for now, his first priority had to be to care for this beautiful, damaged woman.

She shook her head, blinking rapidly, a single tear leaking from her bloodshot eye. Her eyes frantically searched the room before landing back on him. She stared at him uncomprehendingly. Her tongue darted out to moisten her cracked bottom lip.

"S-Soloman's not here... he left me..." she whispered hoarsely, the gun wavering in his face. He could tell she was trying her best to keep holding it up, but exhaustion was claiming her. Every time her beautiful cloudy eyes blinked, they became slower to open. She was having incredible difficulty focusing on him. The other men in the room may as well not even exist to her.

"No, baby," he said carefully, drawing her attention back to him. She jumped a little and blinked at him. "I came for you. I promised. Do you remember? I promised I would always come for you."

Her breathing hitched and her brow crinkled in concentration as she tried to remember. Finally, she nodded. "B-but... you walked away..." her whispery voice cracked and the gun jerked in her grip. He didn't move. He could hear Roman dealing with the men behind him. Roughly. They didn't matter to him. Riley was his here and now, his whole life.

"I will never walk away from you, gorgeous," he assured her, his deep voice washing over her. He could see her tense shoulders gradually relax. "Not in this lifetime or the next. You will always belong to me, Riley Bancroft. Listen to me, baby, I will *always* come for you. No matter what."

She stared at him, completely focused on his face, as though seeing him for the first time since he'd entered the room. She lifted her free hand from the bloody confines of the dress and touched his face. "Soloman," she sobbed, "you came for me."

She dropped the gun between them and swayed. He reached for her, hauling her against his chest. She wrapped her arms around his back. He was immediately struck by how weak she felt in his arms. He cradled her in his lap, holding her head against his shoulder so he could see her face. She gazed up at him from eyes that grew heavier by the second. She lifted her hand, but couldn't quite make it. He captured her fingers in a strong grip and lifted it to his face.

"I… I love you," she whispered.

Her eyes closed and her head sank to his chest.

"Riley," he said her name like a command and shook her a little. Her head fell back but she didn't respond. Her face was as pale and still as death. Her lips had gone blue. For the first time that he could recall he felt tears gathering in his eyes.

"Riley," he muttered and dropped his head to her breast, waiting breathlessly to feel movement in her chest. Her hand was still clutched in his own tattooed hand, held tight against his cheek as he waited for any sign that the woman he couldn't live without was still alive.

CHAPTER THIRTY-THREE

Agony.

Fire.

Unquenchable thirst.

Is this what his angel had felt when he'd locked her in this very same trunk? Slowly creeping death as his lungs burned up from heat and lack of oxygen. Maybe he deserved this horrific end. He had no idea this is what he'd condemned her to. He thought he was keeping her quiet.

He'd lost count of how many times they'd pulled him from the slow baking death. The beatings in between. Violent, bloody, crushing. They made sure to break his bones, hurt him as much as they could without actually killing him. He laughed through the pain. He was fucking psychotic Shank. He could withstand anything and survive. He'd taken a bullet to the guts from the love of his life and survived. He would smile in the face of this slow burning death from her satanic lover.

The lid of his own trunk lifted and the demonic visage of Soloman Hart looked down at him for what he immediately recognized was the last time. It wasn't a look of rage or even one of satisfaction on the mafia king's face that finally forced a quake of fear to slither through Shank's bloodied and battered body. It was the flat, dead look of acceptance for what must be. He slammed the lid shut and walked away, leaving the gangbanger to dream of his angel until death do they part.

CHAPTER THIRTY-FOUR

"Riley, wake up."

Riley frowned. She *really* wished people would stop saying that to her. So far nothing good had come of those words. Despite her displeasure at having her sleep rudely interrupted, she managed to crack an eyelid to inspect the person who dared interlope on her good dreams. She should have known. It was her mother.

"Cilia," she whispered.

Whoa! Was that horrific croak really her voice? Riley's eyes popped open in surprise, an action she instantly regretted when harsh fluorescent light flooded her vision. She winced, closed her eyes and brought a hand up to cover her offended eyes. Then she winced again when she realized her arm was attached to an IV. Carefully, she cracked her eyes back open and stared at the intravenous line leading from her arm to a bag held high over her head. She frowned for a second. Then her memory came back.

"Fuck," she croaked, panic settling on her chest. She clutched the blankets on the bed and glanced frantically around her. She must be in a hospital.

Cilia sat on the bed and looked down at Riley, sadness

saturating her bright blue eyes. Riley hadn't seen that expression since Alan Bancroft had died. Riley's bottom lip wobbled and tears welled up.

"Mom," she cried helplessly, the tears streaming from her eyes and tracking wet paths down her face.

Cilia leaned over and touched Riley's head, gently sweeping her dark hair away from her face. It wasn't a hug, but it was more, much more than Cilia usually gave. It was her way of loving. Her sad eyes expressed how much she felt for her daughter in that moment. Though it was difficult for her to express. Her delicate, light touch soothed Riley in a way nothing else could, calming her.

After several minutes, Riley had herself under control enough to ask after the one person she wanted most. The one person that should have been there but wasn't. "Soloman?"

A cool light touched Cilia's eyes. She said only one word to explain his absence. "Retribution."

Riley frowned, baffled.

Cilia smiled pleasantly and stood, smoothing her coral skirt. "Never mind, dear. He'll be back shortly. He didn't leave your side all night. In fact, when they dared try to mention visiting hours he had you transferred to this private unit where he explained exactly what would happen if they tried to force him to leave. No one was brave enough to ask. He flew in a pharmacology doctor from Atlanta who specializes in both PCP and GHB, both of which that disgusting little man had on his person. I am very impressed with how thorough your Mr. Hart has been with your care. I haven't had to step in at all."

Riley's mouth fell open. She wasn't sure what to process first. Her mother's being impressed by anyone other than her own self was HUGE. Then, there were the type of drugs being forced through her system. She was both horrified and disgusted to learn she'd been forced to take a combination of the date rape drug and PCP, otherwise known as angel dust.

Then there was Soloman's heavy-handed care of her. Apparently, he'd refused to leave her side all night, yet he wasn't here when she woke up. It was confusing. And it hurt.

Cilia watched the flickering emotions cross her daughter's face. "He's also flying in a counsellor from Vancouver. Apparently, she's married to a friend of his and comes highly recommended. For when you're ready to talk about what happened."

Riley pulled her knees up under the covers, hugging them against her chest, subconsciously recoiling away from the idea of sharing her horrific experience. "I don't need to talk to anyone, especially not a stranger."

Cilia nodded and shrugged her shoulders, turning away from the bed. She looked out the door into the interior of the hospital. It was just like Cilia to watch the people and the inner workings of the hospital than to gaze out a window toward something more scenic.

"Side effects of large doses of phencyclidine, otherwise known as PCP, can include distortions of time, space, body image, and visual stimuli. Impairment of higher cortical functions, such as attention, concentration, judgement, motor coordination and speech. Other symptoms can include paranoia, confusion, hallucinations, anxiety, agitation, delusions, bizarre and sometimes violent behaviour…"

"Cilia," Riley gasped, "stop! I'm not some fucking drug addict!"

The cool blond turned to look at her daughter, seriousness reflecting in her eyes as she took in the agitated young woman on the bed. She smoothed the blanket over Riley's legs. "Of course not, dear. But the drugs were in your blood stream and entered your brain. You should talk to this woman about possible long-term effects and how to cope with any side effects. Including, but not limited to, possible flashbacks, prolonged anxiety, social withdrawal and isolation, severe depression, impairment of memory…"

"Holy shit, mother, stop! I'll see her!" Riley yelled hoarsely. Jesus, she'd become so used to Cilia avoiding her that she forgot how much her mother sounded like a damn textbook.

Cilia beamed at Riley, patted her foot through the blanket and turned to leave. "I'll send Katie and Wendell in. They're very anxious to see you, but Soloman has been strict about visitors."

Riley watched her mother leave with a suspicion that she just got played by the master.

CHAPTER THIRTY-FIVE

Three months later.

Riley stood with her back to him watching the sun set over the Pacific Ocean. She was waist deep in the water, allowing the gentle waves to lick against her tanned body. Dark chocolate hair was pulled high on her head in a ponytail. Her arms were wrapped protectively around herself. He could see her black chipped nails splayed against the skin of her back on either side. The thin black strap of her bikini halter trailed down between the angel's wings of her tattoo. She was so fucking beautiful it made him ache deep inside.

He wanted to smile, but he couldn't. Eventually they would get there. But for now, his chest ached too much at how serious his gorgeous girl had become. He almost always knew to find her outdoors at this time of day when he came home from work. Claustrophobia was probably the biggest side effect to her ordeal. He calmly dealt with it by clearing out the local pharmacy of all their sunscreen so she could spend as much time outdoors as she needed. She also had about a hundred new hats to choose from to protect her face from the sun. Hats she never wore, he noted with annoyance, stripping the clothes from his body and leaving them in the sand.

He also watched quietly and never said a word as she opened every door and window in their house, allowing flies and critters to wander through. That was how they'd adopted McDavid the month before. An ugly as fuck snaggletooth Shepard mix that had wandered in looking for a handout and found the mess Riley had made in the kitchen. Somehow the mangy mutt could calm Riley's panic attacks when nothing else could. So the damn dog stayed.

Soloman didn't push her to go to counselling. Surprisingly it was Cilia that managed to talk her into seeing his friend's wife. And the counselling seemed to help gradually heal her trauma. She opened up bit by bit about her experience. Sometimes she cried. Sometimes she raged and threw things. He didn't care what she did as long as she got it out and kept it out.

He waded out into the ocean, splashing a little so she wouldn't be surprised. Some days she got stuck in her own head. He hated the terror that would cross her features when something or someone startled her. He noted the gradual loosening of her shoulders and knew that she was aware of his presence. His lips twitched upward.

She turned her head to the side as he came up behind her and wrapped his arms around her. She leaned her head back against his chest. He loved the way her soft hair fell between them and rubbed against his hard body. Then he saw the necklace. She was wearing his choker. Fuck, that sign of his possession combined with her tiny bikini nearly made him come right then and there. Was she telling him she was finally ready to resume intimacy?

"You're late," she said, her voice softly accusing.

The rage he felt every time he heard her damaged voice was like a fresh wound. Her voice was softer now, hoarse and sexy. But not the Riley he'd originally met. Not the confident, strident woman that told him to fuck off in no uncertain tones. That Riley had been taken. Her voice had been torn to shreds from screams of terror and agony as she slowly baked to death in a trunk.

He never let her know how he felt. He was never anything but infinitely gentle. It cost him. He wanted the man that had hurt his girl back under his hands. He would make him pay. Again and again. For a thousand lifetimes.

"Trouble at Merchant's," he told her not wanting to elaborate. He didn't know how she'd feel about his most recent bout of trouble.

She turned in his arms pressing her full breasts against him. Breath hissed through his teeth as he tried like hell to tame his reaction to her. Knowing what she'd been through, understanding what that sick fuck had tried to do to her, he'd kept his distance. But now, with her in his arms, pressing herself curves against him, nothing could stop his cock from rising up between them.

And for the first time in a long time, a smile curved her gorgeous lips. She clutched his biceps, tilted her head back, pressed her stomach against his erection and grinned with her eyes closed. He held her loosely in his arms just watching her glow in the light of the setting sun. So incredibly down to earth and lovely. He couldn't imagine wanting anything else in his life.

She opened her eyes and looked at him mischievously through her lashes. "Is Cilia causing mischief in your club?" she asked innocently. A little too innocently. The little vixen knew something.

His arms tightened around her and he dragged her up his body. He slid an arm up her back and cupped her head, forcing her face up to his. "What exactly do you know about it, Riley Bancroft?"

She bit her lip to stifle the giggle that threatened to erupt and shrugged her shoulders. He reached into the water for her leg and lifted it high to hook around his hip. She gasped as his thick cock rubbed against her bikini bottom. He pulled her other leg up and cupped her ass in one large hand, sliding his fingers into the material.

"I may or may not know something about a large amount of missing funds," she admitted in a breathless rush, her melted chocolate eyes clouding with lust.

Jesus, she knew about the money. And fucked if he cared. He wanted her so fucking bad in that moment he was about to shrug off six million dollars just so he could slide his cock into her willing heat. Apparently, she had the same thought, because she tangled her fingers in his hair and tugged his head down to hers, spearing his mouth with her tongue.

He groaned and shoved her tongue back into her mouth with his own before orally fucking her with every pent up sexual feeling he'd had over the past three months. He felt like he finally had his girl in his arms instead of a ghost. She felt so good, so alive. He'd been willing to wait for as long as it took for her to be ready. He would have waited forever if that was what she'd wanted. But fuck, three months felt like forever.

He turned in the water with her and started toward the beach with her nibbling at his neck. She breathed sexily in his ear before moaning, "Don't you want to know why she stole the money?"

"No offence, gorgeous, don't want to talk about your mother right now. Want to lay you down on the beach and fuck you until we both can't stand anymore... wait... why would she tell you about any of this?" he finally asked. "That's not like her, right?"

They emerged from the ocean together. He let her slide through his arms until her feet sank into the soft sand next to his expensive suit, which was now going to have to be thoroughly cleaned. She smiled and nodded. "Now you're catching on."

"I'll bite," he growled. "Why did she steal the money?"

A beautiful blush splashed across her face and she looked away from him. It was so unlike his Riley to not be completely forthright that he was shocked for a moment.

Finally, with her eyes glued to his chest, she said, "She's holding the money for ransom. She wants us to get married. It's going to be a wedding gift. You say, 'I do' and she transfers the money back."

He stared down at her in surprise. "And she told you this?" he asked incredulously.

She nodded and laughed a little. "About an hour ago. She left town just in case you decided to be pissed. Understanding people's reactions aren't really her thing, so she likes to be safe, just in case things don't go as planned."

Soloman wanted to laugh. He was beginning to really enjoy his bizarre soon-to-be mother-in-law. He'd have to keep a better eye on his assets around her though. Instead, he dropped to his knees in the sand, surprising Riley. Her hands fell to his shoulders and her eyes widened in shock. She opened her mouth, but he shook his head sharply.

He took her hands in his. "I don't give a fuck about the money, Riley. I would throw it all away if it meant I got to spend the next ten minutes with you. She can keep it. I should have proposed to you the moment I saw you in the garage. You would've thought I was crazy, but it's what I wanted to do. Instead, I scared you, bullied you and forced you to come to me."

She smiled at him and raised her eyebrow. "Are you about to apologize for all that?"

"No," he growled.

She laughed, her belly shaking against him. He loved the feeling. "Of course not," she said, "because you'd do it all over again, wouldn't you?"

"If it meant you belonged to me in the end, then yes, I'd do it all over again. Marry me, Riley?"

She dropped to her knees in the sand and wrapped her arms around his neck. Pressing her lips to his, she drew back just enough to whisper, "yes."

He crushed her against his chest and kissed her with everything he felt since the first moment he saw her. He forced her to feel how crazy she made him. She returned the pressure kiss for kiss. He pushed her backwards to sprawl on top of his suit in the sand. She watched through dark chocolate eyes as he yanked her bikini bottoms down her legs. He shoved the halter top over her head causing her breasts to bounce.

"Want to be gentle with you," he growled. "Can't right now."

She looked up at him with hooded eyes, giving him what he wanted. Permission to fuck her the way he needed to. Her chest rose and fell rapidly as she struggled to catch her breath. She reached for him, dragging him down against her, running her hands over his tattooed shoulders and holding him tightly against her. His fists landed beside her. She rolled her head to the side and kissed the tattoo on the back of his hand before looking back up at him with passion clouded eyes. He reached down and thrust one long, thick finger into her pussy. She cried out and arched against him. Thank fuck, she was soaked for him.

He lifted her leg into the curve of his elbow and opened her up to him. Leaning down, he kissed her gorgeous plush lips and drove inside, slamming home in one thrust. He pierced into the heart of her, forcing his way through tight silken tissue. He swallowed her cries as she arched to relieve the pressure. Hooking an arm underneath her, he lifted her tight against him and began fucking her with long, sure strokes. Soon the tightness eased and pleasure flooded through her. She rocked her hips against him, seeking the incredible sensations only he was capable of giving her.

She dug her fingers deep into his arms, securing herself

against him. Soloman grunted in satisfaction, loving the bite of her nails in his skin. He dropped his head and nuzzled her breasts where they bounced in time with his thrusts. He bit down on the tiny peach bud, drawing a small scream from her throat. She arched up into him as the small bite of pain sizzled through her body and pooled in her clit. He made sure her body arched into his just right so her clit rubbed the right spot.

"Oh god, oh Soloman," she cried out, her eyes flying wide. "I'm coming!"

He grunted and tightened his hold on her, watching every flicker of emotion as it crossed her face while she orgasmed beneath him. The tiny widening of her eyes, the 'O' of her mouth, the flare of her small nostrils and the moan as it escaped from her sexy throat. He wanted to capture the moment forever.

He dropped his head into her neck and bit down just enough to mark her before following her over the edge of bliss with a powerful orgasm of his own. Fuck it felt good to empty himself in this woman again, after all these months of waiting. Slowly he lowered himself onto her, careful not to allow too much of his weight to crush her. She wrapped her arms around his naked back, her fingers gently tracing one of his tattoos. She kept her legs hooked around his hips. He was fine with the arrangement. He'd be ready for round two soon enough.

Lifting his head from her breast he stabbed her with his dark gaze.

"We'll get married tomorrow," he told her.

Her finger froze midway through the pattern she was tracing and her mouth opened in surprise. "That's too soon!" she told him. "We have to wait for Cilia to come back at least."

His hands tightened around her. "Not a fucking chance. You agreed to be my wife, now I'm locking this shit down.

Tomorrow. Your mom had the chance to come to the wedding, she took off with my six million instead."

Her mouth remained open for several seconds while she thought about it. Finally, she shrugged, her shoulders moving underneath him. Her warm eyes glowed and she licked her lips provocatively. "Fuck me again and I'll think about it."

He reached up, took a fistful of her hair and dragged her head back. He kissed a path up her throat to her chin and then claimed her lips. Moving his hips back, he thrust forcefully back into her wet heat, their combined fluids easing his way. She moaned in delight, tightening her arms and legs around him.

"You'll marry me tomorrow, whether you agree or not," he grunted against her lips.

She grinned up at him. "Because you love me and you'll always come for me?"

"Fuck, yes, gorgeous. Always."

THE END

EXCERPT: THIEVING HEARTS – BOOK 2 OF DRIVEN HEARTS

Revulsion hit Katie like a punch in the stomach. It was everything she could do to search for the key to her old apartment in her coach bag, fit it in the lock and open the door. She wasn't sure who she hated more, her ex-husband or herself. She didn't understand how he could feel such disgust for her and her profession, yet summon her here month after month. Oh, she understood the money. Blackmail for money was an easy concept to comprehend. It was the sex she didn't get.

She shifted uneasily in her knee length button up tan coat. Reaching for the belt, she knotted it tighter around her too slender waist. She knew she'd lost too much weight recently. Constant fear and agitation had taken its toll on her figure. She spent every waking moment terrified that the FBI were going to break down her door. All because of the man whose apartment she was about to enter.

Something didn't feel right. Usually she heard the sound of music or the TV blaring. The smell of food would hit her as she cracked open the door and stood nervously waiting for his summons. Colin liked to keep her waiting. Like a dog or a slave. Today she heard nothing.

She pushed the door open further and saw that the interior of his apartment was flooded in darkness. Had he forgotten about their appointment? Impossible. It was the same time every month. Since the day of their divorce a year ago. She would come to him on the 25th of the month at 8 pm, like clockwork. If she didn't, he would make the call that would end her life.

Something definitely wasn't right. Her legs began to shake. She wished desperately that she wasn't wearing four inch heels. Not that it was her choice. Colin chose her apparel for these visits. It rarely deviated. He liked the easy access of the coat, heels and nothing else.

She stepped further into the apartment, allowing the door to close behind her. The sound of the muffled slam made her jump. Her heart pounded in fear and her palms dampened. She smelled something metallic.

Blood.

She bit her lip to hold back a whimper. "C-Colin?" she whispered. Then realized he wouldn't possibly be able to hear her unless he was standing right next to her.

"Colin!" she called in a stronger voice.

When he didn't answer she took a few more steps closer to what used to be her kitchen before the divorce. Before Colin had taken everything from her and then demanded more every month after. A $25,000 payment and her on her back with her legs spread, a willing vessel for him to use as many times as he wanted before kicking her out like some dirty whore. Something he liked to call her during their hours together. She shuddered.

With shaking fingers, she reached for the light and pushed. The bright overhead light blinded her for a moment. She blinked and then turned her head toward the metallic smell, forcing herself to brave the possibility that something might have happened to Colin. She gasped in horror as she took in a pool of blood that was far too big for someone to simply walk away from.

She whimpered and backed away from the kitchen, intent on reaching the door, her eyes glued to the blood. It was almost perfect in its shiny depth, the way it was spread across the floor. No smears, or prints to mar its glassy surface. She forced herself to blink and continue moving toward the door. She would call the police as soon as she got down to the lobby.

Her heels were the only sound in the apartment as she shuffled slowly backward toward the door keeping her eyes on the blood, as though it would somehow attack her. Before she could reach the door, her back hit a solid wall of muscle. She opened her mouth to scream and would have jumped away, but a hand clamped over her lips and another around her waist, pinning her arms to her side. She was dragged backwards into the heat of a very hard, very male body.

She knew instantly the man holding her wasn't Colin. Her ex-husband was the same height as her when she wore heels. And he wasn't near as hard as whoever was pressed against her back. This man was rock solid. Was this man responsible for the massive pool of blood on the floor? Of their own volition, her eyes fell to the crimson lake. She tried to struggle, but the man held her so tight, all she could do was wiggle helplessly against him.

He groaned and pushed his face into the back of her neck, nudging his nose into the short blond hair and breathing deeply. W-was he actually smelling her? He tilted her head to the side and forward a little so she was forced to look down. He ran his nose down the exposed arch of her throat from her ear all the way down to her shoulder. He was definitely inhaling her scent. His lips teased her shoulder and he tugged the sleeve of her coat a little until it moved toward the edge of her shoulder exposing more skin.

Oh god, what was he doing? Was this man going to rape her in her ex-husband's apartment? Had Colin's depraved mind come up with some new kind of punishment? But how did that explain the blood? Somehow, she *knew* deep inside that the blood belonged to Colin. Just as she knew no one could survive the loss of that much. She whimpered against the hand.

Her fear seemed to penetrate his fascination with her skin. He straightened to his full height, which was still several inches taller than her, even in heels. Though his broad palm remained firmly over her mouth, he used his thumb to rub her cheek soothingly as though to calm her. She blinked rapidly as his thumb brushed too close to her eye, her eyelashes sweeping over the rough pad. He groaned again from behind her and tightened his arm in response, pulling her further into the cradle of his thighs. She gasped into his hand, feeling the rigid length of his cock through the back of her coat.

Then she caught sight of the tattoo that ran along the edge of his forefinger. His trigger finger. It said, "For Dexter." Her dead brother's name. She stiffened in his arms, anger suffusing her as she realized exactly who held her. She didn't bother struggling. There was no point. He was too tall and outweighed her by a lot. The bastard also had a ton more street fighting experience than she did and wasn't afraid to fight dirty.

He chuckled darkly from behind her. He knew the exact moment she realized who he was. He dropped his hand from her lips, no longer worried that she would scream bloody murder, and slid it down the front of her body. He wrapped both arms around her waist, still keeping her arms pinned to her sides and dragged her tightly back against him. He thrust his erection into her ass.

"What are you doing here?" she hissed angrily.

"Think that's pretty obvious," he growled, bending his head to speak in her ear. "Come for you, pretty lady."

She shivered against him, her eyes falling on the blood.

"Wh-what did you do to Colin?" she asked, her voice both a plea and a hope.

His body became rigid, his arms so like steel bands around her that they hurt. He didn't speak for a moment. She got the feeling he was controlling himself so he didn't say or do something he might regret. She frowned, her breath catching in her throat. Roman would never hurt her. Would he?

"You don't have to worry about him anymore."

Katie opened her mouth to argue with him, but he brought his hand up to cut her off, pressing his palm against her lips once more. "You don't want to talk to me about your husband right now, Katie. Nod if you understand?"

She shivered and nodded quickly. She wanted to know what he did to Colin, but Roman was like a wild animal. He'd always been dangerous and unpredictable. There was no telling what he was going to do next. Until she was in a better position. Like on the other side of a locked door, her questions could wait. He moved his hand again.

"What happens now?" she whispered, hoping that one question would be okay. Was he going to let her run back to her life now that he'd done whatever he'd come to do?

"You come with me, like you should have years ago when I asked you to."

She gasped and jerked in his arms. "Impossible!" she told him.

She had a job in Milan in just a few days. She absolutely couldn't go with Roman. She knew the odds of his letting her out of his sight. The man had an eerie way of tracking people. The only way she'd managed to escape him all those years ago was because she'd begged him to let her go. And for some reason her opinion had always mattered to the street hardened criminal.

"Not impossible, Katie," he growled at her. "In fact, it's a fucking promise. You're coming with me this time. I'm done living without you."

"No!" she gasped out, lunging in his arms. "You can't do that, Roman. I have a life. I won't go with you!"

"I've been watching you, Katie, my love," he growled at her, lowering her struggling body to the floor as she twisted in his arms. He took her elbows and locked them behind her in one strong grip. He pulled something from his pocket with his other hand. "You live a half-life. I'm done watching from the shadows while you slowly kill yourself. It's time to start living again."

"With you?" she spat out, glaring at him over her shoulder.

"With me," he confirmed.

When she realized what he held, she begged him to stop. She threatened him and tried to kick him with her sharp heels. He ignored her threats and her pleas. He pinned her to the floor, lifted her coat to her thigh, baring the smooth naked skin. He froze when he realized she was completely bare underneath. Then he shoved his hand roughly into her coat to confirm his suspicion, cupping her bare breast.

She gasped and surged up into his hands. He slammed her back into the floor, treating her with a lack of care she'd never felt from him before. He leaned over her, his breathing finally as heavy as hers and growled in her ear, "Knew the fucker was blackmailing you. Had no idea you liked it enough to spread your legs. Maybe I should've let him live and just walked away from your mess."

She screamed and fought to get away from him. He cut her screams off with a heavy hand over her lips and plunged the syringe viciously into her thigh while she beat at his chest. After a few seconds, she stopped fighting, her body gradually going limp beneath him. He pulled her across his lap, cradling her head against his arm, and smoothed the coat over her nakedness.

She watched his dark, sinister face as she drifted into unconsciousness. The only man she ever truly loved. The man she feared above all others. He'd finally come for her.

Keep reading! **Thieving Hearts** *is available now from Amazon.*

EXCERPT: BECAUSE YOU'RE MINE

"She's been hurt."

The three simple words sent a chill through Jay's heart, dissolving his annoyance at the interruption. He dismissed the two men he'd been meeting with and turned to Greg with a raised brow. Words weren't necessary. Greg had been his right hand for nine years. He understood exactly how much Allie meant to Jay.

"Allison was taken to the hospital in an ambulance twenty minutes ago. Preliminary reports say a knife wound to the arm and across her side. The cuts don't appear to be life threatening, but deep enough to need stitches."

Jay's fury rose with each word. Renowned as he was for icy calm and deliberate control, Allie was the only person that could draw this kind of feeling from him. He struggled to contain the rage so he could ask the requisite questions. It wasn't necessary. Greg knew exactly what he wanted.

"She was working in one of the addiction offices at the soup kitchen. Apparently a fight broke out among the clients being served in line. She left her office and tried to intervene on her own."

"Of course she did," Jay managed from between gritted teeth.

He turned his back on Greg and stared out the window of his office to the dockyard beyond. It was just like Allie to think with her heart instead of her head. It was going to be the last time she would be allowed to do that. He'd stood in the shadows long enough. He gave her what she wanted. She'd lived her life the way she'd wanted. Now it was his turn.

"Her husband?" he snapped, knowing the answer, but needing to hear anyway.

Greg shook his head. "She sent him a text while she was waiting for the ambulance. Apparently the little prick's too busy to go to the hospital himself. Said he'd send someone to pick her up and take her home when she's been patched up."

Jay clenched his fingers on the windowsill and narrowed his eyes on a vessel slowly making dock. It was one of theirs. "What did she say?"

"She told him not to worry. Said she wanted to catch a cab back to the kitchen. She has to meet with one more client before she goes home and then pick up her car. She plans on driving herself home."

"His response?" Jay demanded.

Greg hesitated, then replied, "He told her not to keep supper waiting for him, he's going to be working late again. I'm checking into it, but at a guess, he's meeting with his side whore."

Jay felt wrath rise up and knew if Derrick were in the room with him he'd be on his knees begging for his life. Jay had despised the idea of this marriage, yet had allowed it to go forward, since it was what *she* wanted. And what Allie wanted was everything to him.

No more. He would harden his heart to the only thing in the world that could touch him. Her safety would come above all things, including her wishes. It was time. Past time.

"Get the plane ready, we're bringing my girl home."

Allie pulled her jacket tighter around her shoulders and tried to curl her legs into her chest without pulling on her fresh stitches. She tried to calm the shivers that wracked her body, but they kept coming. She was laying on a cot, tucked into the far corner of one of the wings of the emergency room in the Regina General Hospital. She wanted to ask for a blanket, but didn't want to disturb any of the busy staff that were rushing by her tiny curtained cubicle.

She'd been in the hospital for nearly three hours. The first hour had been waiting to get into the cubicle, the next had been waiting to see a doctor and the third had been waiting for her doctor to sign the release forms. She wished she could say it was just an extra busy day at the hospital. She knew better. It was always like this. She'd accompanied people there on more than one occasion.

She squeezed her eyes shut and tried to suppress another shiver. Sighing she ran her hand lightly over her arm, avoiding the heavy bandage on her bicep. Her fingers caught in the tangled strands of long dark hair. She shoved it out of the way impatiently and moaned when she jostled her arm. She wiggled her hips in an attempt to get more comfortable on the small metal frame bed when the curtain moved and light flooded her eyes.

Allie blinked up as a man stepped forward. He wasn't wearing scrubs like the nurses and doctors.

She frowned and blinked in the harsh light. "Derrick?"

She knew she was wrong though. Derrick said he wasn't coming. He barely cared enough to acknowledge her text. It was only her stupid heart that hoped he might rush to his injured wife's bedside that made her send that text in the first place. He wasn't even coming home from work to check on her. That was how much he cared. No, the man standing before her was not her husband.

"Hello, Allie."

Heart thundering, Allie pushed herself up using her good arm. She blinked against the brightness of the light, her mouth opening in disbelief. It was impossible. He couldn't be here with her. Could he? Yet the deep, measured voice could belong to no one else.

He looked so good it made her body ache in a way nothing else could. He looked older than she remembered. It had been five years since she last saw him briefly at Veronica's wedding. His hair was completely grey now, prematurely, she thought. He was thirty-nine. His grey eyes looked wearier, harder than she remembered, framed by lines that weren't there before. His body leaner, as though he didn't eat enough. He exuded solid strength though, despite the lean frame.

"Jay," she whispered, tears filling her eyes.

His eyes caressed her face and the corner of his lip lifted in a tiny smile, softening the always present hard edge. The only time she'd ever seen Jay Le Croix smile was for her or her mother. Never for anyone else. Allie lifted her arms, ignoring the painful pull of her stitches and leaned forward trusting him to catch her as she slid forward off the bed. Strong arms enveloped her, holding her tight. She breathed in his familiar scent as he rocked her against the strength of his body. One hand cupped the back of her head, holding it against his shoulder, while the other hand swept down her back comfortingly. He was careful not to touch her where she'd been cut. Somehow he'd found out about her injuries and come to her.

They stood that way for a long time, looking to all the world like a couple in love locked in an embrace. Finally, Allie indicated she was ready to pull away. Reluctantly Jay allowed her a few inches of space. She looked eagerly up at him, taking in all of his features. Jay ran his fingers lightly through her long, dark brown tresses, automatically restoring some order to the wavy chaos with his reassuring touch. Despite an age difference of ten years he had been her best friend for much of her life.

When Allie had been a child, her mother had watched over the orphan boy as though he were her own. Veronica had made sure he was fed when his foster homes forgot. More than once she'd given him a roof over his head when things got too bad to stay in his placement. When he was old enough to care for himself, he returned the favour by watching over Veronica and her young daughter. He made sure none of Veronica's clients got too rough and he helped Veronica get clean when she was ready to make the choice. When he was able to run a crew of his own, Jay worked his way up the streets until he was able to create enough legitimate business opportunities that he could get Veronica and Allie off the streets.

Allie adored Jay all of her life. Her mother assured her the infatuation would wane. It didn't. With each passing year it only grew until Allie became old enough that Jay began noticing Allie too. Veronica and Jay agreed that Allie was too good for the life he'd chosen. The life that had chosen him. She was destined for better things. When Allie turned eighteen and graduated from high school, her excellent grades and, unbeknownst to her, Jay's maneuvering, earned her a scholarship to a university two provinces away. Allie didn't want to go. But Jay had insisted.

The separation had been difficult. She'd cried for him every night. She'd written him letters and phoned him. He never answered her letters and rarely picked up her calls. When he had, it was monosyllabic responses before abruptly ending the call. Confused and hurt, she'd finally decided to forge a life without him. When she visited her mother, she stubbornly avoided talking about him and almost never saw him. The last time she'd heard from Jay was three years ago to receive his decline to her wedding and an extremely beautiful pearl necklace as a wedding gift.

She'd only seen him twice in the ten years since he'd sent her away. The last time she'd actually seen Jay had been at Veronica's wedding five years ago. He'd walked the bride down the aisle, turned to Allie, held her close for several seconds pressing his lips against her temple and then leaving abruptly. The time before that was seven years ago when he'd come to her apartment out of the blue. She'd just graduated from the Addictions Education program and had accepted a job as an Addictions Counsellor. He wanted her to quit.

"It's too dangerous, Allison."

"Of course it's not! It's perfect for me. It's something that I've always wanted to do. With the way I grew up and my mother's past, its practically the only think that makes sense for me. Why can't you just support me in this?" she'd pleaded with him.

"Support you? I pulled you out of the fucking gutter! Now you want to jump in head first. I refuse to support this shit."

"Jay! You don't get to dictate to me. You shut me out of your life years ago. Now I'm living it the way I want to."

"Tread carefully, little girl. I can wrap you in chains just as easily as I set you free."

But that was years ago. Now, as Allie looked up into the eyes of the man that used to possess her every thought, those same words echoed in her mind. His gaze hardened on her face. "What are you doing here?" she whispered.

"We're going home, Allie."

Keep reading! **Because You're Mine** *is available now from Amazon.*

EXCERPT: PRISONER OF FORTUNE – BOOK 1 OF FIRE & VICE

"Another card for the lady?"

Shania glanced down at her cards uneasily. What had possessed her to attempt a table at the casino? She'd never even touched a slot machine. Of course, she had never been one to balk at risks either. That could explain how she found herself dropping fifty dollars on one game of Black Jack, sitting around a table with a stone-faced dealer and two other men, both older and likely vastly more experienced than herself.

She had to discover for herself what the game that had nearly gotten her husband killed was all about. Ex-husband, her mind whispered. Or soon to be ex-husband, to be more exact.

He was the reason she was here in the first place. She had promised him one last favour before walking away from her disaster of a marriage forever. She would find the owner of this casino and hand over the $2,000 her husband still owed.

Shania shivered in apprehension. Perhaps it was an unconscious attempt to put off the meeting that had lead her to try her luck at a table.

She glanced back at her cards. A queen and a seven. Seventeen.

Shania chewed her bottom lip and thought hard about what to do. She didn't really care about the fifty. She had fully intended to play until it was gone. But she wanted to prolong the moment before she would have to search out the casino owner – the man responsible for Aiden's brutal injuries.

"Another card, please," she asked quietly.

Ace.

Now she held eighteen in her hand. She thought that was high enough and decided on prudence. Lowering her cards a little, she looked up. The casino was brighter and flashier than she expected. It smelled nice too, a subtle blend of fresh citrus and spice. She looked curiously in the direction of the slot machines when she noticed a pair of dark, stern eyes on her. A man, staring intently in her direction.

Shania shifted in her seat and glanced discreetly over her shoulder, checking to see if he could be looking at someone behind her. No one nearby. She dared another glance at the man as the players to her right placed their bets.

He was tall. Very tall. And broad. And intimidating. Which was something, considering Shania's Amazonian proportions. She didn't often find men that could dwarf her. She stood just under six feet with a body that gave curvy a new name. A friend had once called her ass a ba-donk-a-donk. Whatever that meant. But it had sounded like a compliment, so Shania had taken it as such. She'd always felt comfortable in her own body.

The man was clearly interested in her, though she couldn't tell why. His gaze was not one of casual sexual interest, but intense and frightening. As though he recognized her. Which was impossible. He might know Aidan, but not her.

Oh god! Could he be the guy that had beaten up her husband? He certainly looked capable of such brutality.

Her breath caught in her throat as he approached the

table, circling closer, like a hunter after his prey. He stopped a few feet away and continued to watch her. Shania barely noticed that she lost the hand. The man two seats over won. He beamed and scooped up the chips.

"Leave," said the man that had been staring at her so intently.

Shania jumped at the deep voice. She assumed he meant her for her to leave now that she'd lost. She glanced up with a small smile and made to vacate her seat when she realized he was no longer staring at her, but at the two other men she had been sitting with.

The winner got up good naturedly enough, while the other grumbled a bit first. She wondered why they would leave when some random guy told them to. Especially the guy who won. Perhaps the intimidating guy was a bouncer and was shutting the table down? He was certainly big and thick enough. She didn't think so though, with his crisp, well-cut shirt buttoned up his broad chest nearly to his throat and immaculate tailored jacket.

She stood, thinking he intended for her to leave as well.

She gasped as a heavy hand gripped her shoulder and held her fast, pressing her back into her chair. His long fingers felt like a brand, searing her skin through the thin fabric of her jacket. He stood next to her, so tall she had to tilt her head back to see him properly. Up close, the man was a walking nightmare and so sexy he took her breath away.

He didn't remove his hand immediately, but stood watching as the others left the table. She could feel the contact in every part of her body and shivered, wishing he would move away. She wanted to say something, but his imposing presence kept her silent.

He was likely around forty – maybe ten years older than her. His hair was black and cut very short. His eyes also looked black, with no colour to relieve the intensity of his stare. His skin was a medium shade of brown, slightly lighter than her own, and smooth, except for the scar that caused the corner of his eyelid to droop slightly. He was positively terrifying and absolutely the sexiest man Shania had ever laid eyes on.

He trailed his fingers across her back as he rounded her chair, coursing shivers down her spine. He turned the seat next to her to face hers and sat down, his long legs spread at the knees. One of his knees rested against the side of her chair, lightly touching her hip. Shania gasped at the sizzling contact and shifted away from him as subtly as she could.

"Deal," he said, not taking his eyes off of her.

The dealer nodded and began shuffling cards without hesitation.

Shania finally looked at the man next to her in earnest, trying to hold his gaze without dropping hers. God, but he was intimidating! "I lost my last round, I'm finished for the evening. I really do need to get going."

What had possessed her to come here in the first place? She certainly hadn't wanted to when Aiden had begged her to make the trip on his behalf. But he'd looked so pathetic in his hospital bed. And she'd always been a sucker when someone asked for help.

The stranger didn't say anything for a moment, just stared at her until she dropped her eyes.

"If you'll excuse me," she murmured, and made to stand.

"You lost the moment you walked into my casino, Shania."

She gasped, her eyes flying up to his.

He knew who she was! She tensed, preparing to sprint for the door and the relative safety of her car. He tensed as well, as though readying himself to leap on her if she chose to run.

"Stay," he growled at her. "If you attempt to leave, I will stop you, and then we'll have this conversation the hard way. You need to trust that you won't like that, Mrs. Galveston."

Shania shivered and gripped the edge of the table tightly,

a wave of dizziness washing over her. His voice slithered down her spine, alternately chilling her and heating her from within. She was completely, bone-deep terrified of the dark man. She sensed the ruthless power that rolled off of him.

"What do you want?" She said, struggling to keep the edge of desperation from her voice.

He chuckled. Not a mirthful sound, but one of sinister intent.

"I want what belongs to me."

She looked at him, pushing her long dark hair over her shoulder in a nervous gesture, and tried to channel brave. "I assume you mean the money that my…husband, lost in a poker game here last week?"

Dark brows came down in a fierce frown. "You know about that?"

She nodded slowly, moistening her lips. "He told me, after… after… he was hospitalized. I have some for you… it's not everything, but it's all we have."

He inclined his head toward the cards the dealer placed in front of them. "Pick them up, Shania."

The way his voice captured her name told her just how deep she was in it with this guy. He allowed the hint of an accent to caress each syllable. Possibly middle Eastern. She flipped her cards over with a shaking hand.

An ace and a five.

She looked at him from under her lashes and watched as he flipped over his cards with long, brown fingers.

A king and a nine.

"Ma'am?" The dealer inquired.

She nodded and he tossed a card down.

Nine.

The dark man inclined his head at the dealer, who tossed down another card. Risky, she thought.

Two.

"Twenty-one," said the dealer.

The man stood without moving his chair back, towering over Shania, his body touching hers. His fingers wrapped around her upper arm and he lifted her easily from her chair. She reached out for her purse and managed to hook one of the straps just as he began pulling her toward the back of the casino, as though she were somehow on board with whatever he had planned. She stumbled after him through a hallway toward a large door. He shoved it open and pushed her inside.

Shania stumbled and reached out to grab the back of a chair. Before her fingers could make contact, she was seized from behind and spun around. Hard hands gripped the tops of her arms.

"Why did you come here?" he demanded, eyebrows drawn over flashing dark eyes. "You don't belong in my casino."

Shania was suddenly very afraid. A huge, furious man – a debt collector – was confronting her in what could only be his private office, nowhere near help if she needed it. Considering she couldn't make out any noise from the casino, she suspected the room was soundproofed.

"I… I don't understand."

"Don't play innocent with me, woman," he growled, shaking her a little. "I met your greedy fuck of a husband. You clearly aren't here to gamble, because you've never played before tonight."

Again, the barest hint of an accent caressed the word woman, running shivers through her body.

When she opened her mouth to defend herself, he cut her off.

"You hold your cards like a baby, so don't pretend you belong here," he snarled. "The only other reason I can think for your presence in my casino is to make payment for your husband. And I thought I was pretty fucking clear while I was rearranging his internal organs. I want the money he owes plus interest, not some fucking housewife."

Shania stood in shocked silence as his merciless eyes bore into her. He thought she was here to barter herself to pay off her husband's debts? She could barely comprehend the possibility, let alone believe Aiden had suggested it to this brute of a man.

"Ex-husband," she managed to choke out. With shaking hands, she pulled her purse up between their bodies like a shield, unzipped it and reached in for the cash. Pulling it out, she tried handing it to him.

His eyes flickered down, barely touching on the cash, before returning to her strained face. She appeared to be in genuine shock. She brought a hand up between them and tried to push him back, a hand against his stomach. To her surprise, he actually took a small step back.

"I'm sorry, I think there's been some kind of mistake," she whispered, her voice shaking. "Please. Just take the money!"

She chewed on her lower lip and gripped the cash in a shaking fist, glancing up at him pleadingly.

He shook his head and asked in a more neutral tone, "Is it possible you have no idea, Shania, how truly despicable your husband is? What are you doing in my casino?"

"I just wanted to give you the money Aiden owes. And… and I wanted to see the casino. What kind of a game – what kind of a place – could take away a person's life savings in just a few hours."

She straightened, pulling her shoulders back and owning her height, which still didn't touch his 6'4" frame. Her golden eyes glittered with something other than fear as she tilted her chin.

"You're worse than Aiden ever was, with absolutely no morals whatsoever," she said, growing suddenly bolder. "You take away people's livelihood's and then you crush them."

Instant fury washed over his face, but there was an edge

of suppressed amusement as well. "The last person that insulted me... well... I can't remember the last person that insulted me. And that's for good reason. I run a tight club. Here I am law and order, God and villain."

She was suddenly acutely aware of her situation, like a baby lamb bleating angrily at a full-grown lion. She was brave. Or trying very hard to act like it.

He raised a brow at the furious, frightened beauty challenging him. "I didn't force Aiden to come to my club, and I didn't force him to throw down that money. I also didn't force him to gamble away an IOU."

"No conscionable business owner would accept an IOU!" she snapped.

He took a step toward her, thick brows lowering over dark eyes. "Watch your tongue, woman. Just because you trespass on my good graces this evening doesn't mean I'll let insults pass those beautiful lips unpunished."

Shania quickly stepped away from him, trying to keep some distance between them, and bumped the top of her thighs sharply against his desk. She tried to look brave, but was failing miserably on the inside. She wanted nothing more than to escape his presence, run to her little car, drive home, pack up all of her belongings and move away from this godforsaken city and her failed marriage. She silently vowed that was exactly what she would do the moment she was allowed to leave the club. And she feared, very much, she wouldn't be leaving without his permission.

Finally, she found her voice and asked the question that had been burning in her mind since she found out about her husband's reckless behaviour and the subsequent beating.

"Wh... why did you beat him so badly?" Her eyes closed briefly at the memory of Aiden's wounds. As angry as she was at him, she would never wish such pain on anyone, let alone the man she had once loved.

"He gave you everything we had in our accounts,

close to $20,000. He only owed a few thousand more. Wouldn't it have been smarter to wait a month or two until he could earn the extra? It just doesn't make sense to hospitalize him. How can he possibly pay you back now? I sold everything we had left just to get this for you." She held up the crumpled bills clutched tightly in her fist.

For a split second, he just stared at her in surprise and then threw his head back and laughed. "You think he only owed 'a few more'?"

She nodded, starting to feel queasy.

He sobered quickly, boring into her again with an intense gaze. "He owes closer to $200,000. That $20,000 was a down payment to get him in on the games."

Shania gasped and swayed. The money fell to the floor in a pathetic heap as she gripped the side of the desk.

"No! That can't be right... he said..." But she knew without saying it that Aiden had lied to her. "But he doesn't have that kind of money!"

"I know. He tried to barter with me. Offer something besides money."

Shania desperately wanted to put her hands over her ears and sink to the carpet of his office. She knew what he was getting at. There's only one other thing Aiden would consider of any value in his life.

Her.

"That's how you knew what I looked like?" she asked, pain and humiliation choking her already weak voice, rendering it almost inaudible. "You knew about me before I even came here."

He nodded and, reaching over the desk, picked up a photograph and showed it to her. Shania closed her eyes against the image of her laughing face, smiling up at the camera. It had been taken one year ago on her wedding day. She had worn jeans and her nicest top to the county clerk's office. Neither she nor Aiden had wanted a big, expensive wedding.

A thought fluttered briefly through her mind, penetrating the haze of humiliated pain. This man had been keeping her picture on top of his immaculate desk. Not tossed, but carefully, purposefully placed. Why?

It took her a moment to gather her thoughts and take hold of her shaking limbs. Finally, she collected herself and straightened to face the man watching her every move with an unnerving intensity.

"I take it the beating you gave Aiden was your rejection of his suggested debt payment?"

"Yes."

Shania sighed in relief. It was absurd to think he might agree to Aiden's terms, but the confirmation lifted a weight from her shoulders nonetheless.

"Of course, that was before I met you."

His deep tones shattered her composure. "I...I don't understand," she whispered, terribly afraid that she actually did understand.

"You walked into my club tonight, little girl, placing yourself in my power," he said, gliding toward her and caged her against the desk with his arms, leaning over top of her, his lips inches from her face. "I would have let you go, princess, and settled Aiden's debt with him, if you had been a good little wife and stayed home tonight. But you came here, showed yourself to me. Now, I think, I'm willing to take Aiden up on his offer."

"No!" she gasped, turning her face away from him, straining to escape his gaze. "I only came to give you that money. Aiden sent me here to give it to you!" As soon as the words left her mouth she realized she had been set up. Aiden had sent her into the casino with a very specific purpose. He had placed her under this man's power.

A whimper of pain escaped her lips, along with any lasting feelings she might have felt for her husband.

Shania raised her eyes to the man who held her life in his hands, searching his face for mercy. She saw only a flicker of pity, acknowledgement of her pain and fear, before his eyes hardened once more.

He reached out and wrapped long fingers around her neck, tilting her chin up with the edge of his hand until she was forced to look at him again. "Oh yes, sweet Shania. I do believe I will take you as my payment."

"But, that's illegal!" she gasped, trying to sound braver than she felt.

His eyes traced each word as it left her lips. "This is my town, princess. I make the laws. And if I choose to accept the terms of Aiden's debt – his wife in exchange for a clean slate – then so be it. But I'm amused you think you have a say."

Shania tried to shove him away, but he stood immovable, blocking her in against the desk. "But the money… You must want the money!" she tried desperately. "I can get it for you!"

His eyes searched her face. "I doubt that," he drawled. "It was never about the money. Two hundred grand? I make that in a day without breaking a sweat. It's about a fool gambling in my town, trying to cheat me of what's mine. It doesn't matter though, I've made my decision. I take you and Aiden Galveston walks, debt free."

"You can't!" she pleaded. "That's kidnapping… and… and… slavery!"

"Slavery?" he smirked.

She nodded.

He looked down at her, considering. She might be attracted to him, which would make things easier, but it really didn't matter. The moment he had made the decision, she belonged to him, whether she liked it or not. He wasn't particularly interested in what she thought was right. He was far more interested in that beautiful, lush body packed into a pencil skirt, blouse and formal jacket.

He reached past her, brushing his arm against her breast and causing her to jump. He picked up the phone and dialed.

She held her breath as he spoke swiftly into the phone.

"Ash, you can tell Aiden Galveston his debt has been paid in full. He needs to leave town and never show his face here again. And give him a love tap to remind him of my mercy."

He hung up and looked down into the accusing golden eyes below him. Despite the loss of $200,000 he felt pretty damn good about things. It'd been a long time, if ever, since he wanted a woman as badly as he suddenly wanted Mrs. Galveston. Damn if he didn't just purchase the privilege of using that gorgeous, curvy body any way he wanted.

"Khalid," he said, eyes tracing her full, red lips. "Say it," he demanded.

She blinked and sighed before whispering, "Khalid."

———

Keep reading! **Prisoner of Fortune** *is available now from Amazon.*

ALSO BY NIKITA SLATER

If you enjoyed this book, check out some other work by Nikita. More titles are always in progress, so check back often to see what's new!

DRIVEN HEARTS SERIES

Book One – Driven by Desire

Book Two – Thieving Hearts

Book Three – Capturing Victory

THE QUEENS SERIES

Book One – Scarred Queen

Alejandro's Prey (a novella)

ANGELS & ASSASSINS SERIES

Book One – The Assassin's Wife

FIRE & VICE SERIES

Book One – Prisoner of Fortune

Book Two – Fight or Flight

Book Three – King's Command

Book Four – Savage Vendetta

Book Five – Fear in Her Eyes

Book Six – Bound by Blood

Book Seven – In His Sights

OTHER BOOKS

Because You're Mine

Mine to Keep (a novella)

STAY CONNECTED WITH NIKITA!

Don't miss one sexy moment. Keep in touch with Nikita for the latest news and updates about all of your favourite characters.

- Get more info and updates at **www.nikitaslater.com**
- Keep up to date with **my blog:** nikitaslaterblog.wordpress.com
- Like and follow on **Facebook (@SlaterNikita)**
- Follow me on **Twitter (@NikSlaterWrites)**
- Connect with me on **Goodreads**

Sign up for the newsletter today on my website to receive exclusive updates and access to *bonus content and chapters* not available anywhere else!

www.nikitaslater.com
nik@nikitaslater.ca

Made in the USA
Middletown, DE
27 December 2018